THE COURTSHIP OF MAGGIE'S GIRL

by

G. C. Booker

ALSO BY G. C. BOOKER-"WHAT
REALLY HAPPENED"
AVAILABLE ON AMAZON KDP

G. C. Booker

ISBN

9781080188239

TO
WOMEN   EVERYWHERE

PROLOGUE

Maggie Frick turned twelve years old on May 16, 1766 on a small farm in southern Frederick County, Virginia. Two days later the mid-morning routine was interrupted by a posse of men and boys galloping up to the house shouting that ten Indians and a Frenchman had come through Delinger Gap in the Allegheney Mountains at dawn. They had attacked a cabin on Riles Run, she heard some man tell her father, burned it down, murdered the farmer, his wife, and their only son. They were last seen heading east, carrying the couple's ten year old daughter with them.

Maggie's father, the giant Tenante Frick, hastily gathered his family together as the rattle of the vigilantes' hoofbeats faded away. With a horse to bear the load of some of their possessions, he led them along a path through the forest toward "Mueller's Fort" — Jacob Mueller's stone house that was surrounded by a stockade, and was a gathering place for the locals at times like this.

They didn't move fast enough. As they descended toward Liberty (now Swover) Creek, a shot came from the woods on the other side, hitting Tenante Frick in the shoulder and knocking him to the ground. Maggie's older brother grabbed the reins of the skittish mare. Maggie went for her father's loaded musket. With only a patch of dirty white linen showing through the leaves sixty yards away, she aimed and fired the way she had been taught. As blue smoke rose from the barrel, she heard a moan, saw that the white linen was no longer there, and turned to look down at her wounded father.

But the leaves rustled as six of the raiders burst through the underbrush, their hands holding knives and clubs, their voices high and loud in frenzied screams. Maggie hurriedly crouched to retrieve the ammunition pouch from her father's coat pocket; her hands shook as she loaded the gun. There was no time to aim. She hitched the musket up to her waist and jerked the trigger back. The nearest attacker twisted and fell, but the others still rushed toward them.

Maggie swung the gun like a club. Her older brother grabbed a dead tree limb. Rocks as big as loaves of bread were pried from the path by her mother, her two sisters and a little brother, and heaved at the raiders. It was as if all of the rage and resentment contained in the spirits of the hundreds of victims from twelve years of war gathered there at that spot and took over the bodies of the Frick family. The attackers' skulls were cracked, ribs were smashed, arms and legs were broken before the five Indians lay ruined on the ground.

Maggie stared down at the wounded men, her shoulders heaving with deep breaths, her eyes wide in amazement at what they had done. Before a smile of triumph reached her lips, an awareness of their vulnerability seeped into her mind, bringing the first tears to her eyes. She looked to her mother for guidance and protection, but her mother's face was as white as a wedding veil and distorted with fear, making Maggie want to get away from it all. She took a step back, another up the path, then through the gap in the trees where the trail forded the creek she saw the four remaining Indians run to their horses, dragging the girl from the Riles Run cabin with them. Without a thought or a word to the others, Maggie ran to the remaining horses, vaulted onto one, and began to chase.

Maggie's mount carried her quickly up the path, but the Indians, even with their burden, moved faster. At times their heads showed above the rises, usually she just followed the sounds. She never knew how far they rode; she never went back to walk the route the way an aging soldier might, but did remember galloping across fields and trotting through forest, splashing through streams and crashing through briars. She was certain she would never catch them. They began to realize she would never stop.

As she came down a path with dense forest on either side, she saw them through the trees no more than fifty yards away. One was still had the little girl, two others were looking back at their pursuer, and the fourth... He was out of the tree and on Maggie before she knew he was there. He slammed her off her mount and to the ground, smothered her with his body like a blanket. Maggie kicked and punched and tried to grab his arms, screamed, and cursed for the first time in her life, thought better and began to pray. But neither strength nor the Devil nor God could help her. He tried to clinch her wrists to keep her from flailing at him, but she twirled them too fast, so he suffered a weak punch or two, raised the stone hatchet in his right hand and started to swing it down.

The pause at the top was all the time Maggie needed. In just that instant she drove her right arm up with her hand in a fist, except for one finger which went straight and strong to the left eye. The Indian reeled back in shock. With a thrust of her pelvis Maggie bounced him off of her, and scrambled to the side.

Blinded, he tried to stand. Revived, she hustled to her feet. He got to one knee, but a kick to his face sent him back down, and a stomp on his crotch made him curl up in pain.

Only a few knew what happened after that. For the rest of her life Maggie insisted the others simply dropped the girl and fled. But it was said that years later, after the forests were cut to make way for wheat fields and corn, and cabins and homes built in the clearings, human bones would be carried in by dogs, or unearthed when gardens were dug. The ten year old girl would live another sixty years, and although often asked about that day, would never really say.

It was a safer, softer world that Maggie's great-granddaughter Anna Rose Sigler was born into in 1835. The Indian raids stopped after that year of 1766. More settlers moved south from Pennsylvania and Maryland, and from east of the Blue Ridge. A new county was formed, first called Dunmore, later changed to Shenandoah. In the decades following the Revolution the intersections of paths became villages; the stagecoach stops became towns. Churches were built, most primitive, a few nearly grand. There were more grist mills, lumber mills, and wool factories started during those years, and the number of iron furnaces grew to take advantage of the ore deposits on the slopes of Massanutten Mountain, the charcoal from the forests that had to be cut anyway, and the necessary limestone that made up much of the Valley floor.

It was from this industry that Charles Sigler extracted his income. He was one of two partners in The Windmere Iron Company, the engineer who designed the smelting process, and supervised it. His partner Otto Metzger sold the product, got it to market, decided how much they should produce. The morning Anna Rose was born her father was at work, just up Stony Creek from the town, overseeing the construction of a new furnace that would double the yield of the one it replaced.

The family prospered on pig iron. From their house on the Valley Turnpike they could watch the company's wagons make their way toward the ford of the North Branch of the Shenandoah River. Twice a week there would be a parade of eight or more, six mules pulling the load, the words "Windmere Iron Company" stenciled on the canvas.

Stony Creek was also the town's name, although that wasn't official. Many people called it "Shyrock" after the stagecoach stop and eaterie. In 1852, when it was incorporated, it would become Edinburg. It was a busy, industrial place. Stony Creek's current provided energy for three mills in four miles; the Valley Turnpike brought constant traffic through the town. Workers at the furnaces and mills would liven the air with their talk and laughter as they made their way out at dawn; their sluggish footsteps and tired whispers seemed to create a chant when they went home at night.

From the time she could crawl Anna Rose watched it all from a front parlor window. As soon as breakfast was done that was where she would go if she weren't ill and confined to her bed. The sill was just a foot off the floor, low enough for her to peer through the glass even at a very early age. The turnpike was just fifteen feet away — a panorama, a carnival, at first just a blur of sights and sounds, but over weeks, months and years, events and faces became familiar. Anna would squeal when her father's wagons went by, later yell to her mother or nanny, eventually identify the drivers by name. But, with the sensations that the bustle of life in front of her house created— the excitement of the new, the romance of the unexplored — there was also an aura of danger.

When she was old enough to understand, talk of crimes and other misdeeds would make her judge which of those men just fifteen feet from her perch might do her and her family harm. Sometimes the sight of a horseman would make her jolt without knowing why. She wondered if travelers passing by were heading into personal wars, or coming from them, the way the Catawbas and the Delawares used that path to attack each other before the settlers arrived about a hundred years before.

Maggie visited there once a week, at least, during the early years of Anna's life. Richard, the black man who drove the carriage, would help her down with a strong arm. Lucinda, Richard's wife, would lead her up the front steps. Maggie was alone then, except for the house servants and the workers on the farm, some of them former slaves she freed and hired, others whom she purchased, then freed and hired. By the time Anna was eight years old Maggie had outlived four of her five children, and all three of her husbands, including the one she shot and killed.

Henry Fornier was his name. He came to Shenandoah County from Frederick, Maryland in 1794 with three wagonloads of English furniture, and opened a store in the county seat of Woodstock. A "frayed aristocrat," was how he was described. He possessed intelligence, wit, charm, and manners, but always seemed to be looking up the road as if worried about what, or who, might be catching up.

Maggie was delighted by him from the first time she met him. She told her friends about his sensitivity, about the fact that he was the first man to make her laugh, at least on purpose, since her father died five years before. She was 41 when she met him seven months after he arrived in the county. His age was never determined. She had been a widow for four years, reigning over the 3,000 acre estate she inherited from Thomas Bledsoe, her first husband. Her life the previous four years centered around the practical and necessary tasks of running the farm, with no attention to what would benefit her heart and soul.

For days after she first entered Henry Fornier's furniture store she lost all sense. Her conversations would stop in midsentence; her mind would go blank in the middle of a task. She sighed; she laughed at nothing more than what was in her head. For minutes she would stare out into some distant land only she inhabited and controlled. She went back three days later. By then Henry Fornier knew her name and her reputation. He could imagine no better refuge.

It took him another six months to win her. She did not put up much of a fight. Some family members were uneasy with the union. To them he seemed to work hard to maintain a shell which hid something grotesque underneath, but no one dared approach her with their fears. When the two were wed in the backyard of that massive stone house above Narrow Passage Creek on October 11, 1795, over thirty relatives attended, as well as more than a hundred neighbors and friends.

As charming as he was, Henry Fornier had another way with women. Unfortunately, it was brutal and uncaring, and could be called sadistic when that word was coined. Even before Maggie met him his reputation was spreading over Shenandoah County like a fog over the hills — just as extensive, just as nebulous.

Whether Maggie knew about it, or believed it was true, was never determined, but on that warm February afternoon when she somehow heard the servant girl's cries coming from the shearing shed, there seemed to be no hesitation, no dilemma, according to someone who was in the house. She was loading the pistol as she walked across the yard, repeatedly shoving the rammer into the barrel and pulling it out like an act of love. She waited until she was behind him to cock it so he would hear the sound. His head jerked back when he realized what it was. He was thinking of excuses as he got to his feet, as the girl scrambled to the side trying to grab for her dress with her wrists tightly bound. Maggie waited until he turned around, waited until he seemed to understand why this was being done. From fifteen feet away she raised the gun and fired the way her father taught her. The shot hit Henry Fornier in the chest, in the center, and went through his heart. In thirty seconds he was unconscious; in sixty seconds he was dead.

There was no trial. The sheriff was sent for just after the killing, arriving hours later in the early evening darkness. While he sat in a yellow velvet-covered arm chair that, ironically, came from Henry Fornier's store, Maggie calmly and exactly described the events of the afternoon. He went to the barn to look at the body still laying in the dirt, bringing the pine cone lantern down close to examine the wound. The fifteen year old black girl was brought to him, and the marks on her wrists where the ropes cut into her skin were pointed out. The sheriff said little, grunted several times, mostly frowned, told Maggie he would think this out, then mounted and rode off knowing there wasn't a juror in the county who would ever vote to convict Margaret Frick Bledsoe Fornier of anything.

Maggie married one more time, thirty years almost to the day of the shooting, to a Mr. Peter Wirtz. Peter had worked on the farm since 1779, was raised in a cabin on twenty acres at the foot of Kerns Mountain in the Massanutten range, and lived in a cabin on Thomas Bledsoe's 3,000 acre inheritance from his father, who had received it from Thomas the Sixth Lord Fairfax.

Peter tended to some of the sheep on the farm, if that place could be called only that, taking care of a herd of about 200 that grazed in the pastures on the east side of Narrow Passage Creek. Other than his dealings with his fellow workers, and his occasional attendance at church and festivals, he kept to himself in his cabin, never married, never seemed to want friends. He read, according to the few who knew him at all, a skill he taught himself, and sometime late in life actually wrote a book, a history of the first settlement of the area, that was discovered in a wooden box after his death, published five years later, and can still be found on library shelves to this day.

It was a cold, blistery evening in January of 1825 when he walked into the house without knocking, and to the library doorway, waving off a servant who hurried from the back at the sound of his footsteps on the foyer floor. Seventy-one year old Maggie sat in one of the two armchairs that Henry Fornier sold her more than thirty years before. The yellow velvet was by then frayed and faded. Stains from spilled tea and brandy were on both arms. Maggie was wrapped in a blue blanket to keep away the chill, and illuminated by two candle lamps on opposite walls, and the glow of a fire just in front. Her gaze went from the flames to Peter Wirtz as he slowly walked into the room. Her brow wrinkled as she wondered why he was there, but with a long look into his eyes after he moved into the good light, she recognized his expression, knew his mission, and gasped in a breath.

Peter's confession of love took almost an hour. He cited the first time he saw her 46 years before, and related nearly every time since then, describing what she wore, how she looked, what she was doing, what she said. He remembered the temperature of each day, which wildflowers were in bloom, or whether there had been rain or snow just before or just after. He compared her to goddesses from Greek and Roman myths, and told her their stories and how she fit in. He quoted Shakespeare, Byron, Goethe and Strassburg, pronouncing the English words with the heavy German accent that came from his childhood, and the foreign words that way as well.

Maggie was amused at first, startled by his memory, mildly alarmed that her life had been chronicled, perhaps her secrets revealed, concerned about his sanity, and wondered if he carried with him a gun or a knife. But his voice was so strong, so sincere, his expression so affectionate — Maggie gazed at this short, thin, wrinkled old man and knew why he was there. This wasn't a plea or a request. She realized he understood that in a week or a month his life could be gone, and although he might linger before the end, this could be his only chance to reveal to her his devotion, and his recognition of the fountain of energy that had fueled his life.

They married a month later. No one could figure it out. It provided substance for gossip for three weeks before the wedding, and for years after that. Their lives changed only a little. Maggie ran the farm as she had before, with much of the work in those years being done by a Irish overseer named Richard Higgins. Peter still tended to his sheep, and many nights slept in his cabin instead of in the grand house with her.

Their time, when they were together, was spent in philosophical discussions and intellectual discourses that Peter led. Although Maggie could read and write, had been schooled as a child by her parents, she married at seventeen, and thereafter devoted her time to being a wife and a mother, and eventually the mistress of a vast commercial domain.

Peter filled her in on much that she missed, reading to her from the great books of the ages, or quoting long passages from memory. He told her of the customs and traditions of peoples in other parts of the world. She would look at his face in amazement hearing of bizarre rituals, or strange practices, certain he made them up. The diversity of the world surprised her. Her existence had been ruled by the sameness of survival in Shenandoah County, the circle of life repeated over and again.

The marriage lasted four years. Peter stayed out in the cold one day too many, became feverish and weak, began to cough, and was soon bedridden. The physician said he would recover if kept warm and well fed, but pneumonia set in, the coughing worsened; his sweat drenched the sheets. It took all of his effort just to raise his head. Two weeks after falling ill it was obvious the end was near.

Maggie would not leave his side. He whispered to her, his voice rasping, yet tender, carrying the same tone of affection it held for an hour four years before. At times, in what must have been delirium, he repeated parts of that night's confession word by exact word, as if he had written and memorized it the day before.

They spent their last hours together wrapped in each other's arms. As he was fading toward death he began to recite a Shakespearean sonnet he taught her on their wedding night. At first she could not remember the words, but in a desire to join with him one last time, her mind somehow found them hidden in a trunk in her memory. As his strength abandoned him she had to take the lead, bringing forth tears from both of them.

" Those hours, that with gentle work did frame
  The lovely gaze where every eye doth dwell,
  Will play the tyrants to the very same
  And that unfair which doth excel;
  For never-resting time leads summer on
  To hideous winter, and confounds him there;
  Sap check'd with frost, and lusty leaves quite gone,
  Beauty o'ersnow'd and bareness every where;
  Then, were not summer's distillation left,
  A liquid prisoner pent in walls of glass,
  Beauty's effect with beauty bereft,
  Nor it, nor remembrance what it was;
  But flowers distill'd, though they with winter meet,
      Leese but their show, their substance still lives sweet."

◆ ◆ ◆

No one understood why Maggie spent so much time with Anna Rose, what she saw there. The girl was considered by most people to be nothing more than pitiful. She was tall, too tall, as skinny as a sapling. She could never figure out what to do with those long arms and huge hands, so they constantly flapped around her as if she were swatting at unseen flies. In another age, in any age or epoch, any place or culture, she would have been described as plain, if one were nice, or homely, if one were fair. Her nose was too small and upturned, her ears too large. Other children were at a loss deciding what to ridicule first.

Even her mother and father had some concern about her. After a time, after Anna reached an age when most children had acquired some grace, they would grimace or groan when Anna walked into a wall or the low limb of a tree. Her mother tried not to yell when dishes were dropped, and they were always dropped, but she couldn't control herself when Anna's little brothers went crashing to the floor.

To the neighbors she was hopeless as well. At least once a week one woman or another would comment that it was good that Anna had her father's money and Maggie's heritage since it would take all that for her to someday attract a man, and even that might not be enough.

If any of this had any effect on Anna, it didn't show. Other than the bruises and the welts and the scrapes and scratches, there was no sign she believed she was anything other than a normal, happy, well protected and provided-for child. She would play with the same children who taunted her the day before, climb the same old dogwood that ejected her countless times, shrug when a plate shattered on the floor, and grin and laugh when she fell from a chair.

It seemed only Maggie could diminish or elevate her. Every Sunday, and in seven years it was all but twenty, Maggie would arrive in that tattered carriage she could have easily replaced, take Richard's arm, then Lucinda's, and climb the six stone steps to the Sigler's front door. Charles and Rebecca would receive her there. Maggie's daughter, her youngest and only surviving child, Martha Boelt would stand in judgement of her mother from a few feet away, always thinking she should not have made the trip, that *she* and the Siglers should be taking the ride down the road to see her. Martha would look for feebleness and dementia in her mother, try to gauge her health and care, knowing there were demons out there who would rob her, spirits that might infect her, age that would eventually defeat her.

The two youngest children approached first. It was a custom. Junior, four years younger than Anna Rose, would walk stiff and proud to "Granna" and offer a hand as he thought a gentleman should. She would bend her old, hardened back to meet him, but even in later years as he grew, she still towered above him. Thomas, the youngest, named after his great-grandfather, the Bledsoe aristocrat, would crawl, toddle, later shuffle toward her, never quite certain who she might be, at one time thinking she was there to take him away, a beast who devoured little boys. For months when he was three he would have to be dragged to the foyer, his screams and cries escaping out the windows, echoing down the turnpike and turning peoples' heads.

But it was Anna Rose whom Maggie came to see. Eventually the others would drift from the parlor leaving the two of them alone. Anna would sit still and stilted, her hands gripping the arms of the high-backed chair. Maggie would ask about this or that, would listen patiently while Anna struggled to find the correct words, the right thoughts, and show a sincere interest in the stories of a child's simple joys.

Maggie would have her own tales, not of Indian raids or abusive men or poets, but of her life, day to day and mundane, anecdotes of an existence on the farm. At times, there would be harrowing descriptions of storms that seemed designed to blow everyone off that plateau above Narrow Passage Creek, of floods and daring rescues, of fires and tragedies, births and heartbreaking deaths, but it was mostly a chronicle of sheep, corn and wheat, and workers' and neighbors' lives, of her own thoughts and feelings as if she were preparing her great-granddaughter to be her biographer.

Some say it was these visits, Maggie's presence in Anna's life, that caused the changes in the young girl. It was more than the natural progression of childhood, people insisted. Maggie was somehow bequeathing her spirit across the room during those talks, they were certain of that. It was the only way to account for the poise and beauty this frightful child began to gradually possess, like the land slowly going from winter to spring. As one life was ebbing, another was advancing; an essence somehow flowed from one to the next.

There was a reversal in the fall of 1846 when Charles Sigler was killed. He had climbed the platform to ready the next ore "charge" to be lowered, slipped on the rain slick wood, and fell thirty feet to the rocky ground below. The household was in chaos with grief for months; the town mourned the premature death of a decent man. Anna Rose retreated to a world where it did not occur, making up truths and expectations that would bring her father back.

Even Maggie could not make a difference. Anna saw that this "goddess" was now somehow flawed, too feeble in old age to perform another miracle, to rescue her from the greatest danger she ever faced. For a few months, and it would be only minutes in the span of a week, she wondered if Maggie somehow caused it; her eleven year old mind never understanding why she would think that, then dismissing the thought when it became too frightening for her to accept.

But as the poets realized long ago, time allows us to adapt, to somehow find the means to change our outlook to enable us to go on. In two years the tragedy was only a memory, a scar perhaps. The thought of her father might make Anna Rose stop and grieve for a time, but she continued to grow and to thrive. It helped when her mother remarried and they left the house in Stony Creek and moved to a farm four miles to the southwest on the Middle Road, as it is called.

Richard Faraday had 350 acres there, a few hundred

sheep, cattle, corn and wheat fields, a daughter six months younger than Anna Rose, and two sons near the ages of Junior and Thomas.

Instead of a parlor window with a view of the Valley Turnpike, Anna could see much of the Valley from those high fields. To the west, between the farm and the Allegheny Mountains ten miles away, the land fell and abruptly rose, slumped and surged. Cave Ridge and The Knob loomed like prehistoric monuments to the gods. Lesser peaks hid hollows where mystery and adventure might hide. On a clear day, facing east, and swiveling right to left, she could see much of the steep, wooded slopes of the Massanutten range that ran fifty miles from Penn Laird to Strasburg.

Like a filly freed from the stall and allowed to run in the fields, Anna seemed to rejoice in her life as a farm girl. Her muscles became hard and strong, her skin tan. The color of her hair — dun was how it was described — lightened and soon shone like the sun off an October leaf. It would flip around her shoulders as she chased the others in a game of tag, or bounce off her neck when she ran in for meals.

She still grew taller, but her ears slowed their progression, her nose seemed to catch up; firm flesh covered her bones, and downy skin covered that. Anna entered womanhood near her fifteenth birthday, and her figure soon made that event clear. By the time she was seventeen it all seemed to fit together like the pieces of divinely designed puzzle finally solved. Her face glowed in perpetual happiness; a celebration of life was always in her eyes. By the spring of 1852 there was no one around who did not think she was the most beautiful girl in Shenandoah County, if not in the entire Valley.

Thus the war began.

CHAPTER 1

"Do you know who I like?" Hester Faraday asked. She was lying on her stomach crossways on the bed, propped up on her elbows with her feet in the air. The petticoat beneath her dress made a scratching sound as she kicked her legs gently back and forth. Hessie, as she was called, was much shorter than Anna Rose and slightly heavier, with wide hips and larger breasts. Her dark brown hair was wavy and tended to get frizzy when not diligently cared for, going against the current trend of smooth, flattened locks, but her wide, crooked smile and twinkling eyes made the boys and young men see her as devilish and enticing.

If Anna heard the question it didn't show. She was gazing into a full length mirror supported by an oaken stand while dressed in only a quilted, white satin corset which ran to just below the top of her breasts. In front of her she held up a turquoise cotton dress with copper colored trim at the collar and at the ends of both sleeves. The dress was "double -skirted" with the first one ending at mid calf. The lower skirt was a darker blue, fell to the ankles, and was trimmed at the bottom in yellow. With two crinoline petticoats it would be pushed out into the shape of a bell. "Oh, I hate this one, too," she complained. "My mother has such awful taste." She spun ninety degrees to the left so that she and the dress faced Hessie. "Don't you hate this one, too?" Hessie shrugged. "Oh, you said something, didn't you? I *am* sorry."

Hessie got up to all fours on the bed, then rocked back so that she was on her knees sitting on her feet. She leaned slightly to her right and supported herself with her hand. "I was just thinking," she said softly and hesitantly, "somebody I hope is at the party. Somebody I like."

Anna folded the dress at the waist over her left forearm and let it hang there. "Who? Oh, I know. It is..."

"You will never guess." Hessie flashed that big, bent smile, then suppressed it as if she were thinking mischievous thoughts she couldn't control, but wanted to hide.

"David Hertz?"

"Noooo. He cannot talk of anything but sheep and wool."

"Franklin Metcalf?"

"He smells like cows all the time. Besides, he is practically our age. I do not want to fall in love with a child."

"Peter Metzger?"

"Peter Metzger? I thought that you liked him. Everyone says that you will marry him since his father and your father were partners."

"Everyone says that?" Anna tilted her head. Her eyes widened with surprise. "They do?"

"All of the girls around here and in Stony Creek think that. They are afraid to have anything to do with him. They do not want their hearts broken."

Anna seemed to tremble. She took several quick steps over to a stuffed chair and carelessly laid the dress over the back of it, snatched another dress that was hanging from the wardrobe door, almost dropping it before walking back to the mirror. Hessie watched as Anna held the dress up with shaking hands and tried to concentrate on its image in the mirror, but it was obvious her attention was elsewhere.

"Are you in love with him? You seem —"

"No," Anna said emphatically, "I am definitely not."

"Yes, yes, you are," Hessie said loudly, in between laughs." I can tell. Oh, my. It is true."

Anna could not keep her composure any longer. Her shoulders slumped. She bundled up the dress, then dropped it to the floor. As she knelt down onto the bed she ran both hands through her long hair. She sat with her legs tucked under her. "How do you know if you are in love?"

Hessie let out a laugh that sounded like the first notes of a song. "You are in love with him if you act the way you are acting just at the mention of his name."

Anna's lips went tight in a forced grimace, but it was evident she wasn't going to be able to keep them that way for long.

"Peter Metzger, Peter Metzger, Peter Metzger," Hessie chanted until Anna couldn't fight it. She gave into the giggle she was holding back, and let herself fall to the right so that she was laying on her side. She tilted her head slightly to look at Hessie, then tilted it some more to gaze up at the white cotton canopy of the bed. "Oh, it *is* what I want so badly. But it would be..." She paused. "It would be so *scandalous*."

"Scandalous? Why? Your father and his father were in business together."

Anna slowly sat up. The expression on her face suggested she had just awakened from a pleasant dream and now had to face the reality of the day. "My mother *despises* Mr. Metzger. He tried to cheat her when he bought Poppa's half of the foundry after he died."

"I have never heard that." Hessie scooted around so she was facing Anna.

"No one knows except us," Anna whispered. "I assume your father does, and Mr. Rutherford. He — "

"The lawyer?"

"He is another one that my mother does not like or trust. She hired him to help us. He said he looked at the books, and thought it was a fair offer, but my mother was sure something was wrong, that the price was too low. She said all the men in the county know each other and help each other out. Sometimes I think she is too suspicious. I cannot imagine — "

"Well, what happened? Did she get more money?"

Anna smiled. She seemed relaxed for the first time since this discussion started. "Granna went to see Mr. Metzger."

"Maggie?" Hessie let out a cackle. Her face was beaming

like a victor's. "What did she do?"

Anna shrugged. "She just went in to see him. That was all. To talk to him. She did not threaten him, I do not imagine."

"Still, Mr. Metzger must have been terrified."

Anna's face took on a look of sweet innocence. "Terrified? I do not know why. Granna was..." She stopped. Her brow wrinkled as she thought. "She was 93 then, I think. She was not much stronger than she is now. I am sure she practically had to be carried into his office."

"Yes, but still, everyone says that she possesses spirits. She can make things happen without even being there. There are some people around here who think everything bad is caused either by God's vengeance or your Granna's. If I were you, I would let them believe that."

Anna shook her head slowly. "That is simply foolish. I do not know why anyone would think that. It is just superstition. She is nothing more than an old woman." A smile slowly crept onto Anna's face like morning sunlight spreading across a room as she silently acknowledged the aura of protection that came from being Maggie's great-granddaughter. It wasn't something she had been conscious of before moving to the Faraday farm, perhaps she started to become aware of it after her father died. At times she had a sense of insecurity knowing that, despite the rumors, her Granna would not live forever. In the back of her mind somewhere she worried that Maggies' death would be like the crumbling of a dam, and all of the waters that had been held in check for all of those years would come rushing toward them. There were people who blamed her great-grandmother for a number of things, and in their delusions might come seeking revenge. "I mean, she has not harmed anyone for over forty years," Anna insisted.

"As far as we can prove, anyway." Hessie said with a laugh. "But face it, it might scare some of the boys away. They might be afraid of doing something wrong and getting hit by lightning or having a tree fall on them."

"Well, those are not the boys that I would want to have

anything to do with. Anyone who is afraid of her is too foolish for me to fall in love with."

"Peter's father was. Didn't he give your mother more money after Maggie went to see him? He must have been afraid of her."

Anna shrugged. "That does not mean that Peter believes that. Besides, maybe Mr. Metzger did what he did because he realized that he was not being very nice. People do nice things, don't they, not just because they are afraid of what might happen if they do not."

"You sound like a preacher, or a philosopher."

"I do, don't I?"

"And a poet. Think — you are in love with a man your family hates. That is just like that play 'Romeo and Juliet.' This is so romantic. I never thought when we became stepsisters that having you around would be so much fun. I cannot wait to see how this turns out."

"You mean like Peter and I lying dead together somewhere. Yes, that *would* be fun. I would become as great a legend as Granna. She would be so proud of me." All of the muscles in Anna's face seem to droop at the same time, the way they always did when she was shocked into dismay.

"Well, maybe it will not happen that way. Maybe —"

"No, we would just have to live somewhere else, I suppose. I would not be able to see my family again. I do not think I could bear that. Junior and little Thomas lost to me forever? I could not live without them. It is hopeless."

"Well, maybe by the time you are ready to get married it will not be Peter you will be in love with. You will find someone better."

"No!" Anna protested. "I want to get married now, as soon as possible." Her voice became stronger, the words quickened. "I can feel it. It is, it is something inside of me. Granna calls it my 'biological destiny.' Every time I think about Peter and I together, it is, it is just the best feeling I ever had. I cannot describe it. Someday you will fall in love and know what it is like.

We would have a big stone house somewhere, and servants, and he would go to work at the foundry, some foundry, *his* foundry. It would be perfect."

"It would be just like your..." Hessie stopped. She knew Anna didn't want to hear what she was going to say. Yes, it was hopeless, Hessie was thinking. The girl was hopeless. When she considered that Anna was only six months older than she was, she knew she might have to be married soon as well. At Anna's wedding everyone would ask if she were to be next. She had seen *that* before. To avoid looking like a spinster or a free woman she would have to find someone, too. Anna had to be stopped, or at least slowed down, until Hessie got out of there, out of that house and off that farm, or she would find herself chained to a man and babies, always attending to someone else's needs as if she were just another servant girl, assuming she didn't die giving birth before the age of twenty. The world was too large, too grand, she was too special for her to spend her life as just another woman in some sheep-infested Virginia county. "Well, I may be in love, too," Hessie said, instead of what was on her mind.

"You? I am sorry. You did try to tell me, didn't you. I am so sorry, going on about myself and Peter." Anna laid down on the bed, supporting her head with the palm of her right hand. "Who? Who is it?"

Hessie shifted positions several times before she spoke, ending up sitting just the way she had before she moved. She took a deep breath, delaying revealing the secret as long as possible, making Anna's eyes grow wide in anticipation. "It is..."

"Tell me!"

"Oh, I shouldn't. It is just too... "

"You are going to kill me with this."

Probably not, but I might change you, Hessie was thinking. "Okay. Okay. Are you ready?" Anna nodded several times quickly as if her head was being pulled by strings. "I will just blurt it out. Here it comes. Ian Froth."

"Ian Froth!!?" Anna exclaimed as she gasped in a breath. A

squeaky, little giggle escaped as she exhaled. Trembling fingertips went to her lips as all of her rosy-white skin turned flaming red. "But he is a..." she whispered, "he is a fornicator."

Hessie let out a single laugh like a crow's call as she collapsed onto the bed. "You sound like a preacher again. That is simply is not true. I mean, nobody has ever seen him do anything. Those are just rumors because he is *so* handsome, and all the women seem to like him."

"And because he is nearly thirty and not married. And because women have been seen coming out of his blacksmith shop at night."

"It is simply not true. If it were true he would have been arrested by now. Besides, so what if he has been with a woman or two? All men do that kind of thing, don't they?"

"Peter doesn't," Anna said with a slight turn of her head. The voice was husky and strong. The words seemed to have been marinated in venom.

"Okay. Peter doesn't. He should. Do you want him to know nothing of women when you get married?"

"How can you say these things? No, I, uh, ... Oh, this is so... It..."

"I think that it is important for a man to know how to treat a woman." Hessie stared at Anna as a predator does at a prey. "We should be happy. We are not cattle to be bred, or new carriages or horses to be shown off, or slaves to be used for our labor. Ian Froth likes women. He wants to please them, and knows how, from what I hear."

Anna squinted her eyes in confusion as if she wasn't certain she was hearing the words correctly. Her muscles were tense as if trying to break ropes that bound her. Her head slightly tremored. "But being in love makes a woman happy, doesn't it?" Her voice was high and shaky. "That is all that matters."

Are you sure you are Maggie's girl, Hessie thought. "Are you sure you are Maggie's girl?" she said.

"What does that have to do with it?" Anna said loudly,

then realizing she could be heard out in the hallway, whispered, "What does that have to do with it? Maggie was in love, her first husband, she was in love with him. They were married when she was 17. I doubt that he was the kind of man who had experience pleasing women, and she probably didn't care. She told me those were the happiest years of her life, having all of those babies, raising them. Just because she shot Mr. Fornier you think that she is, she was the kind of woman who, uh, demands that a man pleases her? She did what she should have done with her life, what she had to do, what God intended her to do. I don't think she ever cared much if she was being pleased."

"Maybe if she knew what she missed she would feel differently." Hessie's speech slowed. "I have heard that when a man makes love to a woman just right —"

"You have heard? You have heard?" The words snapped like a whip. "Who do you know that has ever —"

"Edina."

"Ed, your cousin?" Anna gasped. "Has she —"

"*No, she hasn't.* Ian just kissed her once. Last year. The day before she turned seventeen. At least that is what she said it was, just a kiss. She said it was the most wonderful feeling she ever had. She said that whenever she wanted to she could remember it and get that same feeling back. For weeks."

"Is she in love with him?"

"No, I do not think so. I just think she likes to be kissed by him. I think she would like to be kissed by him again."

CHAPTER 2

"'Fare-thee-weel, thou first and fairest! Faire-thee-weel, thou best and dearest! Thine be ilka joy and treasure, peace, enjoyment, love and pleesure! Ae fond kiss, an then we sever!'"

"Burns again?" she asked.

"Aye, Rabbie Burns."

"Don't you know any other poets?" Mary Wainwright chuckled, looked down to fasten the last four buttons of her dress. She was a plump woman of 32, but taut, with large, heavy, firm breasts. Her face was pudgy, round and creamy white-skinned, pleasantly framed by dark brown hair that had been gathered at her neck earlier, but fallen onto her shoulders during the afternoon's activity. She had to brush her wavy locks away to get to the last button. "Do you see my hair ribbon, dear?"

Ian Froth tilted his head and scanned the bed for several seconds before turning his gaze back to Mary. "Nae, nae, Aye don't, Mrs. Wainwright." he said, leaning back against the pillow. The beige blanket covered his body from the waist down, revealing sculpted, hard muscles on his arms and chest. His rooster red hair poked out in several directions. He was stroking the short, red hairs of his beard with his left hand as he watched Mary Wainwright finish dressing.

"Could you at least give a look under the covers, dear?"

"Ae, there be nothin there but a tossel o iron."

Mary giggled. "Yes, you are a blacksmith, aren't you?"

"That aye am."

"An not a very popular one, from what I hear. There have been complaints that your shop is closed when it should be open."

"There are many farms aye need to visit. My work is nae always here."

"With your wagon in the shed, an your horses in the stalls?"

"A man needs his rest in the een." He smiled smugly.

Mary's expression turned stern. "Well, your rest may be eternal if the men ever catch you. My husband for one seems suspicious at times, an he *will* shoot ya if he finds out."

"For puttin a smile en his wife's pretty face, an a lilt in her voice? His gratitude should be vast."

"You should be wary. The more they suspect, the closer they're gonna be watchin. You should get a wife an put an end ta this gossip."

"Aye have a wife — Mr. Wainwright's."

"An several others, I'll wager, an a few daughters now an then, as well. Trust my words — you need to be married.. Maybe it will put some guilt in you."

Ian pulled the blanket off and swung his naked legs over the side of the bed. "Aye have thought o that myself, my dearest. You want a wager — in six months time, that gilpey Anna Rose Sigler will be Mrs. Ian Froth."

"What!!?" Mary had taken a step toward the bed to retrieve the red ribbon that was now revealed once the blanket had been moved. Ian's statement stopped her two feet away. Even in her shock she had a huge smile on her pretty face. "That... That... She is just a child. Yes, I grant you, a beautiful child. But Maggie's girl? That witch will turn that iron tossel of yours ta clay, an you inta a frog."

"That is bibble. She is but an auld lady, nothin more. Why gave her such power? She caent control the weather, the beas, us. She caent even keep herself from gettin aulder each day. Have you swatched her all bent an satteral, stiff? No, she is nothing more than an auld lady."

"An old lady who has turned her great-granddaughter into her likeness, from what I hear. Except the girl is young an healthy. You may think you can win a battle against Maggie, but Anna Rose will be more than you can handle."

"Ah, my dear Mrs. Wainwright, you taeke o love as if it is war. It be pleesure an hope. She will welcome me."

"Oh, you do think a lot of yourself, don't ya? Why her? There must be someone else who will please you, someone easier to catch. Or is it the chase that excites you?"

"Nae nae. It nae be the chase. It is, as you should know, the beauty. You nae know what female beauty does ta a man. It is everythin. Billies kill an die to possess it. A bonnie lass should be the prize to the man who seek her the maest. The Lord hath put her here ta be with me."

Ian nodded to show his confidence. Mary, staring closely at his eyes, and nowhere else, looked for a flutter of uncertainty, but he seemed to actually believe what he said. He was taking himself too seriously, she thought. Yes, he could please women; she was familiar with that. He could make them feel as if they were the most beautiful, the most desirable object in the world, just by his response to them, remove any self-doubts and insecurities. He could take them from the dreary existence of their ordinary lives, make them feel as if they could fly, or live forever, at least for an hour, and sometimes for days after that. But eventually they would have to return to the commonplace, to face the threats of the world, their need for the real and substantial trappings that make life possible, protection against danger that gives them peace of mind. He could do none of that.

She worried for him. He had no idea what he was facing. His expectations would be false, his reactions all wrong. It would be as if he were stumbling around on a foggy night. It might be interesting, she thought. It might be deadly. She told herself not to stay around long enough to find out which.

CHAPTER 3

"Did ya see her, boy? "Woodrow Clapp asked. "Did ya see that girl?"

"Yeah, Pa, course I saw her. She was standin right in front of me." Alvis Clapp pulled down on his stringy black hair with both hands as if putting on a hat. "Ouch," he muttered when he hit a snag.

"Whew, that is one pretty girl. Tall, jist like Maggie. Thank the God in heaven she didn't git that Prussian nose, though, ya know." From further back in the mill a black man let out with a loud curse. Woody turned to look in that direction, frowned, shook his head, then went back to what mattered to him at the time. "Now, that's a girl you oughta marry. What is she --- sixteen, seventeen? That's old enough ta git married. Hell, yer ma weren't more an 14 when I married her."

Woody was a little under six feet tall, but massive, as if he always beat everyone else to the dinner table, and consumed most of the calories himself. He didn't notice that his short, skinny, twenty year old son was turning bright red and burning with embarrassment. Woody again swiveled toward the cussing, which continued like an epic poem.

It gave Alvis a chance to escape. He barely rose from his chair and scurried out the double doors to the loading platform, moved to his left and backed up against the wall. "Well, jist stop the damned thing!" he heard his father yell. "Disconnect the damn wheel!"

It was one of those May days that erases the castigation

of the winter and the early spring. It was just mid-morning yet the temperature was well over seventy degrees. The leaves on the trees and the shrubbery were now mature and boldly green in the bright sunlight. Extravagant yellow wildflowers invaded the weeds at the edge of the woods that lined the lane from the Columbia Furnace Road, adding to the spectacle of pinks, whites and reds of the dogwoods and wild apple and cherry trees that grew on the hills on the other side. Stony Creek, brawny and bronze from snow melt and spring rains, gushed proudly as it poured its way down the trench toward the town two miles away.

Alvis didn't notice the sound of the water, or the birds that frolicked above him, or the breeze as it puffed through the treetops He was too occupied with fighting the panic that had overtaken him. He wasn't sure why it was there, but was gradually grasping that it had something to do with his father suggesting he should marry Anna Rose Sigler. His mind wouldn't calm enough for him to comprehend that he was being goaded into a battle he couldn't possibly win. He was familiar with the consequences of failure in his family; they had been constant companions for most of his life. He knew that another bout of shame would make him see himself even smaller. If he lost here he would end up far from being the force of nature and society he perceived his father was, and forever have to cower before him and everyone else, always being what they needed him to be, never what he wanted.

He had to do something, but didn't know what. The wall he leaned on wasn't enough to protect him from his father. Woody could come storming out any moment and start bellowing about Anna Rose Sigler as if she were a hurricane that threatened their lives. Alvis would want to put his arms over his head to keep the humiliation from getting to him. He had to get further away. He took two steps to his right and nodded to look through the doorway. He couldn't see his father, but could hear him. From the words he could tell that a gear shaft had split, and would be splintering to kindling if left in place. It would take Jim all day to carve a new one and install it. With the wheel down there wasn't much they could do. Actually, there was plenty they could do, but it would have to wait. His father wanted him to marry Anna Rose Sigler. He had to figure out a way to do that, or his life was done.

It took Alvis fifteen minutes to retrieve his horse and saddle it. He glanced toward the mill one more time, stopped and listened, sensed only inactivity, so he walked his gelding out through the field behind the house, went through the gate and onto the road.

Clapps' Mill occupied a seven acre cut of land that was bordered by Stony Creek on the bottom, and the road from Columbia Furnace to the town of Stony Creek at the top. The creek paralleled the road just before the mill, then curved away from it to the south, looped back to run southeast again just beyond it. It was on this sloping land between the road and curl of the creek that the Clapps made their home.

Besides the grist mill, which was fed by a race that came off the creek where it made its turn, there was also a saw mill that was powered by water coming down the tail race. This building was now abandoned, having been poorly designed and cheaply built; they spent more time in repair than in operation. It was surrounded by logs that would never be cut, mounds of slab wood from the year they had it running, and stacks of lumber, warped and weathered and soon to rot.

Between the two mills and the house up toward the road were two acres of junkyard — old wagons, cracked grindstones, farm machinery that was broken and rusting, burnt out cook stoves, discarded furniture, empty flour sacks, feed bags, and trash that was simply carried from the house and dropped.

The dwelling itself had been grand and full of promise when it was built forty years before. It was designed to be the envy of the neighborhood, and had been while Woody's father Wylie was still alive. Its first and second story porches looked to the south, toward Stony Creek and the billowy, often haze-covered fields on the other side, and the low, mysterious forested hills beyond them. But the white clapboard was now in need of paint, and had been for years, the roof leaked, shake shutters would add litter to the yard in strong winds; both porch floors had holes in them that grew larger with each rain, and the mortar holding the foundation together was turning to sand, and releasing at least one stone a month.

Alvis' ride took twenty minutes. He started out slowly, his horse at a walk at first, his mind still running at full speed like a man under attack searching for a weapon to aid in his defense. He didn't know where he was going. He thought about heading to the southeast, riding down the Middle Road to the Faraday farm, as if that might help, but made a quick assessment of himself and Anna, and realized that the images hadn't improved since he left the mill. So he rode to the north, galloped through the village of Bedford, didn't slow down to make the turn onto the Chapel Road, and went another mile. He pulled the gelding to a halt, tied it to a rail and climbed through the fence.

Twenty year old Stephan Otterbein saw Alvis coming through the field, stopped the two oxen, and let go of the plow. It tilted but stayed upright. Stephan ran his hands through his shoulder length blond hair, then folded his arms over his bare chest as he waited for Alvis to reach him.

"Voodrow mad, too?" he said with a smirk when Alvis was close enough to hear.

"'Agin,' not 'too.' Jeez. Learn English." Alvis breathed a long breath in through his nose. It made a whistling sound. "You won't guess... Anna Rose came ta the mill with her stepfather an Hessie this mornin. Don't know why. Pa owes him money or flour or somethin. They went off an talked." Alvis shoved his hands into his pockets, then pulled them out , but couldn't figure out anything else to do with them so he put them back in. "Anyway, after they left, Pa said he thinks I should marry her. I should marry Anna Rose Sigler."

Stephan's cackle came out like a series of gunshots. He stopped when he saw that Alvis did not join in. In fact his friend's face was tight with alarm. "Oh, this not vitz?"

"No, it ain't a joke. The old man actually thinks it's possible."

"It possible. It possible. You are man; she is madchen. It possible."

Alvis looked away, obviously annoyed. "Yeah, maybe if I was the only man left."

"Then ve, uh, toten..."

"What, toten, kill, kill all the others?" Alvis shouted. "That's no plan!" We..." He suddenly stopped, his shoulders and arms lost their nervous twitches, and came to rest; his head cocked a bit as if he were thinking about it. He shook it slowly from side to side. When he faced Stephan again he seemed composed. "Ya know, it jist might work." He squinted as if looking back inside of his head. "We..."No! Wait a minute, " he said. "We'd never git away with it. That's stupid."

"You want marry Anna? You like her?"

"Like her, like her?" Alvis' voice cracked and squeaked. "My God, you stupid dutchy, I would be the best man in the county. My God." His hands came flying out of his pockets and swirled all around him as if he were trying to fly. "Think about it. Okay? Think about it. I marry the best girl, the best girl around, the prettiest girl, Maggie Frick's grand... Whatever the hell she is. Okay. What would their opinion of me be then? Huh? Huh? They'd realize I ain't the village idiot like they think."

"You be as great as Voodrow."

"Yeah, I would be." Alvis yelled. "Yeah, I'd be jist like Pa. Yeah. Yeah, ya know, we kin do this. We kin do this jist like Pa would. We won't hafta kill nobody, but yeah, like Pa always says, 'Whatever it takes.' Yeah, whatever it takes."

"Ve lie an cheat an steal jist like Voodrow."

"Yeah. Yeah." Alvis started hopping up and down. "Yeah, if we hafta. Yeah. Whatever we hafta do, I'm gonna marry Anna Rose Sigler."

CHAPTER 4

Peter Metzger pulled on the reins to halt his horse, swivelled in the saddle, and looked all around. He didn't see anyone. The road was empty for a quarter mile to the curve up ahead; there was no one behind him; he didn't hear a horse coming up the hill he just climbed. To his right was a rolling field of new corn plants. Nobody was working there. He could see the shake roof of a cottage in a hollow just beyond the cornfield, about a hundred and fifty yards away, but only the roof. If anyone was home and looking out a window, they shouldn't be able to see him, but he was certain that no one was home, not on that day, so it didn't really matter.   Satisfied that he was alone on the road and not being watched, he dismounted and hurriedly led the mare into the woods on the other side, swearing at every obstacle, every bush and branch that got into his way, every rock he tripped over. The whole way down he muttered to himself, raging at whoever it was who set his horses loose the night before, and made him spend most the morning looking for them, and therefore late that day. He hadn't figured out if that act of vandalism had anything to do with what he was there for, but it all seemed to be coming together to make him more agitated than he wanted to be.

The woods ran for seventy-five yards from the road, nearly flat for the first half of the distance, then ramped steeply down from there. At the start of the descent Peter tied the reins to a low branch of a hickory tree, removed his tan linen riding coat, draped it over the pommel, lifted a two foot long, cylindrical leather case that hung from the saddle by thin straps, forced off the cap with his left hand, and tilted the case nearly upside down, catching the telescope with his right hand. He took the time to wipe the lenses at both ends with his riding coat sleeve before heading down the hill.

Peter found this place two weeks before when he realized he was going to have to do this, when he knew there was no other way. If it bothered him to be this secretive, he wasn't aware of it. Perhaps it was because two weeks before, when he came across a boulder just the right size for his rear end, next to a split trunk at just the right height for his telescope, just far enough up the hill to keep him hidden, he felt as if God approved of what he was doing, and was helping him to get what he deserved.

Between him and the house three hundred yards away was a pasture with a herd of sheep scattered throughout it. He didn't look left or right to see how far the pasture ran. That didn't matter. He came to observe what was happening around the house, and when he finally looked down there he cursed again for being so late.

The masses had arrived, they had definitely arrived. It was as if all the citizens of Shenandoah County were on the lawns around the house and in the fields beyond them. He had wanted to get there early when just the family was celebrating Maggie's birthday. It would have been easier to pick Anna out of that group than it was going to be now. Once he saw the color of her dress he could have easily followed her throughout the day. Besides, by getting there late he probably missed seeing her talk to quite a few suitors. He might have rivals he didn't even know about. The horses getting loose is what ruined this for him. He was trying hard not to give Maggie credit for that, but it suited her needs so well he couldn't get it out of his mind.

Peter brought the telescope up and rested it in the crook of the tree, raised his head slightly and began to spy on the party. It was as bad as he thought it would be. There were at least five hundred people there, he figured. Faces were hard to distinguish. He could make out gender and age, height and weight. Normally it would have been easy to find a six foot tall, beautiful blond girl in any crowd. He shouldn't need a telescope for that, but all the Frick/Bledsoes were tall, a few were blond girls, and half the people were hidden by someone else, or were on the other side of the house.

Five hundred, at least. That's what he always heard. He had never been to one of these; it was a new event. For years it was just the family coming to the farm on May 16, or the Sunday closest to it. They alone formed a horde. Twelve of Maggie's grandchildren were still alive, about 40 great-grandchildren, maybe fifteen great-great grandchildren, not to mention their spouses, her distant cousins, and the like.

That thought depressed him every time it came to mind. Peter moved his head away from the telescope to glance left and right at the pasture trying to figure out what 3,000 acres looked like, and how many sheep she might have. He gazed at the house wondering what was its value. A third ownership in a carding mill, half interest in the wool factory in Mt. Jackson, a dairy, a slaughtering house, a wagon company — what was all that worth divided by sixty or seventy, or so? Probably not much more than he had now.

But Anna Rose was Maggie's favorite; everyone knew that. There was a popular assumption that the bulk of the estate would go to her, but he wasn't certain that was true. It would be just his luck to marry her, then discover she received only an equal share. Maggie had a will, he found out from contacts in Woodstock, but he couldn't find it the night he broke into her attorney's office. He figured it must have been in the safe he couldn't open, and Charles Miller wouldn't talk about it the night they got drunk together. He leaned toward the telescope thinking he was just going to have to take a chance that Maggie and God would do the right thing.

Peter began to scan the crowd, randomly at first, hoping he would get lucky. For a moment the appearance of all those people captivated him. It seemed so democratic. Here at the grandest home in the Shenandoah Valley was every type possible, a sample of all the human flavors of the earth — sod kickers and shepherds, Presbyterians, bankers and clowns, mill owners and mill workers, teachers, preachers, wool sorters and wool buyers, crooks and cranky old widows. At that distance the children seemed to float across the grass as they chased a ball or each other; their bright, colorful clothes looked like flags waving in the breeze. Peter didn't have the time to be entertained by it. Somewhere in the midst of it all was his savior. He had to find her.

He began to search in a more deliberate manner, starting with the tents. The nearest one, and it was just a massive piece of canvas supported by posts all around, contained several tables of food. In what was left of the area were dining tables and chairs, some occupied, many empty. Most the guests seemed to come in, get what they wanted, then return to the lawn. He went from person to person, face to face, cursing when his view was blocked. He realized he wasn't just searching for Anna, but trying to get an assessment of the situation, to see who was talking to whom, looking for conspiracy and conspirators, knowing that any plot to marry Anna would start at an event like this. Then *she* walked into the tent.

Peter gasped. His heart began to race. He brought his head back from the lens and watched her with just his eyes from 300 yards away. "She is so beautiful," he whispered. "Why did she have to do that? It is going to be so much harder."

He peered through the telescope again as Anna walked to a food table, picked up a plate and spooned something onto it. He perused the occupants of the tent to determine if she went in there for some reason, to see someone, but there were no young men in there, none with her, and she didn't seem to be glancing around. He did spy Frederick Rutherford, a fifty year old widowered attorney from Woodstock looking over the shoulder of the man he was talking to, watching Anna as she moved down the table. Yes, he was a possibility, a slight possibility, but since he kept a young, black mistress in a house a block from his, he could easily be beaten.

Peter turned his attention back to Anna, saw Hessie walk over next to her, and Anna lower her head while Hessie whispered something into her ear. Anna's eyes seemed to widen, her head jerked quickly to look out the tent at something or someone, and a big smile was evident even at that distance. Anna then turned back to the table, Hessie walked from the tent and disappeared into the crowd.

"Oh, no," Peter whispered. "What was that all about?"

What that was all about was Hessie telling Anna that Ian Froth had arrived and was asking about her. Anna's eyes widened in excitement, her skin turned red with embarrassment, a nervous smile formed on her lips, then grew. Two weeks before she might have just shrugged with disgust, but Hessie, realizing she went too far in her promotion of the man worked hard to soften his image, pummeling Anna with her insistence that Ian Froth was simply a hard working, handsome blacksmith whom women adored and other men envied and spread rumors about. She told her the kiss Edina received was on the cheek, not on the lips, and it was because her birthday was the next day, nothing more. Whether Ian Froth knew anything about pleasing women was still a mystery to her; she had just been speculating. It took her most of two weeks to finally calm Anna down, to make her consider Ian as an acceptable suitor. What finally started melting the ice was Hessie saying to her, "Wouldn't it be nice to be courted by the handsomest man around. It will give you something to remember, something to tell your grandchildren." That made Anna shrug, then smile, but she giggled and laughed when Hessie added, "Besides, it will make Peter *mad* with jealousy. He will have to marry you just to end his torment. Once you have rejected Ian, he will require me to make him happy again." But it was Anna who came up with the idea that convinced her she did indeed need Ian Froth. "Maybe if my mother thinks I am serious about him, she might let Peter court me."

After Hessie left the tent, Anna had trouble concentrating on what she was doing now the plot had begun. She stared at the table of food for seconds before remembering why she was there; her hands shook as she forked ham onto her plate. By the time her plate was full she had lost her appetite. She considered just putting it down and walking outside, but was concerned with how that would look.

At times that day Anna felt as if she were the main attraction at this event, not Maggie. Everyone seemed to be spying on her, seeing whom she talked to, who talked to her. She hadn't made a public announcement that she wanted to be married, but was sure they all knew somehow. It made her nervous realizing that any conversation she might have, anytime she moved her eyes, any gesture, would be taken as a sign. The public would be making up their own truths, and she, being who she was, would be the topic of gossip until she finally made a choice, and maybe forever afterwards. She was starting to understand that she was going to have to get used to it, to learn to contend with gossip as if it were an adversary. They would be making a judgement of her, and what she was like, and she would begin to see herself in their eyes if she weren't careful. She had to fight off the feeling that their opinions mattered. She knew what they would think if they believed she were seriously considering Ian Froth as a suitor, and that bothered her, but felt it was something she had to do if she and Peter were ever going to be together.

"My, my, you certainly have become a lovely young lady." Anna's thoughts were interrupted by Frederick Rutherford's voice. Her head turned slowly around as if her muscles were exhausted. This was about the tenth time she had heard those words, and each time it was from some man her mother's age. She wasn't sure who this one was; he looked familiar, but she couldn't remember where she met him, or his name. He smiled at her with tobacco on his teeth and whiskey on his breath.

She smiled back. "Thank you," she said as if she meant it.

"I am Frederick Rutherford. I am your stepfather's attorney."

The one who keeps a mistress in a house a block from his. Hessie told her about him a week before when they were discussing the strange practices of some of the men in the county. Anna was never sure where Hessie got her information; she suspected that it came from her cousin Edina, or perhaps from another girl at the academy Hessie attended. It didn't matter. She wished she didn't have to talk to this man now. It was improper for him to approach her without her mother or stepfather around. Maybe she should have brought an escort with her into the tent as her mother suggested, but knew those boys who were hovering around her would take it as a sign that she felt something, and would probably get in her way for the rest of the day.

"Yes, that *is* right," she said trying not to sound too cold. "I do remember you now." She looked at his face as a courtesy. His appearance shocked her. In his eyes was an expression of love, of lust, of something. His mouth was formed by a giddy grin as if they were sharing a secret. For an instant she wondered if he knew she had been thinking about Ian Froth, and took it as a sign that she might now be available to the likes of him.

In her excitement caused by the start of this adventure, Anna suddenly believed God was trying to tell her something, that with every action she takes there is going to be a reaction in the world around her. It wasn't just gossip she should fear, but the ebb and flow of people's emotions, and the deeds that will be caused by them. No, it wasn't God telling her this, it was Maggie. Her mind began to search all the conversations they had, trying to find out if she should have already known this somehow.

It was beginning to seem so chaotic to her, so complicated, so beastly. She felt inadequate to function in it. What had been such a perfect plan now seemed nearly impossible. There were too many things that could go wrong, too many trappings she hadn't accounted for, forces of man and nature she couldn't control. She wanted to get back behind that gate of protection her mother and grandmother provided, to her safe, familiar garden of childhood and innocence, and forget the whole thing. She wasn't ready for this — for love, for romance, for marriage. The excitement, now that it had started, was going to be too much for her.

Anna excused herself from Frederick Rutherford. She walked away before he could protest. She left her plate on the table nearest the entrance without concern for what anyone would think. She was just about to turn to her left to go out of the tent when something caught her eye, slowed her, made her stop, then take two steps back and stare across 300 yards of pasture to the hill to the north.

What Anna noticed was the reflection caused by the sun being at just the right position, and its rays hitting a telescope lens that was cocked at just the right angle. The beam of light hit her eyes as she started to walk away. It took her just an instant to realize what it was, who it was, and why Peter was there. She put the trembling fingers of her right hand to her lips to hide the smile she couldn't control, then ran all of the way back to tell Hessie what she had seen.

CHAPTER 5

Peter didn't expect this reaction in himself; the bolt of emotion surprised him. He thought he would be able to remain cool and aloof, watch her, and plan things out, but once Anna left the tent after talking to Hessie, and then to Frederick Rutherford, he couldn't control the anxiety that was growing like water beginning to boil. The unknown was making him nervous; what he suspected created terror. Questions, answers, scenarios were rushing through his mind like a herd of cattle stampering. He couldn't keep a thought in his head long enough to analyze it. For instance, why did she stare up the hill at him? That didn't make any sense. He was certain she couldn't see him, not at that distance. He hadn't told anyone he was going to be there; she shouldn't have known. Was it a feeling she had, a guess, a lucky accident? Was she trying to send him a message? Was God? Was Maggie?

Peter leaned back and tried to relax. This shouldn't have been this difficult. He was sure she liked him. A month before he made a point of being across the street from her seminary when she came out after school. Her reaction was a giddy smile; she turned and nervously whispered something to the girl next to her. Granted, it wasn't much, but at least the right emotion was there. He started working on his plan after that, figuring he could get Hessie to act as a go-between, meet with Anna somehow, and by the time her mother found out they would be too much in love for her to object.

Now it appeared that Hessie was working for someone else. Rutherford, maybe? That didn't seem right, but then this was Maggie's girl, and the rules in that family might be different than they were for everyone else. They could deal with the world and society in any manner they chose, and everyone else would have to follow. He knew from the start it wasn't just a young woman's heart he had to win, but the submission of the most powerful clan in the county as well. He was beginning to realize now that he was foolish thinking it would be simple and easy, but had he faced the truth of the situation, it would have seemed too daunting for him to go on.

He had to know what was happening, what Hessie said that agitated Anna, why she suddenly left the tent. He leaned toward the telescope again, but from where he was he could get only bits of evidence. He could see patches of green cloth in between bodies near the far corner of the house; he couldn't tell if they were from her dress. The strands of blond hair could have been on anyone's head. He was certain there was something happening that was out of his view, and therefore out of his control. A good businessman cannot make decisions without the right information. He had to get closer. He had to see.

The mansion and estate of Solway Court occupy, as all know, a plateau above Narrow Passage Creek, the name of the stream coming from the skinny strip of land between it and the North Fork of the Shenandoah River near their confluence where they parallel each other for a few hundred yards. The Valley Turnpike runs over this thin peninsula after fording the creek on its way north, about halfway between Stony Creek and Woodstock. From where the creek passes by Solway Court it is approximately a mile and a half in a straight line to the North Fork, although its actual meandering path is more than twice that distance. Woodstock is two miles to the northeast of the house, the town of Stony Creek a little more than that to the south. The house doesn't sit on the highest point around; that would be the hillock where Peter Metzger was perched on a boulder while he spied on the party he couldn't attend.

Eighty-two years before this day Thomas Bledsoe decided that ridge was too narrow and too rocky, so he built the house just east of there, closer to the creek, approximately forty feet lower than the high point, about thirty feet above the creek and 250 yards from it.

The house itself was eclectic in design; an almost square Federalist box with neo-classical influences that did not quite fit. Measuring seventy feet by fifty, two and a half stories high, with six thirty-five foot tall pillars in front, it was huge by any standard. At the time it was built it was so large and so grand that the locals considered it to be "auffallend" to use their word, or "gauche" in French. Instead of siding the house with stones right from the fields, Thomas Bledsoe imported a crew of workers from central Pennsylvania to chisel them into identical dimensions, then sort them by color and tone.

The framing timbers, the flooring and the paneling came from the forests and mills in the county; he raised the income of many loggers and sawyers, but that did little to lessen the resentment the Germans felt over this "Tuckahoe," as the Tidewater English were called. They remembered that his father challenged their leases and purchases of land when his grant from Thomas the Sixth Lord Fairfax was validated fifteen years before. Materials were constantly delivered late or not at all; a wall on the south side was constructed with too few pegs and should have collapsed in a year, but somehow did not. Oaths and threats were written in hidden places that wouldn't be discovered until the property was renovated after the Civil War. When the day's work was done, and the laborers gathered around pitchers of beer or jars of whiskey, they would gripe about the tyrant who came from the east to disrupt their lives and make them feel inferior.

Thomas Bledsoe did nothing to make himself more likeable. He was as aloof as he thought an aristocrat should be. Every sentence and phrase that came out of his mouth sounded like a command or a complaint. Ruddy-faced, red-haired, broad shouldered and tall, he looked superior and imposing even in his mid-twenties, but his eyes were deep pools of verdant liquid that made a few suspect there might be some feeling, some passion, perhaps even a little sensitivity. It wasn't until he met Maggie Frick that anyone realized how unguarded he could be.

It was Easter Sunday in 1771. The Fricks had ridden seven miles to the Lutheran church in Woodstock for the occasion, and were on their way back home in the late afternoon, hoping to get there before the storm that was hovering over the Alleghenies reached them, keeping an eye on the clouds as they climbed the hills, and worrying and commenting in the valleys.

They didn't move fast enough. The storm, which seemed to have been sitting in place for an hour, quickly advanced. It hit them as they were crossing Narrow Passage Creek, releasing an unrelenting torrent and blowing the rain sideways. The steep, opposite bank of the ford soon became as slick as ice; the horses slipped and slid; the raging winds spooked them; they tore from their harnesses, turning the wagon over and spilling the seven Fricks into the mud.

They got to their feet, made a quick assessment to determine that no one was hurt, instantly wondered why God would have done this to them, then, drenched and covered with mud, trudged up the embankment, fruitlessly searched a few hundred yards of newly cleared pasture for their horses, then walked to the two story stone cottage where Thomas Bledsoe was living until the mansion was done.

Maggie would never understand the allure Thomas felt the second she walked in the door. Her face was spotted by remaining blotches of oozing muck, her hair was matted and dripping; she kept her eyes low and unfocused with a look of defeat. With her spirit muted she should have been the least attractive female on earth, but there was a jolt the second he saw her, and felt her presence. Even had they introduced themselves immediately, he wouldn't have known who she was or what she had done. Perhaps if he had had a single social conversation with any of his workers he would have known of her reputation, but the facts of her life weren't necessary for a commotion to start within him that made his mind to heed only that.

Peter left his telescope resting in the crook of the tree and walked through the sparse woods, paralleling the fence line. After 60 yards he saw that the food tent, most of the back yard, and the several hundred occupants were blocked by the house, and the sight of him hidden from them. There were a few children playing in the side yard, but they wouldn't know who he was or understand what he was doing. Still, to be careful, he charted his way through the field before climbing over the fence and starting across.

Peter, or Brozie, as he was known to his good friends, stood a little over six feet tall, large in those times. As a young man he shoveled ore in the mines, felled trees in the forest, and worked as a laborer at his father's foundry, so his naturally slender frame became muscular over the years, giving him a limber, yet dignified posture, long strides and a firm steady walk. His hair was sun-bleached blond, covered his ears and the back of his neck. A bushy moustache hid his top lip.

From childhood on Peter had ambitions of becoming a military officer, sought an appointment to West Point in 1844, but it went to another boy, so he spent two years at the university in Charlottesville studying mathematics and the classical languages before returning home to help his father at the foundry. It was about six months later that Charles Sigler died, so he soon became his father's partner, the engineer at the company, a fact that made some of the more superstitious employees believe that he somehow caused Charles Sigler's death, even though he was a hundred yards away at the time in another building.

Girls and women found his ruggedness appealing, his brash, confident manner irresistible. In his late teens and early twenties a few lured him to their beds or up to a barn loft, but he soon felt as if sex were a waste of time since the fifteen minutes of pleasure didn't make him smarter, stronger or richer.

Peter was no more than twenty yards into the field when he began to regret doing this. He was too exposed. Someone was going to come around the house to check on the children, see him, and run to tell Maggie. He would be forced from the property at gun point; the gales of laughter from the people who knew what his father tried to do would resound in his head for weeks, the story would be told for months, and although Anna might think it daring and dashing, they would be on the lookout for him forever after that.

His father, what a fool. For the sake of a few thousand dollars he risked Peter's chance at fifty times that, not to mention that he eventually cowered before Maggie's power, giving that witch a greater sense of her dominion than she deserved. Of course, at that time Anna was only eleven, he had just turned nineteen, and he dreamed that his fortune would come from smelted iron, seeing he and his father taking over one foundry after another until they controlled the iron industry in the entire Shenandoah Valley. But over the years as deals failed, when they lacked the cash to go after others, as their competitors became larger and passed them, he lost his dreams, and his honor, and soon realized that marriage to Anna Rose Sigler was his only chance at great wealth.

He was going to get caught, he was sure of that. He still had 280 yards to go. Someone could come up the lane, or be watching from the house. There were four trees scattered in the pasture, but only four. There was no way to go from one to another, no way to hide on the way there, no other route he could take. He had to figure out a way...

"Baaah."

There must be some way across. If he could only...

"Baaah."

If the sheep would keep quiet maybe he could think this out.

"Baaah."

Peter didn't need a flash of lightening to get him to move. In an instant he was up to a sprint, running toward a gathering of forty of the beasts just off to his right. Unnerved, they began to flee; their short, quick steps divotting the ground, spitting bits of sod in their wake, their torsos rocking like barrels on a wagon while their heads switched back in panic to glance at their pursuer. But as swiftly as they moved, Peter was quicker. He soon caught up, dropped down into a crouch, and using what the children call a duck walk, a very fast duck walk, stayed in their midst as they whipped left or right trying to get away.

Enclosed in a moving woolen womb he had no idea where they were taking him, whether it was closer to the house or further from it. He hated relying on luck, on God, on Maggie's sheep, imagining them delivering him right to her side. When, over the trampling of a hundred and sixty cloven hooves, he thought he heard the sound of children's laughter and squeals, he imagined he was their entertainment. "Come look, come look," they were yelling, and five hundred people were probably rushing into the side yard to watch Peter Metzger running with the sheep. His spirit now shredded, he lost his strength, lost his balance, and fell on his face as the herd went on.

He prayed that he wasn't near the house. He didn't dare to look up. He hoped he wasn't on the top of a rise looking like a prone statue to folly. At least the grass was mid-May high, over a foot in most places. That should hide him for now. But it would be five hours before it was dark, before he could get away. This was such a failure. It had to be Maggie's doing. For an instant he wondered if she somehow put the idea into his head. She was probably sitting under a tent on the other side of the house, rocking gently back and forth, seemingly unaware of what went on around her, her ninety-eight year old eyes barely making out the images, her ears hearing hardly any sounds. But Peter was sure she knew where he was and what he was doing, and although the smile wouldn't reach her lips, it was in her heart, and it warmed and comforted her.

◆ ◆ ◆

Over the seven hours the Fricks stayed at Thomas Bledsoe's cottage, Gretchen and Tenante observed him with concern. They watched as his gaze followed Maggie around the room, answered many of the questions he posed to her, and politely but firmly refused his offer to ride with them back to their farm to make certain they were safe.

It wasn't until they were home that Maggie realized what happened there. She had been oblivious to his stares and attention. It was only her mother's comments the day after their return that made her think back to what she saw, to what was said. Thereafter, she looked upon his attraction as a prize she had won, an honor that was bestowed. Although it made her smile and begin to see herself a little differently, she had no sense that it would ever change her life. Most women would been delighted, perhaps thrilled and giddy, that the richest man in the Shenandoah Valley was interested, but Maggie felt none of that. She hadn't yet considered getting married; she wasn't quite seventeen, thought herself to still be a child, and always assumed she would remain on the family farm forever.

Thomas Bledsoe showed up a week later. Nowhere in his demeanor was the authority and power he usually displayed. He was meek, seemed to be apologetic for being there, close to not having control over his voice or facial muscles. Tenante Frick saw him ride up, walked out the front door and met him in the lane, keeping a hard expression of disapproval, barely hearing what Thomas was saying, intent on presenting a wall between this man and his daughter as if the visitor were a villain who planned on doing her harm

Thomas would not go away. Even when he didn't receive discussion in return to his questions, shuffling his feet and shifting his weight during the long silences while he thought of something else to say, he remained in place in front of the house, glancing at the door and up at the windows, hoping she would come out, or at least show him she was watching.

He was there for a half an hour, unsure if he should ask about her and make his intentions obvious. He imagined what they thought of him, what all the Valley Germans thought of him, and although he believed it would make his quest more difficult, he would never admit it was hopeless.

He finally gave up and left with one more glance up toward the house. On the ride home he wondered what he should do, could do, never considering that he should do nothing at all. By the time he reached his cottage he had composed a letter in his mind he would write that night. It took him five hours, a half of a bottle of brandy, and about a half of a mile of pacing to finally get his thoughts down on paper.

He began the communication with a proper request to see her, doing his best to describe his emotions and intent. He came close to apologizing for being English, for all the transgressions of his race, and tried to explain away the legal difficulties caused by Thomas the Sixth Lord Fairfax and his father, pointing out that a union between himself and this German "princess" might help to heal those wounds, then thought that seemed too cold and political, did not include it in the second draft, but put it back in the third. He included a summary of his financial position and his plans for the future as if it were necessary. The next day, shortly after the workers arrived at dawn, he sent one of them off on horseback to deliver the letter to Tenante Frick.

Tenante Frick was appalled by it. He crumpled it up and tossed it away, but later became nervous without knowing why, then realized that such a proper request could not go unanswered if he wished to be thought of as polite and civilized. He strode from the barn to the house, retrieved it, tried to flatten it out, and walked into the sewing room and handed it to his wife.

Maggie was the third one to read it. She went from dismay to joy to confusion to outright fear over the next few days.

She wasn't ready for this adventure, for any adventure, saw no need to rearrange her life, but couldn't escape the elevation in stature the idea presented. It seeped into her mind when she wasn't careful, making her feel what it would be like to be a part of the aristocracy, a fairy-tale world inhabited by princes and princesses, of beauty and power, where, at least as far as she believed, she wouldn't have to defend her survival every minute of every day. It was easy to go from there to mystical and magical, to imagine the mundane indignities of a hard existence on a seventy acre family farm somehow gone. A week after the letter arrived she was able to contemplate her life as anything she wanted it to be, to see the fantasies as valid and believable enough to transform her emotions, as if her existence had already been changed.

Thomas Bledsoe came to dinner on Sunday, April 27, arriving about three o'clock on an afternoon that showed how grand spring could be. His behavior that day couldn't have been better had it been rehearsed and memorized. Over dinner he told them the story of his life, and of his ancestors' lives, relating anecdotes about minor power struggles from centuries before that made them laugh, and about major ones that awed them. He described the events that involved a great-great uncle named George Jefferys, a judge who presided over the trials of the conspirators of the Rye House Plot, the attempt to assassinate Charles II in 1683, his role in the subsequent persecution of Whigs over the next two years, and his brutal judicial defense of James II after he became king.

Thomas was careful to monitor their reactions, altering the narrative when he perceived that the details were too graphic, too disturbing to Mrs. Frick and the younger children, then looking at Tenante Frick with an expression that showed he understood they both knew the battles all men face.

It didn't take long for the word of the courtship to get around, considering Thomas' prestige and Maggie's reputation. Most of the men were outraged that he intended on picking this German flower. An assassination was planned over pitchers of beer, but never taken further. The women were enchanted, agreeing that Maggie *was* the only possible choice for the English prince, thinking it would end the aura of supremacy and subservience that characterized the relations between the two tribes.

Thomas Bledsoe and Margaret Frick were married on June 19, 1771 at the Lutheran church in Woodstock. Although only a few invitations were sent out, the news soon spread. The wedding became a festival, a street party made up of people throughout the county and from other parts of the Valley. The attendants had to fight their way through the crowd. Women and girls reached out to try to touch Maggie's dress, called out, "God bless you, Maggie." She didn't understand why they were there or what they wanted. She never really knew who they thought she was, and wouldn't for the rest of her life.

When Thomas arrived and descended from his coach, he, too, was unsure of why the crowd was there. Even though the gathering consisted mostly of women, he saw only the men who brought them there. He quickly pulled himself back inside, slumped onto the seat and ordered the driver to get away. They were four miles up the Valley Turnpike before he told the driver to stop. For an hour, while Maggie grew nervous, then cried, Thomas was thinking it all out, deciding whether this was right, acceptable and just. During that time, while the crowd outside seemed to groan in mourning that something had gone wrong, Thomas Bledsoe came to the realization that it didn't matter if it was reckless; there was something compelling him to marry Maggie Frick. He knew he had to give in to it, or risk living a life of regret and sorrow. He ordered the driver to start up, screamed at him to hurry, then trembled the whole way down the pike worrying that he was getting there too late.

Peter knew he couldn't stay in the middle of the field unless he wanted his dreams shattered, his life ruined. He raised his head slightly, and expected to see Maggie staring back at him with a grin on that old, gray, corrugated face, but there was nothing there but pasture grass. He looked around, was relieved to discover that he was in a bowl, a depression deep enough to hide him if he stayed on the ground, but not if he sat or stood. He wiggled forward ten yards to get to the lip to check where he was in the field, and saw that the sheep had carried him closer, halfway across and still hidden from the tents and the people in the back yard. So, with the grass as high as it was, unable to come up with any other plan, Peter began to crawl toward the house inch by inch.

◆ ◆ ◆

It is a pity that the art of photography wasn't sufficiently advanced so a cameraman could have captured the expression that took over Rebecca Faraday's face the second Ian Froth handed Anna a bouquet of daffodils. It was as if she had just eaten something sour and rotten — her mouth was puckered, all the muscles in her body were tense as if she were under attack.

Anna couldn't have been happier about her mother's reaction, or her grandmother's, or her stepfather's when he paused in the conversation he was having and looked over. It was as if they all thought their world was soon to change for the worse, that their army was losing the war, and the enemy was about to be among them. Anna was just sorry that Peter wasn't there to see it, but at the time he was staring out into the pasture trying to figure out a way to do just that.

Ian made a point of looking dashing. While most men appeared as if they were attending church or court in their finest great coats and top hats, Ian was dressed to be noticed. He wore a light blue, high collar shirt with a black bow tie that matched his black satin waistcoat, or vest, black/gray checked trousers and a black cotton cape that was lined with red satin.

On his head was a black riding cap that had a short brim, and a hard, moderately high crown.

Anna had settled on a forest green cotton dress, with three-quarter length sleeves trimmed in yellow lace on the arms and at the high, buttoned collar. This one was triple skirted, with the tiers separated by chocolate brown flounces. Her footwear was low heel brown boots with side gussets and laces from the insteps to the ankles. On her head was a yellow bonnet, deep enough to hide her face in profile, held on with a forest green ribbon tied under her chin.

Ian brought with him two bouquets, and after giving Anna one, and offering his respects to her mother and grandmother, and smiling through the disgusted grunt that came from her stepfather, offered his arm in a bold gesture, and led her further back into the tent where Maggie sat. A crowd of men and boys off to the side who had refused to let Anna out of their sight seemed to have suddenly lost their enthusiasm for romance like soldiers who showed up for a battle unarmed.

Ninety-eight year old Maggie sat in a high back armchair that came from inside the house. Her eyes, even with glasses, weren't strong enough to see Anna or Ian clearly. She did, of course, recognize Anna by shape and walk, but was unable to distinguish much about the man whose arm the girl held. She could tell that he did have red hair and a red beard; she frowned at the sight of that, never having gotten used to the new trend of full beards on men. Beyond that she couldn't tell if he were young or old, handsome or homely, weak or powerful, but there was something about his demeanor — he seemed free when most men were conservative and restrained by the society around them. He was almost beastly, she sensed, controlled by his own feelings, not anyone's rules. Maggie gasped in a breath as an image of six Indians stampeding toward her and her family from Liberty Creek came into her mind, but did not understand why. It induced in her a strong need to be protective. She grasped Anna's hand and pulled her closer, taking her away from Ian's side. "He seems like a nice young man," she said for about the fifth time that afternoon.

Ian looked down at this frail old woman, remembered what Mary Wainwright had said, and decided she was wrong. There was no more power left there, if there had ever been any. It was just superstition. Such were the Germans, he thought. True, she was a great woman, an Indian fighter at twelve, had married the most...

There was something about the way she was clasping Anna's hand that bothered him, pulling her to her the way she was. Her grip seemed too tight, as if she were using more strength than she should possess to keep her great-granddaughter next to her and away from him. In an instant, without looking at Maggie more closely, he felt the force of the child who galloped through the forest to rescue the ten year old girl from the Riles Run cabin. Into his mind came the legend that years later human bones were carried in by dogs or unearthed when gardens were dug.

He couldn't shake the image he now had of this woman, this killer, who would do anything to protect her great-granddaughter. He didn't know what she knew about him, but *he* was aware of what he had done, and realized there were witnesses to his acts out there, women he had been with, women he convinced were the most beautiful around, women to whom he promised his love and devotion. Once the word got around that he was courting Anna Rose Sigler they would become rejected women, scornful women, women Maggie might listen to. A few of them might even insist it was all his doing, that they were forced somehow. He knew what Maggie's punishment was for that.

Ian was only slightly aware that Anna was telling Maggie he was a blacksmith in Stony Creek. Maggie was nodding to show she understood. As deaf as Maggie was Anna had to shout; her words were heard by everyone within thirty feet, by people both inside and outside the tent. Ian sensed they were turning around and staring at them, making comments. He imagined that some admired his courage for courting the girl; others were probably amused by his foolishness. By the time Anna finished talking and this sacrament was done, so was Ian. He truly feared for his life then. He didn't say a word to her as they walked back toward the entrance to the tent, didn't glance over at Rebecca Faraday, Martha Boelt or Richard Faraday, but assumed they were enjoying his fear. He was ready to deny he ever sought the girl, ever even considered it. He was searching his mind for excuses for being there, but there was no escaping that he was there to court Anna Rose. If he wanted to be alive in a week, he would have to leave the county, maybe even the state.

Anna thought she understood what Ian was feeling, why he was so quiet. She was charmed by his sensitivity and compassion, and surprised that he too lamented that Maggie was now so old and frail, and would probably not live much longer. She had been a hero to many people, the Germans mostly, and it was nice to see that a Scotsman could admire her as well. As soon as they were clear of the crowd and she could talk to him without being overheard, she turned to him, and with sincerity in her beguiling green eyes, said "I am so glad you came. I hope you will please stay with me for the rest of the afternoon."

There was no escaping it all right, no escaping her. He closed his eyes, his head went back when he realized he couldn't leave, and that he might die soon if he stayed. When he opened them she was still there, still the most beautiful girl he had ever seen. Standing there looking at her he felt as if this is what his whole life had been designed for, this is what he always sought. It was a shame he wouldn't live long enough to enjoy it.

God was with him, Peter thought. Not only was there no one in the front yard when he reached it and stood up for the first time in an hour, the door was unlocked and the foyer was empty as well. He was almost discovered by lingering too long just inside as he surveyed what he could see of the house, and was held in place by its elegance. He had been there once, fifteen years before, two years after Anna was born. Maggie invited the Siglers, the Metzgers and others to the house for Easter dinner. Even then he wanted this to be his house, or to be able to build one just like it. He remembered how awed his father had been by the mansion, and how he seemed to worship the memory of Thomas Bledsoe, a phenomenon Peter would never forget.

With one last look around Peter slowly started up the stairs, then took them two at a time when someone opened the front door behind him. At the top Peter was in a hallway with the stairwell sitting in the middle of it. There were rooms at each of the four corners, and one room in between them for a total of eight. To his left were three doors that opened into the northside rooms. This is where the master bedroom, sitting room and nursery were located, although he wasn't aware of that. He had no need to go into any of those rooms; they looked out over the pasture he just crawled across.

Peter knew there were guests staying at the house. Maggie had grandchildren and great-grand children in Richmond and in Baltimore, in Fauquier County east of the Blue Ridge, and elsewhere in the Valley. He had to be careful not to walk in on anyone, but they probably wouldn't know who he was even if he did. He met some of them back when relations were good between the two families, but that was years ago, and he figured no one would remember who he was.

He last saw Anna in the back yard as she exited the food tent. That's where he would start. He held his breath as he took soft, quiet steps toward the door just ahead, leaned his head down to listen for sounds from inside, but heard only the murmur of the people in the backyard. He turned the knob and slowly pushed the door open, stuck just his head inside, and saw no one. On the floor next to a chest of drawers were two leather portmanteaux and a cloth valise. A red dress lay on the canopied bed, and more clothes could be seen hanging in the open wardrobe. Fortunately the curtains had been pulled away so nobody would notice if he had to move them. Peter walked to the window and kneeled on the floor.

Anna wasn't there, he saw after scanning the crowd for five minutes. From eighteen feet up only the short were hidden from view. He could see into the food tent and the one off the corner of the house, and she wasn't in either of those. Nor did he see Maggie or the Faradays. They were probably together in the third tent holding court, and keeping an eye on the gaggle of men and boys who were flocking around Anna. That's what he had to do.

Peter exited that room and went to his left to the corner room, barged in and was lucky it was empty. He glanced toward the window in the back wall and saw that the scene wasn't much different than it had been in the first room, so he went to the other window and kneeled on the floor. From there he could see into the tent in the south yard, and saw Maggie, at least some of her, as a heavyset woman leaned over and yelled something in her left ear. Closer to the entrance Rebecca Faraday and Martha Boelt comprised half a quartet that sat facing each other discussing whatever it is women discuss. Richard Faraday was one of three men who were standing, smoking pipes and probably talking about sheep, corn, or the price of land or slaves. Around the outside of the tent, sitting on logs, was Anna's "army," about twelve boys and young men. Peter knew everyone of them. "Pathetic," he whispered, realizing he had been foolish thinking she might choose somebody over him. But then she wasn't there, so these were the ones she had already rejected, and were waiting around to see if she might change her mind. It was who she was with that he had to worry about.

There were more people just below him, almost up against the wall. He would have to stick his head out the window to see them all. He knew he couldn't get away with that. He leaned forward as far as he could, looked left toward the back yard, then right, then left, but didn't see... It was just green cloth and a little bit of a chocolate brown flounce he noticed, but it was the same shade of green as Anna's dress. She was sitting down. What he saw was her skirt at the knees with what seemed to be a plate of food in her lap. Peter pressed his face so hard against the glass that his skin was deformed. He could peer with only one eye, but could now make out blond hair showing beneath a yellow bonnet, and when she turned her head to look at somebody or something to her right, that angelic face as well.

"There she is," he whispered as he leaned back so that he was sitting on his feet. Whoever she was with was hidden, and would be no matter what he did. Maybe if he went into the next room he might see better, but probably not, they would still be too close to the house. His only choice, he realized, was to go downstairs and hope he could see them from a window there. It was taking a chance, he knew, but it was torment to get this close and still not be able to find out.

This was Maggie's doing again, he thought — him having to work a little harder, take a bigger chance. The belief that she had that power frightened him, weakened him, made him cuss to drive it away. He got to his feet still holding the illusion she could somehow dominate everything in the universe, at least everything in her universe, and he wondered how he was going to get downstairs without being caught. He thought for nearly a minute trying to figure out if there was a better way. He wanted to stay in that room where he felt safe, and soon realized he had to. He returned to the window, kneeled down, pushed his face hard against the glass hoping things had changed and... "Jesus!" he swore as he scrambled to his feet. "Ian Froth? That's who she's with?" Afraid he exclaimed loud enough for everyone to hear, he took two steps back, whispered. "Has she lost her mind?" Then said as he started to pace, "This cannot be. This cannot be." He stopped, his back stiffened, he smiled. "No, this cannot be," he whispered firmly. "That is not what I saw."

He stepped to the wall next to the window and leaned his head toward the glass. The people were in much the same places they had been before, except Anna and Ian, who had been standing further out into the yard, could not be seen. Peter scanned the crowd left and right, and just inside of the tent, bent to look further back, and suddenly found himself staring straight into Maggie's eyes.

"Oh, Jesus," he swore again as he scurried backwards. "She saw me. Oh, Jesus! Oh God!" He began to pace again as he searched the room for something that might cure his panic. He glanced out the other window toward the backyard, but didn't know what he was looking for, so he turned away and paced back. Slowly, gradually, he approached the window again, making certain he didn't get too close, peering through the glass into the tent, having to stoop to get low enough to see to the back, and seeing that Maggie was still looking right at him.

He stood still and thought it out — maybe he was too far into the room to be seen; her expression hadn't changed; she didn't seem to be alerting anyone or giving orders. He calmed, but his mind wouldn't let him get closer to the window, near enough to start looking for Anna again. He began to sweat as he fought the dilemma that paralyzed him. He couldn't stay there; he couldn't get closer. Even if Maggie couldn't tell it was him, she might point and ask. If there were only a way to... Peter mindlessly walked to the wardrobe on the other side of the room and opened it. It too was filled with clothes — women's dresses, men's trousers and coats. He closed it, stepped toward the window again, but only a short way before his fear stopped him. "I have to do something," he breathed.

Like water finding the quickest way downhill, or any moving object that chooses the path of least resistance, Peter did the only thing that day that made sense to him at the time, that made the terror subside. He pulled a sky blue dress out of the wardrobe, held it up to check the size, draped it on top of his head, and pulled it down over him. He turned toward a mirror next to the window, looked himself over, and felt he was now safe. "No, wait, a bonnet," he whispered, rejecting a yellow one, choosing a green one and tying it on, then using both hands to shift it into place. Satisfied that he was as pretty as he needed to be to fool Maggie, he walked to the window, and began to search for Anna Rose.

"Hey, ain't that Peter Metzger up there wearin a dress?" For some reason Peter didn't hear the words that came out of Alvis Clapp's mouth. He was staring to the left where Anna and Ian had been a few minutes before. But the words "Peter Metzger wearing a dress," was, for any who knew him, and they all did, a contradictory phrase, a thought that turned on itself before it was done. The receiver couldn't be certain the words really fit together, so stares and attention first centered on Alvis like a vortex, then were diverted by the direction of his gaze, and the enthusiasm that took over his face like a badly needed summer rain. While Peter was looking left, everyone who had been alerted on his right was looking at him, or at what they thought was him, with the sun hitting the glass and bending back into their eyes, with the distance and the angle obscuring the sight, making them take the time to think about it all.

As the wave of news was moving right to left, Peter's gaze was going the other way, still searching for the woman he feared was on the brink of keeping his life ordinary. He caught the tide midway, didn't recognize it at first, then, realizing that those faces he was rejecting were looking up at him, began to wonder why. The germ grew quickly from slight recognition of his plight to a full scale and undeniable realization that several hundred of his neighbors were watching him standing in one of Maggie Frick's bedrooms wearing some woman's dress.

For an instant the action was frozen like a scene painted by a fine artist. Peter was looking down into the yard, straight ahead, his bonneted head bent slightly forward, his yellow moustache glowing in the midday light, hands on the window trim on either side of the upper sash. The crowd below him — men, women, a few boys and little girls stared up with their heads back at different angles, cocked in different positions, smiles, frowns, no expressions at all, but with eyes wide open, all of them.

A black man named George Johnson, a worker on the farm, was in mid-stride among them, one hand supporting a plate piled with food, the other gripping tightly a tankard of beer. In three seconds both would be on the ground. Alvis Clapp was suspended above the log, his legs just having pushed him up; his mouth agape as he started to shout again, a look of violence in his eyes, evil and unrestrained, a coyote who had cornered a lamb. Stephan looked at Alvis, coiled and ready to strike. And the others — "Anna's Army," men and boys who had spent the afternoon wishing they were somebody else, were now starting to be glad they were not Peter Metzger.

In an instant, impulses traveled from Peter's eyes to his brain to his legs, moving him back so fast that the forces that kept him balanced and upright were late. He fell to the floor, tried to get up, but didn't know how to work legs encumbered by a skirt, so all he could do was thrash around on the floor like a trout tossed to the bottom of the boat.

"That *is* Peter Metzger up there in a dress!" Alvis shouted again as he stood up and sprang forward like a mountain lion, colliding with George Johnson, making him spin like a top and drop his food and drink. Ignoring that, Alvis stood just below the window looking up, his hands on his hips, his body trembling with anticipation. When he took two steps back to get a better angle he bumped into the throng that was forming behind him like a lynch mob. Seeing there was now no one at the window, Alvis, deciding he should be their leader, shouted, "Come on, boys, we gotta find him."

"There's nobody there," some man said skeptically as a half a dozen of Anna's rejects started toward the front door.

"That wasn't Peter Metzger, was it?" A woman asked meekly as if afraid of the answer. "It was probably one of Maggie's relatives, wasn't it?"

The posse stormed into the house as if they were on a moral crusade to put the universe in order. Alvis, with Stephan right behind him, took the stairs two at a time, pulling on the banister to maintain his speed. When he reached the upstairs hallway there were only two others left; two remained just inside the front door, knowing if they did find Peter Metzger up there wearing a dress, he was going to be angry about it. Besides, this was Maggie's house. Nothing good was going to happen here.

Alvis couldn't figure out which way was what, which windows looked where. He figured he would take the doors one at a time, starting with the one that was just ahead, the first room Peter entered a half an hour before. Seeing that it looked over the backyard, he turned away, but not before peering into the open wardrobe at the clothes, fingering the dresses, glancing at the red dress on the bed and the luggage that sat on the floor.

Instead of turning left, he went to his right to the door of the room that was last used as a nursery 65 years before. Over time it had been filled with old clothes Maggie no longer wore, but wanted to keep, furniture that came from other parts of the house and stored there, and other items that were brought up and left. Alvis could barely open the door, at first thinking that someone, Peter Metzger probably, pushed on it from the other side. Figuring he found him, had won this fight, and was about to eliminate the most serious of his rivals, he put his shoulder to the wood and heaved.

The door, which had been held in place by a child's rocking chair wedged against a dresser leg, quickly gave way when the chair slid free, allowing Alvis to fly into the room unrestrained. He stumbled forward and down, smacking face first against the corner of the dresser, cracking his nose, causing blood to drip, then gush, and him to exclaim, "Oh, Gawd, by nose."

The others, unable to see Alvis after he burst into the room, heard what they thought were the first rumbles of a fight. No longer caring about revealing another's secret, they raced each other down the stairs; their shrieks and whimpers bringing people out of the back rooms. Alvis, his face and hands covered with blood, staggered like a wounded soldier down the stairs and out the door.

CHAPTER 6

"You fool," the voice hissed from somewhere in the barn. You let him get away."

Alvis slowly swivelled his head from side to side peering into the darkness. "I broke my nose, okay?" he pleaded in a shallow, nasal tone. "Ain't much I coulda done after, less I wanted ta bleed all over Maggie's house looking fer him. She woulda had me stuffed an put on the wall. What's so serious? Least now Anna thinks he was up there wearin a dress. Stop bein mean ta me. It's not like I shoulda known that was gonna happen an bin ready fer it. Peter Metzger in a dress? Where are you?"

A match scratched across a rough cut board. It crackled as it burned. An uneven yellow/blue flame jumped out and illuminated the barn with a dim, moving light. Hessie lifted the oil lantern and hung it on a nail that had been driven into a beam. "Yes, if it really was him. Maybe, just maybe, if you found him up there we could have ruined him. It would have taken Anna years to get over it. Now she doesn't know what to believe. The fact that you were the only one who saw him makes her think it wasn't true. Let's face it, Alvis, if you told her it was Wednesday, she would assume it was Thursday."

Alvis' face burned bright red. "Why?

"Because you are a weak, sniveling whiner. Fortunately, you are also conniving, have no manners and no morals, so I need you. But do not get me wrong—this alliance is for the sole purpose of keeping Anna from marrying Peter, or anyone else for that matter, for several years. Whether she eventually marries you or not, is none of my concern."

"She will."

Hessie snorted. "Yes, certainly, Alvis." Her voice became loud and defiant. It echoed off the rafters. "Alvis, the only thing you could offer Anna another man cannot — is public ridicule." Alvis turned sideways, brought his arms up as if trying to deflect the words away from him. "Oh, and by the way," Hessie said, continuing the attack, "if your friend Stephan ever grabs my breast again, I will make certain that he ends up actually *being* the girl he looks like."

"He didn't mean nothin by it," Alvis said quickly. "He was jist playin. He —

"Well, you tell him. I do not care what he does with those whore cousins of his, but around me he better watch himself."

Alvis nodded and swallowed hard. "Okay, okay. What now?"

Hessie paced a few steps away, out of the circle of light. Only a slight outline of her pale yellow dress was visible. Alvis wondered what she was thinking, what she thought they should do next. He saw no reason for her to run everything; he had plans and ideas as well, and they were as good as hers. He was the one that set the Metzgers' horses loose the night before Maggie's party. Of course, he didn't know Peter wasn't welcome at Solway Court, so maybe it was a waste of time. But then again, maybe it was the horses getting loose that somehow led to Peter ending up in Maggie's house wearing a dress. Maybe he *could* do this as well as Hessie. Maybe he didn't need her at all. True, Anna talked to Hessie, told her who she liked, so only Hessie would know who they had to stop. "Okay," he said, not realizing he was speaking out loud, "we do need her, but she's gonna hafta stop insultin me all the time."

"Are you finished?" Hessie walked back over while Alvis was muttering to himself. She gave no indication she heard what he said. "For now, we do not do anything. We do not do anything to get into Peter's way. Anna may be suspicious of you after what you did, or what she thinks you did, trying to get everyone to believe that was Peter up there. She will assume that anything bad that happens to him is your doing." Hessie stared at Alvis until he showed he not only understood, but would obey. "If you think God will get you for interfering with true love, wait until you experience Maggie's revenge.

❖ ❖ ❖

Peter spent the next several days in shock. He was careful when he went out, when he met anyone on the street, or talked to someone at the foundry. He knew what they were thinking, what they were wondering about, and any slip from him, any sense of embarrassment would make him seem guilty. He could feel people staring at him as if searching for a clue, but he was as composed as he could be under the circumstances. It helped that Alvis came down the stairs with a broken and bloody nose. It looked as if God punished him for bearing false witness. For now that was probably all that was saving him, but it wasn't enough to keep him from being scared and jumpy about something else. It was what had happened later, after everything calmed down, that unnerved him, was making him stop and ponder life several times a day. He was never sure how long he lay there under the bed in the room on the west side of the house that afternoon. It seemed like hours, and was, he realized The party was in the side yard and in the back; he couldn't really hear it, was never certain if it still went on, but at times, when he considered getting out of there, he would be startled by a voice or laughter, thought he detected the low buzz of conversation. He knew he couldn't come out of hiding while there were still people around. If he were seen in the house or near it, they would know Alvis had been right. He would have to wait until dark, until everyone had gone home and Maggie, her relatives and her servants had turned in for the night. That would cause another problem if there were guests using that room. Maybe after they went to sleep he could wiggle out from under the bed and get through the door without them hearing, without anyone hearing, without a dog being alerted and starting to bark. Who did he know who didn't have dog or two to watch out for intruders like him? He couldn't think of a soul.

So he was stuck there. Maybe forever. In a few weeks someone would wonder about the odor in the house. The servants would began to search for it. Eventually they would find Peter Metzger's decaying body under the bed in the front room. At his funeral people would know he *had* been standing in the window wearing a dress, had died in shame of it, and that is how he would be remembered forever.

It was that that made Peter finally realize he had to do something to get out of there, or his life was done. He made it inside without being observed, as far as he knew; he hoped he could leave unseen as well. Of course there was the possibility that Alvis or someone else was out there waiting for him, sitting on the floor in the upstairs hallway expecting a door to open and Peter to emerge. He thought of going out a window, but it was a long way down. The only porch was in the rear, so the only roof he could drop to was there in front of everyone in the food tent. He might, by hanging by his hands from a window sill, lessen the distance he would have to fall, and he thought about that, but hadn't yet gotten up the nerve.

It was while he was thinking about it, after the initial shock of realizing that he might be trapped had subsided, sometime after he began to believe rational thought might save the day, that the door opened. The sound seemed muted, faint, far off. The door opening hadn't let in other sounds, so there was no great blare when it happened. He somehow sensed it the way a dog might perk up at a noise nothing else can hear. His body tensed as he perceived approaching footsteps; his mind wondered where else he might hide. But the mattress skirt was never lifted, no face with wide eyes intruded into his cave. Instead, he felt the pressure of a body on the down mattress above him, heard the slats creak with the weight of one person, then another, and listened to giggles and groans, whispers and sighs.

Propriety told him he had to leave, and kept him there. It was an act he never witnessed before, not from above or below, from across a room or through a barn door, at least not an act by humans. The times he participated he never wondered what he looked like or how he sounded. He had, of course, been concerned with being alone and unwatched, which is what he wished this couple had done, whoever this couple was. He didn't care. He just hoped they finished soon so he could go back to figuring out how to salvage his life.

It could have been anyone, one of Maggie's kin, a great-grandchild and their spouse, newly-wed and enthusiastic, more than likely. Then again, it might be someone he knew. It might be a scandal that would take everyone's minds off of him, make *them* the center of attention. He hated to do this, to use them to save himself, but it was information he might need someday, might need that day. Peter knew they would be too occupied to know he was there, wouldn't detect him wiggling out from underneath, and probably wouldn't see him as he lifted his head and looked up toward the...

The dress cloth was forest green cotton. It had been removed, and dropped to the floor, so when he pushed the bed's skirt away, that was there as well. He didn't understand what it was at first, or might be. It was simply a blindfold he had to remove, a screen that was in his way. It wasn't until he had a clear sight of the bed, and saw the yellow hair cascading down the side that the possibilities shocked him like a kick to the head. He put his hands up to the sides of his face as if trying to keep the tremors from shaking him apart, then slunk back underneath, with screams of terror vibrating in his mind.

For the next half an hour Peter Metzger went through a personal revolution. Every breath, every whisper, every moan and groan that came from the bed, sounded as if it came from Anna Rose Sigler and Ian Froth. It so defined them he couldn't find any means to deny it. This innocent child, this beautiful innocent child he hoped to manipulate into being his wife, and turning over Maggie Frick's fortune to him, was laying half naked under Ian Froth just above his head. That should have been his control over her, was all he could think. If there was justice in the world, and a God in the heavens, he should have been her seducer.

Peter sobbed that evening under the bed. It wasn't a jealous cry; the thought that an intimacy he sought, an exclusive bond with a woman he desired, was another man's joy. It was the loss of his sense of power. His belief in what would get him through this life was stripped away in that half an hour. He now had to face the world without weapons or armor. Turn a latch and a door opens, swat a horse and he runs, heat ore and make iron — nothing was true anymore, or some of it was and some of it wasn't. It would take him days after that, weeks, months perhaps, to learn again what he could control and what he could not. But he would never get over the fact that he had it wrong, and might be wrong again. Every belief after that day, for the rest of his life, he would hold precariously like fine china in shaking hands.

"Didn't your cousin Melanie look nice Sunday?" Rebecca Faraday asked Anna at dinner two days after the party at Solway Court. "I think being married has made her even prettier."

"Yes, Ma'am," Anna replied without looking up. "I suppose she is."

"Are you upset that she was wearing the same color dress as you were?"

Anna shrugged. "Not really."

"Are you unhappy that she got married first? You should not be. After all, she *is* two years older than you are."

"Oh, I don't know." Anna sighed. She mindlessly stabbed at a pork chop with her fork, pushing it around her plate. She didn't bother to lift her eyes, so she didn't know that her mother, her stepfather and Hessie were all watching her.

"I was certainly surprised to see Ian Froth at the party and showing an interest in you," Richard Faraday said after more than a minute of silence. He took a gulp of beer while he waited for Anna's response. When there was none, he continued. "The rumors are that he likes harlots more than he does nice girls. Thank goodness he did not bring one of them to the party."

"Yes, thank goodness," Rebecca added instantly. "We must remember that we live in a well-ordered society that must have rules."

"Or we would be at war with each other all of the time," Richard said. "It is a pity Mr. Froth does not understand that. He seems to think that we can live like beasts in the jungle and it doesn't matter. It is a shame that—"

"I don't know why people pick on Ian Froth all of the time." Hessie clanged her knife and fork down on the plate in case her words weren't loud and desperate enough to get their attention. "Just because women like him doesn't mean he is out to ruin the world."

Richard looked at Rebecca as if asking if it was his duty as Hessie's father to correct her, or Rebecca's as a woman. He decided it was his job. "I am afraid that it is more than that. There is good evidence against the man. I shall not go into it now." He nodded at the four young boys at the end of the table. "There has been some talk about asking Mr. Froth to leave Stony Creek and the county. I am not certain why it has not been done yet, although I suspect that it is because we want to be fair about it."

"Or maybe it is because if every man that does what he does was forced to leave, there would be only women left in Shenandoah County."

"Hester!" Rebecca exclaimed.

"Young lady, you know that is not true. Most of the men in this county are fine and decent husbands and fathers, upstanding citizens."

"Like your attorney Mr. Rutherwood?" Hessie knew she shouldn't have said that. In an instant she seemed to cower before her avenger, until thirteen year old Junior spoke out with a laugh. "Or Peter Metzger wearing a dress?"

Anna's face seemed to fold back into itself. It was a reality that would diminish her if she let it exist. "That isn't true!" she yelled, trying to drive it away. "It wasn't him!"

"Mr. Miller said it was," Junior insisted brashly. "He was right there and could see the window clearly."

"Well, that is not entirely true, son," Richard said. "He was in the tent with me and Tom Schiller. I doubt that he would have been able to see. I think, when he finally got out into the yard and looked up, there was no one at the window. I am afraid we have only Alvis Clapp's word on that, and to be honest with you, I would not trust a Clapp's word on anything."

Anna nodded in agreement. She decided sometime the day before that no one actually saw Peter in the window, except perhaps Alvis, and she knew what he was like. Still, it created a dilemma. Her great joy that day came from the belief that Peter had been watching her from the woods. It might make sense that he decided he had to move closer, and the only way he could do that and not be detected was to... She knew if she believed one thing, then she had to believe the other, and she hadn't decided which she needed more.

"'O thou, my muse! guid auld Scotch-drink! Whether thro wimplin worms thou jink, or, richly brown, ream owre the brink, in glorious faem, inspire me, till I lisp an wink, to sing thy name!'

Aye, Mrs. Wainwright, that be Rabbie Burns again. Mrs. Wainwright? Mrs. Wainwright? Anna Rose, sing my name. With my wagons in the stalls an my horses in the shed?"

'Adieu! A heart-warm, fond adieu! Dear brothers of the mystic tye! Ye favored, enlighten'd few, companions of my social joy! Tho' I to foreign lands must hie.'"

CHAPTER 7

It was a dreary day for May. It was wet, but not really raining. A fog came in the night before, arm in arm with a cold front, then became heavier, so the air was little more than tiny drops of moisture that accumulated and slid from the edges of roofs, and off the leaves. The temperature would not get above 55 degrees that day; the sun would not show.

When Elias Lutz awoke at dawn, and looked through the cabin window at the unbroken mist he smiled, realizing his decision not to cut the hay the day before had been the right one. It would be lying on the ground getting ruined. Something told him not to do it. It hadn't been the presence of clouds; the day before was sunny and warm, the sunset clear. But there must have been some sign this was coming. Perhaps it was instinct that told him what to look for and what to think, like a squirrel that knows a winter will be long and hard, or birds that can tell when a storm is approaching.

Elias, who went by the nickname of Sonny, was only twenty-three years old, so it wasn't age and experience that guided him the way it did his father and grandfathers. True, he had worked on the farm as long as he could remember, and probably before that, had been through the cycle for twenty-three years, watched, been taught, learned, corrected, and scolded, but it was more than that. There were few farmers around of any age who could do what he did, could do it as well.

The Lutzs came to Shenandoah County from central Pennsylvania in 1761. His great-grandfather and great-grandmother were indentured workers on a farm there, married barely out of their teens, and purchased twenty acres on credit in a valley that would later be named Garlic Hollow, about five miles to the southwest of the town of Stony Creek. The trees they cleared from their land the first year were used to build their cabin. The rocks they pried from the fields formed the hearth, the chimney, and the first of their stone fences.

Although the soil was rich, the forests filled with game, survival was always a question. Too little rain, or too much, pests both large and tiny, exhaustion and disease conspired to make them feel that they were being driven away. Instead of depressing their spirits, making them want to hide from it all, it bent and shaped them as they attacked it head on. It was a battle they should never have believed they could win. There were no doctors to cure their ills, no pills to soften their pains, no relief from cold and heat, no escape from discomfort; it was always there. They had church and prayer, each other, a little whiskey now and then, some friends and festivals, but every dawn the struggle was there in front of them like a beast that had to be slain. It was everyday, for months and years, the same tasks, redundant and ordinary. Boredom or laziness could drive them down, or at least keep them in place. In a few years the twenty acres gave way to fifty, and the wheat and wool from that land provided a hundred acres by the time they were forty, and the three surviving children were grown.

By then the neighborhood had changed as well. The small holdings were combined by those who did it as they had, while the others went to work on large estates or moved into town, learned trades and opened shops. The market for wool and wheat improved, transportation became easier. No one earned much cash; there was enough for tools and some furnishings, cloth for clothing when that came into the stores, but food was always plentiful, and horses, cows and sheep multiplied on their own, as did the Lutzs.

Gottfried and Sarah Lutz produced Frederick, Jacob and Benjamin, and two others who died young. Frederick and Johanna Frick (Maggie's second cousin) issued Sebastian, Karl, Anna and Gottfried II, and one more. Karl married Elisabeth Meyer in 1824. Her father Elias owned three hundred acres on Painter's Run just on the other side of the hills. Sonny was born on October 15, 1828, a cold, windy, frightening night. He was the third of four, and there would still be four into their adulthood, a blessing that seemed to invigorate the family even more.

Karl and Elisabeth were given thirty acres by Elias Meyer at the time they wed, half of it fertile, sloping pasture, the rest hearty forest filled with strong hardwood and cedar. Over the years Karl would spend many sleepless nights out in the fields with a musket by his side to keep predators away from his sheep. He would broil in the summer heat to raise crops to keep them fed, and work himself to exhaustion and through agonizingly tired and stiff muscles on shearing days in May. His efforts allowed him to buy more land from his father-in-law, and from neighbors, and in turn lease some to Sonny and to his older son Charles when they were old enough to go out on their own.

It was never really greed that drove the Lutzs. They never seemed to want more land than they could work by themselves. Slaves were available for a price they could afford, but it wasn't a subject they ever discussed. It seemed to be a feeling they sought, a recognition that they were doing all they could. They had a center that came from legacy and need, and it was there they wish to dwell.

Sonny climbed out of bed that Wednesday morning making a mental list of the chores he could do that day. With cutting the hay no longer a possibility there weren't many things he was compelled to do. The corn had been planted, but it was too early to thin the plants or attack the weeds. The animals didn't need feed; they could get to water themselves. The two dairy cows, of course, had to be milked, and the eggs from the hens brought in. The henhouse always needed cleaning. It was a nasty job he usually put off, but it was something to keep him from being idle that day. But then there were fences that had to be mended — rotting rails and posts he could replace. That would suit him, he decided. The wet ground should be soft; it would be easy to pull out the old ones and dig up the ruined stubs. That should be enough to keep him busy for most of the day.

That's what he did that morning, and planned to do that afternoon, until he had the urge to finish his lunch with cookies. The only place to get cookies he really liked was Steenbergen's Store in the settlement of Painter Town, near what is now known as Hamburg. As he went to the trouble to saddle his horse, he realized how much he must have wanted those cookies, and smiled for the first time all day.

It was a short ride. He could have walked the distance in a half an hour. The trip to the east took about ten minutes. As he tied his horse to the post he nodded to a middle aged, heavy black man sitting on the bench of a wagon. His name was David, Sonny thought, and he worked for Mr. Faraday, or was owned by him. He ran into David once in a while at one mill or another, gathering places for farmers and their help. He didn't know Mr. Faraday well even though the farm was just three miles away, and Sonny would pass it on those rare occasions when he went into Stony Creek or Woodstock. The Faradays were Lutheran and Episcopalian, the Lutzs United Brethren, so he didn't see them at church. He was aware of several children in the family, and knew Mr. Faraday remarried to Maggie Frick's granddaughter five years before. Had he ever listened in on the gossip between the women at family get-togethers, he would have heard of Anna Rose, would have known of her beauty, and would not have been blindsided when he walked into the store.

She was at the counter paying for hard candy that came from Baltimore, and a peach pie Irma Steenbergen just baked. Flanking her were thirteen year old Junior and ten year old Thomas. Hessie stood a few feet away mindlessly looking over bolts of cloth while her brothers Stansbury and Fitzhugh counted their change to see if they had enough money to buy a bow and arrow set Nicholas Steenbergen had made.

The door was open, so it must have been the sound of

Sonny's boots on the porch floor that made Anna turn and look. What she saw was a hard working, prosperous, confident young man who just by his even walk and his composed carriage appeared to find no danger in the world, or none he couldn't defeat. His manner wasn't aggressive, nor was it passive. The presence of others didn't make him hesitant or defensive, didn't divert him from what he was there to do.

Perhaps it was that that made her smile at him — an quick, involuntary reaction, a demonstration of admiration perhaps, maybe just of approval or respect, unconscious and unintended, but for that instant sincere, although a minute later it would be forgotten. Sonny nodded at Stan and Fitzhugh, and at Hessie who frowned as if he were an adversary, then turned his eyes to the young woman at the counter. His glance caught her smile, and stayed there. He gazed for just a second or two, looked deeply to measure her spirit, and felt a rush of familiarity, of affinity, as if she were a traveler he just met on the road and discovered was going in the same direction and had the same destination. Swiftly, automatically, uncontrollably in him rose a deluge of drives and urges, not just of procreation, but of protection, production and provision. All the forces that challenge yet define a man surged into his consciousness and commanded his attention.

Sonny would remember speaking after that. He knew he greeted Mr. Steenbergen behind the counter, said hello to his wife who worked in a kitchen in the back of the store. He was aware when Anna and the others walked out the door, and would forever recall the sound the two horses made as the wagon started down the road. He would never forget the tightening in his stomach as he felt he did something horribly wrong by letting her get away without a word from him. It must have shown, perhaps he glanced at the door, he might have stared, since Mrs. Steenbergen smiled gently at him, a perceptive smile, as if she knew what was on his mind and in his heart, and approved.

Sonny gobbled the six cookies on the way home, devoured one after another. The crumbs bounced off his chest like a rock slide. When he reached the lane to his farm he pulled on the reins, and looked back up the road at the route he would take to the Faraday farm. He sat there for more than a minute wondering what he might do, running several scenes though his mind, his emotions driving his thoughts, his fears holding him back.

He was ruined for most of the day. Up until then it had been only Sundays and illness that kept him from his work. He did put his horse away and removed the tack, but it was in a haze as if he were in unfamiliar surroundings. He walked back out to the field where his shovel and digging bar leaned against a rail, picked one up, then the other, but couldn't remember what he was there to do. Giving up, feeling there were more important things to tend to, he put the tools down, walked back to his cabin, plopped himself down into a tattered stuffed chair, and stared at the wall.

"Hey, mister. You okay?"

"Who is he, do ya think?"

"How should I know? I ain't never seen him before. Don't be such a simp."

"He ain't dead, is he?"

"Gaaa, he's breathin, ain't he? If yer dead, ya don't breath, stupid. He's jist sleepin."

"Well, what are we gonna do?"

"HEY, MISTER! YOU OKAY?"

Sonny went back out that afternoon at about 4:30. He jolted into consciousness and practically ran out the door. There were still more than two hours of daylight left; he had work to do. He was annoyed he wasted half a day thinking about a simple encounter with a girl he didn't know. True, he did need to figure out who she was, but that took just a few minutes once he recalled that Charles Sigler left behind some children. She was tall, so she had to have some Frick in her. She must be Maggie's great-granddaughter, he came to realize. It was that idea that paralyzed him for several hours, made him sit there and process it all like a man about to cross a rickety bridge over a raging river and wondering if it were safe. He never knew what made him finally get up out of that chair and head out the door, but in a few minutes he was back at the fence, swaying a rotted post back and forth to get it loose.

"Don't know why yer botherin ta put another one in. Ten, twenty years, it'll rot too. Jist hafta replace it agin."

"Well, tell you what, Johnny, why don't you come back tomorrow and start building me in a good stone fence."

"You got the money, I kin *find* the time."

Jonathon Stubbs was forty years old, short and stocky with an untrimmed, dirty beard. He left home at the age of fifteen after his mother died, and his father began drinking full time. He crossed the Blue Ridge at Chester Gap, lived in Front Royal for a few years doing odd jobs, then kept on going west. He worked at a wool carding mill in Woodstock for a while, then wandered away from there when he felt confined by the four walls and the orders of his bosses. He did chores for Sonny's grandfather Elias Meyer, his other grandfather Fred Lutz, and anyone else in the neighborhood who was willing to pay him a few cents an hour for rough carpentry work or farm labor. He lived in a simple cabin down in the mud on a branch of Painter's Run with an Irish wife and three of his four unruly children. His oldest son Paddy recently left the county after being slashed from ear to mouth by a black girl he tried to molest on a lonely stretch of the Middle Road a year before.

Johnny was always drinking, his pants pocket usually bulged with a jar, the smell of alcohol was on him like fleas, but his demeanor never seemed to change.

"So what are you doing over here?"

"Boredom. Was gonna help yer Pa cut hay today..." Johnny motioned with both arms into the mist. "Took a nap in yer brother's barn. Thought it was too early ta head back ta Mattie."

Sonny smiled. He knew what Johnny meant. He had heard most of his monologues about his wife. Sonny jerked the post loose and pulled it out. He held it in front of him with the top just below his chin as he stared out into the field. "Tell me," he finally said after a minute of silence. "What do you know about a tall blond girl at Faraday's? Is she a Frick?"

Johnny took a step away as if this was something he didn't want to get involved in. It was only Sonny's stare that brought him back. He was shaking his head slowly as he spoke. "Anna Rose Sigler. Yeah, she's a Frick, is she ever. Saw her a few months ago at Steenbergen's. Pretty girl. Real pretty. If Mattie hadn't turned me gainst women I mighta bin real happy ta see her. Paddy used ta sneak up ta her farm jist ta try ta lay eyes on her. He's probly lucky ta still be alive an livin in Winchester. Why?"

"I saw her at the store today." Sonny's voice shook like a leaf in a strong wind.

"Oh, jeez. You poor boy. Clarisa wasn't enough ta make ya shy?"

Sonny jerked in a breath; he frowned. Clarisa Mott was his passion four years before. She was a year younger than he was, short, slender with wavy red hair. She had a smile to stop progress, a laugh that might keep the world from spinning. He spent the winter after his nineteenth birthday building the cabin two hills away from his parents' house so they would have their own place to live. It was an tortuous three months — colder than any anyone could remember, more snow than they had in years, winds that could have driven the entire county across the Blue Ridge, seemingly God-sent as if the heavens disapproved of his intentions. Sonny ignored all the discomfort, and finished the cabin in March. In April she married Forest Thomas Lee. In June they moved to Richmond.

"I am thinking about adding onto the cabin this summer. Or maybe building a real house. What do you think?"

Johnny smiled as his head jerked to the side. "Jeez, you got it bad. This summer, huh? You ain't got enough ta do?"

"And I want to get more land. Another hundred acres, or so. And hire some help."

"You really need ta do all that?

"Yes. I spent the day thinking. We do fine, have all these years. We make enough money, have kids, raise them, but it is just, sort of, sort of ordinary, common. We could be doing better. A lot better."

"Yeah, ya could. Always thought so. As smart as you Lutzs are, ya coulda owned all the land round here an had a buncha people workin fer ya, steada doin it yerselves."

Sonny let out a quick laugh; he looked away. "Yeah, well, I do not know what we would do if we didn't work, but yes, there is no reason why we cannot be as considerable as anyone."

"You doin all this causa her?"

Sonny tapped the ground with the rotted end of the post, looking down at the thump it made. "No, I don't know. I just saw her today. I did not even say 'hi'" He brought his head back up. "It just made me realize, I guess, just how far we are from... I don't know. No Lutz has ever been to school for more than three years. I do not think anyone in the family has gone further away from here than Winchester. We could be doing a whole lot better compared to the rest."

"Yeah, ya could. Shoot, there ain't a more commendable family in the county. You all are hard workin, righteous. Far as makin more money — she's got plenty. Guess she's gonna git some of Maggie's when she dies, an that could be any day now from what I hear."

The words slammed into Sonny so hard his head tilted back. "I couldn't live off *her* money," he protested, "a woman's money. That is not right."

Johnny had to walk away from that notion. "Jeez, boy," he yelled, spinning around, "that's every man's dream — a rich, beautiful girl. Where the hell were you brought up?"

◆ ◆ ◆

The groan was barely audible through the closed door, but it got Crouse Stubbs to put down his Bible and get up out of his chair. Bad knees kept him from moving quickly; his girth made him rock from side to side. He stopped at the door, put his ear up against the wood. The groan came again, accompanied by muttering he couldn't understand. He turned the latch and pushed his way into the room.

Ian Froth wasn't aware that he wasn't alone. He was lying on his belly with his arms up at his head. The queasiness in his stomach made what he could see of the room spin so fast he couldn't recognize images. He thought he was back in his shop in Stony Creek, and the pounding in his head came from his hammer on the anvil. The muttering that Crouse heard was Ian telling himself to stop.

"You're awake."

The sound of another voice made Ian shudder, wonder where he was. The words came from an avenger. He rolled over instantly to defend himself. "What?" he asked, realizing his mind wasn't working as it should. "What?" he repeated, feeling so weak that he knew he had to obey, but didn't know what he should do. He saw a short, heavyset man about sixty years old with shoulder length gray hair and a gray beard that reached his chest. He wondered if that was what Jehovah looked like.

"Glad ta see yer still with us. Been that drunk myself, fore I found the Lord. Weren't sure you was gonna make it, but I guess God wanted ta keep ya alive fer some divine purpose."

"Drunk? Alave?"

"My grandsons found ya lyin by the road this morning. You was so far back in the weeds that people probably rode on by without seein ya. The boys was throwin rocks at squirrels an hit ya. Ya gotta little bit of a bump on yer head there. I am very sorry for that ta have happened, but they's jist kids. Oh, an yer wagon an yer horses, we found them, too. They was bout a mile down the road. Seems like all yer stuff is still there. You're a blacksmith, are ya? Where ya from?"

Did a herd of cattle just stampede through the room? Maybe if he lay very, very still it will all go away.

"She must have been a real purty girl for ya ta go an do that ta yerself, is what I'm thinkin."

"Anna Rose." Ian wondered who said that. "Sigler."

"German girl, huh. I'm part German myself. My pappy's side. My great-grandfather was one of those Germans they brought in ta work down in Fauquier. Hard workin people, the Germans. But I know how ya feel. Ta my way a thinkin there ain't nothin worse than losin a woman. My Adele left this world, oh, I guess 25 years ago, or so. I was like you, jist tryin ta git over the heartbreak of it any way I could. Then my boy left. Jist went out the door. Guess I was a little mean back then. Might have even hit him a time or two. Oh, Lord, forgive me my tresspasses." Tears rolled slowly down Crouse's cheeks. "But I recovered with the help of the word and the love of our God in heaven. An ya know what I think, I think He delivered you here ta me sos I kin save ya. That's what I think."

CHAPTER 8

"I am not taking any chances," Hessie spit out.

"She didn't say anything?" Alvis kicked a small rock into Stony Creek. He looked up toward the road where David sat on the wagon. "What's he thinkin, starin at us like that?"

Hessie glanced over. "He doesn't care. I paid him a quarter of a dollar. He does what he is told, same as you. No, she did not say anything all the way home, and that has me worried. The way he walked into the store, I thought *I* might want to marry him."

"Hey, my way of thinkin, I don't know what we can do, if ya wanna git truthful bout it. We'd hafta take on the Lutzs, an the Meyers, too. That's two tough clans." Alvis scratched the scab on his nose. "Might as well jist shoot myself right now."

"We don't have to take them on. We just have to keep her confused and stupid, unable to make up her mind until we can figure out how to get rid of Sonny. And I'm still a little concerned about Peter."

"With what happened at the party --- ain't that enough?"

"Like I said, I am not taking any chances. If we get confident and lazy I am going to end up married in a year, and you will lose the delusion that Anna will ever have any thing to do with you."

"What does 'delusion' mean?"

Hessie shook her head slowly from side to side as if trying to dry her hair. "It means pretend, Alvis. Make believe. Something you want to be true, but will never be."

Alvis gasped in a breath, then let it go with a puff. He

seemed to take several steps, but remained in place where he stood. "I don't know why ya hafta be so mean ta me all the time," he pleaded. "I thought we was friends."

Hessie's frown was hard, but her icy eyes softened, her shoulders slumped. As she made a quarter turn away she ran her hands through her hair. "That is what I am trying to avoid," she whispered with her eyes opening wide as if the thought terrified her. "I'm sorry," she said, turning to face him, smiling at him, trying to look sincere. "I will try to keep things like that to myself. How does that sound?"

Alvis stared at her still annoyed.

Hessie ignored that. "You do know that Ian has disappeared," she said, "and without him we are doomed."

"Disappeared? Whatta ya mean?"

"I mean, his wagon and horses are gone, and so are his clothes, his books and most of his tools. His landlord Mr. Rittenhouse said he did not tell him anything. He — "

"How do ya know all this?"

"That is not your concern. What *is* your concern is finding him and getting him back here. I am pretty certain he is not in the county. He could be anywhere else. I cannot go riding around looking for him by myself, and my father is not going to let David drive me every day."

Alvis put his hands up to his shoulders. His head shook in short, quick tremors as his mouth formed words that made no sound.

"Very eloquent, Alvis. What is it that you are trying to say?

"How the hell am I supposed ta find him?" Alvis shouted. "That's what I'm tryin ta say. He could be anywhere. He coulda gone in four directions from here. He— "

"Well, he probably did not go west. There is nothing but mountains there. He might have gone up to Winchester, or down to Harrisonburg or Staunton. He is a blacksmith, he has to make a living."

"Why did he leave, do ya think?"

Hessie showed she didn't want to be bothered with questions that didn't matter, then realized that perhaps this one did. She thought about it for a few seconds. "I, uh, am not sure," she whispered as if talking to herself. "I wonder if there are any women missing from town, any wives who left their husbands, or daughters who have run away." She stopped to think again. "I need to talk to Edina. In the meantime, ride up to Winchester. Don't bother stopping in Woodstock or Strasburg. I know he is not there. He probably could not have opened his own shop, so he would be working for someone else. Just ask around."

"Ya want me ta ride all the way ta Winchester on the slight chance that he's there?"

"My God, Alvis, most men would do anything for a girl like that. Wars have been fought for less. Men would ride through rain and snow and the dark of night for the woman they love, and I cannot get you to go to Winchester."

The carriage moved down the lane tossing gravel in its wake. A brown-white-tan beagle ran from the southside yard barking furiously at it, followed by a smaller black dog which added to the clamor. As the carriage turned to the front of the house, and stopped, the two remained ten feet away still protesting the intrusion.

"Marble," Anna sang out as she swung down to the ground, "come here, girl." She bent over and slapped her knees. "Come here, Kip," she called out slowly in a husky voice. The dogs quieted and sprang toward her as she crouched. Marble shoved her face into Anna's and began licking her cheeks. Kip leaped off of the ground trying to get close. Anna reached down, cradled him with one arm and brought him toward the side of her head. "Oh, stop squirming," she insisted.

"They sure love you," Rebecca said, stepping from the carriage.

"They're good dogs," Anna replied as she stood. Kip still

lapped at her face. Marble wagged her tail and wiggled.

"I do not know why Momma does not get some real dogs," Martha said, taking Rebecca's hand and cautiously getting down. "After what happened in Tom's Brook last week she should consider getting dogs who would protect her. Who would be afraid of those little things?"

"Oh, they're sweet," Anna said, bending to put Kip on the ground. He leaped toward her several times without touching the skirt of her dress. "Why would Granna need mean dogs?" she said with a laugh in her voice. "She — "

"Dear, we have told you not to say things like that," Rebecca said forcibly. Martha turned away and was walking toward the door, but it was apparent her back stiffened. "She does not have mystical power; she is not a witch. She is just an elderly woman and should be treated that way. Please try to remember that."

Anna blushed the way she usually did when she was scolded. "Yes, ma'am," she replied. "Oh, you two," she said turning back to the dogs.

The door opened before the three reached it. A young servant girl named Emily with curly red hair stood in the foyer holding onto the latch.

"You do not need a door knocker the way those two bark," Rebecca said as she entered.

"Yes, ma'am," Emily replied.

"How is she today?" Martha whispered as Emily closed the door.

Emily glanced toward the open doorway of parlor to her left. "She's had a very good morning, ma'am. She got up early, said her prayers, an ate a big breakfast. She's in here." Emily walked to the parlor entry and put her left hand out.

Maggie was sitting on the sofa wearing a dark gray dress. Her long white hair was tied in a bun on the back of her head. On her lap and covering her legs was a green blanket even though the outside temperature had already reached seventy degrees. In her palsied hands she held a small, red-bound book a few inches from her face, peering at the pages through thick glasses. She didn't hear the sound of the footsteps as the three walked into the room. It was only Martha moving into her line of sight that made her realize they were there.

"Oh, you think it is okay to sneak up on an old lady, do you?" There was only a trace of a German accent in Maggie's voice, which was high and weak. She seemed to be forcing the sounds out, which were nearly screeches. Her ears were so poor that she could barely hear herself speak, so many of the words were slightly mispronounced. "You could have scared me right into an early grave."

"I am sorry, Momma," Martha shouted, not smiling at the joke. She leaned down and kissed her mother on the cheek with a hand on her shoulder, as did Rebecca. When Anna approached, Maggie took her glasses off and put the book down on the cushion. She placed both hands on Anna's side as her great-granddaughter bent to kiss her. "Darling, you look as pretty as ever." Maggie leaned back, picked up another pair of glasses off of the sofa, put them on and looked at the three of them one at a time as they scooted armchairs over closer to her. "What are you doing here? It isn't Sunday again so soon, is it?"

"Yes, Momma, it is." Martha had a severe expression on her face as if her mother said something shocking. Martha was the only one of Maggie's children who wasn't taller than average. Everyone thought it was this deficiency that caused her to take everything so seriously. She would turn 67 that year, had lived with the Siglers since Daniel Boelt died in 1838 at the age of fifty-seven. She had three other children: a son George who lived in Baltimore, another daughter named Sarah, and ...

"Alfred came to see me." Maggie said. She had trouble keeping her head erect, so by the end of the sentence she spoke with her face aimed toward the floor ten feet in front of her. "It wasn't last week, I don't think. That is the problem with me never doing anything. Every day seems the same. It must have been the week before." She nodded in agreement with herself.

"Alfred did?" Martha seemed agitated. "I wish he had —"

"What, come to see you?"

"Yes." Martha and Rebecca said in unison.

Maggie looked at Rebecca with accusation in her eyes. She turned back to Martha. "You know how he feels about slavery. *Everyone* knows how he feels about slavery. It is a wonder he has not been arrested for it yet."

"He could have sent word that he was going to be here," Martha said. "He did not have to come to the farm. I would have ridden over."

"What?"

"I said I could have ridden over to see him if I had known he was going to be here."

Maggie shook her head slowly. "I am afraid he has gotten worse. He is being harassed, is that the word, yes, I think, by some of the people in Martinsburg. It has affected him." Maggie's head shook with short, quick tremors. "It is not a, a feud between gentlemen, he said. 'No longer a feud between gentlemen,' is how he put it. He spoke of war, of violence someday."

"Alfred?" Martha exclaimed. "He was such a gentle boy."

"Oh, my," Rebecca muttered.

"I think Alfred now sees you two as the enemy. When I mentioned you he simply frowned and turned away as if he did not even want to hear of you." Maggie's chin dropped down to her chest as if speaking the two sentences exhausted her.

"My own son." Martha's eyes closed. She leaned back, then turned away.

"Is he all right?" Rebecca asked. "His mind..."

"What?"

"His mind. Is he all right?" Rebecca put a hand to her head.

"I cannot tell, dear. He is certainly noble to believe in what he does, and want to do something about it, but I am not certain it is a fight he can win. He has become Don Quixote, I think."

Martha and Rebecca semed confused. Maggie looked at Anna and smiled. Anna smiled back.

"Are Polly and the children all right?" Rebecca asked.

Maggie swallowed before she spoke. Her voice was even weaker. "They have gone to Philadelphia to her father's house."

"Do you think they had to?" Rebecca asked.

"Does he still have the church?" Martha said before Maggie could answer the first question.

Maggie sat in silence as if she didn't hear either one. Rebecca was about to ask again when Maggie brought her head up and said, "He seemed distraught, but would not tell me why exactly."

"Why did he come to see you, do you think? He is not having financial difficulties, is he?"

"I do not know why he came exactly. To talk, I suppose."

"He came to see you for strength, Granna," Anna said. "He —"

"What, dear?"

"I said he came to see you for your strength. He is... He needed to be reminded how, uh, how strong you are. We all need that."

Maggie just stared at Anna, causing Anna to shift in her chair. Slowly a smile crept onto Maggie's face, a youthful smile, as if her mind had gone back sixty years and it transformed her. "Do you know why your middle name is Rose, dear?"

"Yes, ma'am. You told me before. It was because when I was born I was as red as a rose."

Maggie nodded. She continued to stare at Anna, who became more comfortable under her gaze. She smiled at her great-grandmother as if they were sharing a secret. "Are you in love?" Maggie asked.

If Anna hadn't been aware her mother and grandmother were looking at her before, she was now. The question didn't surprise or shock her. Because of her affection for an enemy of the family she had prepared herself for something like this. Her response was direct, steady, and quick. "No, ma'am, but I hope to be someday."

Maggie checked with a look at the other two to determine if Anna was telling the truth. "Will you have to be in love to be married?"

That question did surprise Anna. "Of course," she blurted out before she realized it. Then, thinking her reaction was rude, said, "I mean, yes, ma'am, I would imagine I would need to be."

"Were you in love with Charles when you married him, Rebecca?"

"Yes, yes, I was. I was very much in love with him."

"And you and Daniel?"

Martha hesitated before she spoke, which revealed more than her answer would. "Yes, I think I was."

"Why are you asking, Granna?" Rebecca said.

Maggie dismissed the question by turning away in silence. They were used to her pauses, even though every time she became thoughtful and silent they feared she was experiencing some physical difficulty and wondered if they should help.

"You were in love with Mr. Bledsoe when you married him, weren't you, Granna?" Anna finally said. "You told me that you were." Anna had a strained expression on her face as if the answer would mean a great deal to her.

"No, what I told you was that I *loved* Thomas. I do not recall telling you that I was in love with him when we were married. Of course, that was a few years ago, and my mind is not as good as it was. I am sorry if I misled you."

"Momma, you never told me this. You did not love Father when you married him?"

Maggie shook her head several times in silence as she looked at the floor. "By the time you were born we had been married for quite a few years."

"Twelve years, Momma."

"Twelve years, if you say so. Yes, I loved him then, and had for a while. But my marriage was arranged. I —"

"Arranged? You never told me this."

"Oh, my goodness, dear, of course it was arranged." Maggie's formed her right hand into a fist. She brought it down on the sofa arm several times as she spoke. "It was arranged by God, by the heavens. It had to be, don't you see? It was for the well-being of everyone, the Germans, the English, everyone, myself included. I was able to go from a hard, hard life on a small farm to this. Think about how much better my children's lives have been because of it. It did not matter if I loved him. He was a nice man, thoughtful and kind, at least to me. That was all I needed."

"How could you marry a man you didn't love?" Rebecca asked. "How could you...?"

"Oh, my dear, it was not awful. It could have been worse, much worse. In some cultures a girl is sold to her husband. She has no say in the matter. At least I could have objected. There are places in Africa where girls are dragged away by members of another tribe, never to see their families again. Barbaric. Aren't you glad that you live in 19th century America where a girl is allowed to fall in love?" she said, looking at Anna.

"Yes, ma'am."

"Love. The way it is for you young people today is not something I understand, but I am happy you have that freedom."

"Weren't you in love with Mr. Wirtz?" Martha asked.

Maggie smiled. "Oh, I had a special fondness for Peter, of course, a gentle, sensitive man like that. But I am not sure it was a real love, not the way young people fall in love today. It was not a physical..." She glanced at Anna who was starting to blush. It kept her from saying what was in her mind. "It is risky, isn't it, dear?"

"Yes, ma'am."

"There is a chance of rejection, of heartbreak. You reveal yourself, your true self, to another person, and they might renounce you. They could destroy all the beliefs you have about yourself. It would be humiliating, I would think."

"Yes, ma'am."

"And of course, there is the possibility you could choose the wrong one and have only yourself to blame."

"Yes, ma'am."

"We probably should have sold you to the Metzgers back when we had a chance. It would have been so much simpler."

All of the muscles in Anna's face instantly lost their tone. She wondered how much Maggie knew, if she could read her mind somehow. Maggie didn't have to. Even with her failing eyes she could tell what Anna was feeling. She didn't contemplate what she should say next, or how she should phrase it to avoid hurting Anna's feelings. She sensed there was a danger there. It was her intent to drive it away as quickly and as forcefully as possible. "I guess you have heard the talk about young Peter being up in one of the bedrooms wearing a dress, watching the party."

"Yes, ma'am, but I do not think that it is true. That was just a boy playing a prank on everyone, I think."

"Oh, but it *was* true. When Gayla returned to her room later that day she found one of her dresses lying on the floor, along with a bonnet."

"Well, that does not mean Peter was there." Anna knew that she was giving it away by being defiant, but she was starting to drown, and grasping at anything that would save her.

"It was a blue dress and a green bonnet, dear. Only a man would wear those two together."

"Maybe Alvis Clapp put them there. He was the one, the only one who saw him."

"Anna, why are you defending him?" Her mother's voice had the tone of an interrogator.

Anna's whole body seemed to be shaking as if she were being blown by a strong wind. "I, uh," she said in a voice that trembled. "I just do not think…" She couldn't finish the sentence. She drooped back into the chair and stared off to the side hoping it would all go away. It didn't.

"Do you know that he crawled across the pasture on his belly to get to the house?"

Rebecca wanted to add, "Like the snake that he is," but kept quiet, thinking Anna would now realize it was Peter up there, and her affection for him would quickly dwindle. It had the opposite effect.

"He did? He did that for me?" she said, suddenly revived,

sitting up straight, her face beaming. No longer fearing exposure, she let all of her emotions show.

"Anna, have you forgotten what his father tried to do?"

Anna had never defied her mother before, at least never openly. She never had any reason to. Up until then everything had been fine. But the vision she had of her future was beginning to crumble. It had been fragile when she arrived there that day, had been for the week before. It was taking a great amount of imagination to hold it together, as it had to form it in the first place. She hadn't yet begun to understand how much of the fantasy she constructed to suit her needs, and how little was based on truth, that Peter Metzger was just an image, an outline she filled in.

Anna feelings for Peter were formed years before; she was ten or eleven, she couldn't remember. He had just returned from Charlottesville when the Metzgers came to dinner. She watched and listened as he talked to her father and mother about his experiences there, showing off his grasp of Latin and Greek, describing the great men he met. He was a brash, obnoxious boy before he left; he was a sophisticated gentleman on his return. It was as if he brought back the entire outside world with him to Shenandoah County. She imagined his knowledge was boundless, his mastery of the universe unmatched.

But it was only after her father died that she began to fashion a future that included Peter, that had *him* as her protector and provider. It was *his* strong arms she felt around her. The aroma of iron, sulphur and limestone came from *his* clothes. She knew, at the ages of twelve, thirteen, fourteen that that existence was far off and only vaguely possible, but it sustained her, made her feel that somehow her life would get better, or at least, never be worse.

During the time between her father's funeral and Maggie's 98th birthday party, Anna saw Peter about a dozen times, usually from a distance, on the streets of town as she rode by in a carriage, or on the road on Sundays when the Metzgers were heading into Stony Creek for church, and the Faradays were going to Woodstock. If she felt her mother wasn't watching, or if she wasn't with her, she would turn her head and stare until he was out of sight. Thereafter, for a day or two her heart would race, her mind would rush with thoughts of him, of them. She would imagine conversations they would have, repeating them over and over, changing them now and then, but never doubting it would someday be that way.

Only once did she actually speak to him. In October of '51 the Faradays had ridden into Stony Creek to shop. The six children went off on their own, wandering down the sidewalk looking in store windows, pointing things out, wondering what their few pennies would buy. Peter came out the hardware store carrying a pane of window glass wrapped in brown paper. He turned left into the midst of them before he realized who they were. He was just inches away from Anna when he recognized her. It had been almost five years since the dispute over the sale of her father's interest in the foundry had been settled by Maggie's visit; his guilt was buried deeply and almost forgotten. He couldn't control his smile; she beamed at him with emerald-like eyes. His right hand went to her left shoulder and grasped it. In her dreams his next movement would have been him leaning his head in and kissing her, but he said only, " Good to see you again, Anna," and nothing more.

"Yes," she managed to say before he continued up the sidewalk and was gone.

Anna was despondent for the rest of the day, blaming herself for not saying more, for not doing *something.* She had to work hard that evening to put her vision back together, running the encounter through her mind again and again, seeing things differently, putting an expression on his face that wasn't there before, an inflection in his voice she just then heard. By late the next morning the scene was redrawn like an artist unsatisfied with a work and making it perfect, and she could go on with her life as she had planned.

In April he was there when she came out of school, across the street talking to some other young men. She saw him before he noticed her. She watched as his eyes scanned the parade of girls going toward waiting carriages and wagons, or heading up the street into town. He had come for her, she decided. If not that day, then someday soon.

"Do you know that he asked my attorney about my will?"

"What?" Anna heard the question and understood it, but felt an urgent need to deflect it away from her.

"Young Peter tried to get Charles Miller drunk so he could find out who I was was leaving my money to. I would imagine it was a hard task, as much of my brandy as Charles drinks when he is here."

"Oh." Anna knew there was something there that was upsetting her, but she hadn't yet figured out what it was. The conversation was moving too fast for her. She felt as if she were on a runaway horse that threatened to throw her off, and the scenery was blurred. She wanted to slow it down to a walk, to look at it all for a while, to control it, bend it and shape it so it would come out to suit her, but her mother wanted to keep it going.

"Why would he do that, Granna?" Rebecca asked even though she knew the answer. "What good would that do him?"

Anna again became the center of attention. She was aware the question was directed at her, but had several sentences she had to run through her mind before she could understand what was being discussed.

"Don't you see, dear?" she thought she heard her mother say. The question struck her like an electric shock. Her body jolted, then slumped. The realization came on gradually like storm clouds approaching from the west. When she finally understood, and could find no means to deny the truth, there came the first tears of what would be several days of a cleansing rain.

CHAPTER 9

"Are you sure ya want me ta go through with this?" Johnny asked as he rested the pick on his shoulder the way a soldier would carry a rifle. "I swing this thing down an start diggin, there's no turnin back."

Sonny's face jumped into a grin. "Yes, unless we take a shovel and fill in the hole. Let's get this started. I want to finish digging the footing tonight."

"Tonight?" Johnny looked at the string Sonny had run to mark off where he wanted the foundation. He shook his head slowly to make a point. "Gonna be dark in a coupla hours. Hope you kin dig fast."

Sonny swung the pick down without answering. He pushed on the handle to lift up the sod. "I'll go get us a lantern when we need it. How does that sound?"

"Okay, if you say so." Johnny started breaking up the ground as well. Not as strong as Sonny, the blade did not penetrate as far, so it took him two swings to accomplish the same thing. "What I gotta do jist ta stay away from Mattie," he muttered. The blade clanged when he hit a rock. He turned the head of the pick over and probed the ground with the point of it until he found the edges. It took him a few minutes to clear the dirt away and lift it out. He tossed it to the side. "Guess we're gonna need a few of those for the foundation, ain't we?"

"And the walls. The whole house is going to be stone. The best houses are stone."

"You know anything bout laying stone?"

"I have seen it done. It should not be that hard."

"Okay, guess we got that part taken care of. So you figured how you're gonna git ta see her? Jist gonna ride up an knock on their front door?"

The questions stopped Sonny. He rested the head of the pick on the ground and leaned on it. "I have not really thought that far ahead."

"Maybe the word will git around that yer building this nice big house jist ta impress her, an she'll come down ta see you."

Sonny frowned. He lifted the pick high and swung it down hard, then again. "For one thing I am not doing this to impress her. I am doing it because I need something other than that little cabin to live in. And as far as seeing her goes — like I said I have not thought that far ahead." It was only a few minutes before Sonny stopped again with something on his mind. He waited until Johnny finished lifting another rock out of the ground before he asked, "Have you heard of anyone else courting her? Other than Paddy, of course."

Johnny walked over and picked up the shovel that was laying on the ground. He dug out the loose dirt and flung it to the side. "How deep you want this thing?"

"Um, about two feet. Do not worry too much about that now. Just get it close. We will level it off later."

"Okay." Johnny continued to shovel dirt.

"Do you want to tell me why you did not answer my question?"

Johnny shrugged. Sonny was facing the other way and did not see it. He stopped working and turned around. Johnny had his back to him and was shoveling dirt like a tornado.

"Who *is* he? What don't you want to tell me. Is she is practically married already, or something?"

Johnny pulled the shovel out of the trench. He turned around with a look of resignation on his face. He rested both hands on the top of the handle and stared sternly at Sonny as if giving him one last chance to end the discussion. Sonny just stared back. "Okay, you asked," Johnny muttered off to the side.

"Jist goin by what I saw at the party —"

"The party? Maggie's birthday party? You went to that?"

"Free food an good German beer. Woulda crawled on my hands an knees ta git there."

"Yeah, okay. Who was Anna with?"

Johnny took a deep breath as he wondered if this was something Sonny really needed to know. It might make him end this foolishness. He didn't need the work that badly, and knew as long as Sonny was caught up in this whirlwind, he would be brought along as well. His life would be a whole lot easier if Sonny lowered his sights some, so if this scared him away from her that would be fine. "Ian Froth."

"Who?"

"Ian Froth."

"Who is he?"

"Blacksmith in Stony Creek."

"Red-headed boy?"

"Yeah, that's him."

"So, is he her beau? Could you tell?"

"Uh, I dunno." Sonny was taking this better than he thought he would. "I was in the food tent most the time. They came in an got some food, sorta stood round outside fer a while, then walked away. Fer some reason I didn't think ta follow em ta see what they was up to."

"You are older and you get around more — does that make it serious? I mean, is that telling everybody that they are a couple, and all the rest of us have to stay away?"

Johnny face was taken over by a wide grin. He looked as if he were going to break out in laughter at any moment. "I tell ya, you Lutzs got more rules than anyone I know." His voice became louder and more forceful. The words sounded like a command. "It don't hafta mean nothin if ya don't want it to."

Sonny nodded to show that he agreed with that. "So what is he like? Ian Froth. I don't remember hearing much about him."

"Well." The word was so drawn out that it seemed to last almost a minute.

"What?"

"The boy's supposed ta have some trouble keepin his sword in the sheath, his horse in the barn, that sorta thing."

Sonny's brow furrowed as he pondered what that meant. When he understood, it turned him a quarter of the way around. "Jeez. Is it true? A lot of rumors are not, not factual, you know."

"Things like that ain't none of my business, but where's the smoke there's usually somebody burnin green wood, an purty much what everybody says is that Ian Froth *likes* green wood."

"So you think there is somethin going on there, between them?" Sonny looked as if he were expecting bad news. "I mean, would she like a man like that?"

"Not sure. This is Maggie's great-granddaughter, so she could purty much do as she pleases. I mean, it's not like they was sneakin round. It *was* out in the open. If they was doin somethin they should be ashamed of... My way of thinkin, ya don't draw attention ta yerself if ya don't want people ta know what yer up to. Ya see what I'm sayin?"

Sonny nodded.

"Guess that sorta thing matters to ya, don't it."

"Yeah, it means a lot to about every man, doesn't it? How about Mattie? Would it bother you if she'd been with some boy before you were married?"

Johnny snorted. The question seemed to have made him lose interest in continuing the conversation. His mind went to other things. Sonny noticed and went back to digging. He was surprised when Johnny spoke. "I probably shouldn't be tellin ya this, but, uh, I think Mattie had a little bit of experience in that regard fore I married her. I don't think she liked it much. She don't like it much when I'm with her, ya know. Sorta wonder how we got four kids."

Sonny nodded with short, quick thrusts of his chin. He turned to go back to the digging.

"Sorry. That was probly more than ya wanted ta know."

They worked in silence for nearly an hour. Since they

started just after supper, it was now approaching dusk. The dull light seemed to make the timbre of the tools louder and more precise. The clangs, when they hit rocks, echoed off of the hills, making it sound as if there were gangs of men working all around them, as if there were others doing what they were doing, and for the same purpose. The idea of competition made Sonny swing the pick harder and faster, as if he was trying to outwork his own shadow. He would grimace when the blade did not hit the exact spot or when clumps of dirt would fall from the shovel. He knew he could do better, go faster, be more efficient. He began to believe that any error was a sign of impending failure, defeat due to his own flaws, and knew it would not only mean he would never get Anna Rose, but he might stop being a Lutz as well.

"Ya know," Johnny finally said, coming up with an excuse to rest his arms and slow Sonny down a little bit. "If ya want, I'll ask around, see what I kin find out bout her an Ian Froth. Hate ta put my nose in other people's business, but if ya really think that ya wanna marry this girl..."

"You would do that for me?"

"Yeah, well, ta my way of thinkin, you marryin Anna Rose Sigler would make us all a little more highly thought of."

Sonny smiled. He swung the pick down hard, then again. "Nah," he said as he pried up the dirt. "I think, what it is, is that we have to get a little more highly thought of first."

CHAPTER 10

The blast of thunder made the walls shake and the windows rattle. Anna had never heard it so close. Her room was on the back of the house, facing east toward the Massanuttens, so she didn't see the storm approaching from the west. It wouldn't have mattered if she had. She was lying on her bed at the time, her face turned away from the window, her arms wrapped tightly around her as if she were trying to hold herself together. It was about six o'clock in the evening on June 2, a Wednesday, a week and a half after she, her mother and grandmother were at Maggie's. On the floor beside the bed was a book of poems by written by Elizabeth Barrett Browning that was published two years before. The cover was speckled with several days of dust.

That book was a gift from her mother the previous Christmas. For a week afterwards she did nothing but read it, and read from it, going up the hall into Hessie's room, or down the stairs to recite to her mother. The poems which she appreciated and understood as she would letters from a friend, poems that showed love *was* as exciting, captivating and acceptable as she imagined, only haunted her now as if they were written for other people, and she was left standing alone off to the side and could only observe their joy.

So Anna spent the last ten days wondering what was wrong with her, reviewing her life as people do at times like that, searching for some clue that would have predicted this sorrow. She couldn't figure out why she felt unworthy of happiness. She had done nothing extraordinarily wrong, there was no considerable sin in her past, no transgression she felt she should be punished for, at least none by her. At times there was a rage inside of her that seemed to be aimed at her great-grandmother, but something, morality perhaps, stopped her from directing her wrath toward frail Maggie. She really wanted to blame her mother for it all, but had yet to figure out how or why.

Like all addicts Anna found it impossible to live without her narcotic at first, so for a few days after they were at Maggie's she convinced herself the others were wrong, perhaps even lying, that Peter really did care for her, deeply and sincerely, and her life would be as she dreamed. She could sustain that notion for most of the day, keeping away the gloom the truth created, but with it came a feeling of alienation from her family, from Maggie, leaving her lonely and untethered, and she couldn't bear that either. So each day her fantasy dimmed a little more; the duration it was in her mind and heart lessened. She began to share the resentment of Peter the rest of her family held. At times it was even greater than theirs, creating a feeling of betrayal, as if by not living up to her view of him he deliberately misled her. By the Monday of that week her affection for Peter was nearly gone, her plans for them to be together erased from her consciousness. But there was nothing to replace it, no joyful look ahead at the future, no expectations of a wondrous life, no dreams at all, which is why she was curled up on her bed and miserable.

A few miles to the north Alvis was thinking this was just what he needed — another sign God hated him. He had no doubt the storm he heard coming his way was intended soley to do him harm. Thus was his life. If he wasn't being beaten on by one thing or another, he was lost in worry about what was approaching. But this took him by surprise. Between dreaming about Anna Rose and trying to find Ian Froth, he didn't have the time the time to predict how God was going to punish him next.

This could be serious, he was thinking. He had so much whiskey in him that staying in the saddle all the way home was going to be a struggle as it was. Now he had to worry about getting hit by lightning, or the thunder spooking the horse and him getting thrown. He knew why this was happening — the moonshine he and Stephan spent the afternoon drinking had washed away his doubts, made him as bold as Arminius. He was feeling as if he could fight off Anna's suitors as if they were Roman legions. It was with this confidence he started home. He should have known it wouldn't last.

He was about halfway there when the rain began to pour down. He didn't care. He might as well just ride through it. He certainly didn't want to go back to Stephan's farm. He left when he had for a reason — dinner at the Otterbeins' was a battle. Mother and father and surly sister going at each other the entire meal in German he barely understood, unrelenting carnage as they slashed back and forth with insults and threats the same way they stabbed at their food. He would rather catch pneumonia and die than to go through that again.

But when the top half of a tree broke under the strain of the wind, and toppled into the road fifty feet in front of him, Alvis shuddered, and yanked back on the the reins. He had to get to someplace safer. Turning his horse around, he rode back about two hundred yards, and headed up the first lane he came to, realizing he was at Luke Putt's farm. He stared at the house wondering if he should go up to the front door and ask to come inside, but made an assessment of himself and his condition, and dismounted outside of the barn. He knew if Luke Putt saw him pulling open the heavy door he would understand and not care that he was trespassing. Reverend Putt was like that. While some people crossed the road to avoid a Clapp, Luke Putt would walk right up, offer a hand, say, "How ya doin, Alvis?" Alvis usually resented ministers, especially Baptist ministers, like he would a case of warts, but Luke Putt was different. He didn't walk around with an expression of divine condemnation on his face. He never really seemed to disapprove of anything. Of course, there was a good chance he had no idea of what went on around him. It made him seem like a fool at times, but he was too nice a man for anyone to make fun of.

Inside the barn Alvis made himself comfortable best he could wearing clothes that were heavy and dripping. He found a spot where the rain didn't leak through the shake shingles, took off his shirt, and hung it on a hook on the wall, then sat in the dirt with his back against a stall divider.

The storm continued to rage. The thunder exploded like cannons; the lightning made the cracks in the siding look like flames. Alvis missed it all. Shortly after sitting down, the effects of the liquor began to drown his energy. His head nodded to his chest, he fell over to his right, and there he lay fast asleep.

It was an hour before supper at the Faraday house. The rain began to fall as regular, slow, heavy thumps. Anna could feel the dread that came on whenever she thought of having to face her family at the table. Moments later, as the body of the storm blew in, a deluge battered the slate roof, and sheets of water ran down the outside of the glass, she hoped it would be enough to postpone the meal, maybe cancel it, and she could stay in her room and on her bed for the rest of the evening, if not for the rest of her life.

The land, shadowed by black clouds, exploded into brightness, revealing the fields and barns for an instant, a quick view, then back to obscurity and mystery. The blasts were so loud, the light so bright, that Anna felt compelled to get up off her bed to watch it.

It took only a few minutes for her to be drawn into the fury — the raging wind, the enormous power of the electrical discharges as they slashed toward the ground, the explosions of the air around her. With each crash of thunder her body would shudder, a whelp would escape from her lips. It was as if she were viewing a battle between heaven and earth, standing on the edge of the arena while the combat raged. But just a spectator, her emotions rose as if *she* were under attack. With this rush of feelings came thoughts she was able to suppress the past week and a half, thoughts that did not rise up while she lay very, very still.

Once unleashed, these ideas came at her so fast she could not defend herself against them. In a flash of lightning, with the yard and fields revealed, she saw how foolish she had been. Then, standing in darkness she realized she had been playing a child's game, had been pretending the way a little girl would make up stories with her dolls to suit her needs at the time. "Oh, my," she whispered. "Oh, my."

Her life had been like this storm, she now understood. Those flashes of light were the times she and Peter were together, and the darkness was the fantasies these encounters produced. "Haven't I read this somewhere?" she whispered.

Anna turned from the window and walked around to the other side of the bed. She picked up Elizabeth Barrett Browning's collection of poems, and placed it in on her lap as she sat on the mattress. "Where is it? Where is it?" she repeated, turning page after page, squinting in the darkness to read the first few lines of each sonnet, until she got to number 26.

"'I lived with visions for my company," she read aloud, "instead of men and women years ago.'"

Then silently, "and found them gentle mates, nor thought to know a sweeter music than they played to me. But soon their trailing purple was not free of this world's dust, their lutes did silent grow, and I myself grew faint and blind below their vanishing eyes. Then thou didst come — to be beloved, what they seemed. Their shining fronts, their songs, their splendours (better, yet the same, as river-water hallowed into fonts,) met in thee, and from thee overcame my soul with satisfaction of all wants; because God's gifts put man's best dreams to shame."

Anna lay back on the bed as the storm continued to rage, just a background to her thoughts. "'Then thou didst come — to be beloved...'" she whispered. "'Their shining fronts, their songs, their slendours... met in thee.' Will it be that way for me? Will I ever meet God's gift to me?"

Steam rose from the ground as if the earth was on fire as Alvis led his horse out of the barn. His legs and back were stiff from having slept in the dirt. He stretched, but couldn't work out the knots in his muscles, so he walked unevenly; his right leg hopped. The alcohol made his stomach queasy; his head ached so badly just the scratching of his footsteps annoyed him. He took one last look toward the house, didn't see anyone at any of the windows, mounted, and started down the lane. When he reached the place in the road where the tree had fallen, he found a path around it, didn't try to move it, didn't consider going to the mill and retrieving an axe or a saw to cut it up. This was someone else's stretch of road, he figured; let them worry about it. He just wanted to get home.

But as Alvis neared the road that ran along Stony Creek he began to feel the dread of having to face his father and explain to him where he was all afternoon. He was too tired and too hungover to think up any good lies. His only escape was to kill some time, to ride upstream a few miles, get home after dinner, after his father had a few beers, and was less likely to smell the whiskey on Alvis' breath. Besides, after Woody had been drinking he was easily confused, would usually accept anything Alvis told him. Alvis was hungry, but that would have to wait. He had no choice.

He turned right, instead of left toward his house, riding with his head down, trying to stay awake. Up ahead somewhere came noises, voices, he realized, muted by distance, but to him sounding like screams, frantic and desperate. It was probably the O'Learys, he told himself, those Irish drunks. If husband and wife weren't going at each other, then their four filthy kids were out running wild. Usually he was amused by their antics; they were more pitiful than the Clapps, but as bad as he was feeling the intrusion of their clatter was irritating. Besides, the young ones had a tendency to call him names and taunt him when he rode by. Once he insulted them back, and their father rushed around the side of the house yelling as if he were about to shoot him. There was no sense in trying to go around them. There was nowhere else he could go. The creek ran hard up against the road on one side. On the other side were steep, impassable slopes. He would ignore the O'Learys best he could. After a half a mile or so he'd be out of their range and safe.

But there was one thing he hadn't counted on. The storm must have been worse than he thought. All the rain seemed to have fallen into the Stony Creek valley. When he came around a curve a few hundred yards short of the O'Learys, he discovered that the stream had overflowed its banks, and the road was flooded. Alvis mouthed a curse, shook his head. It was hard to tell how deep the water was. It covered the road and climbed part way up the hill on the other side. It rushed and it swirled, but there was a chance it really wasn't as bad as it seemed. Alvis stared at it, examined it, thought about which held the greatest danger — drowning or facing his father. He urged his horse forward.

It was hard to tell who had the least sense, Alvis or his mount. The rushing water reached the fetlocks as soon as they rode into the pool, and five feet further in it was up to the horse's knees, but Alvis kept on kicking it in the flanks and the gelding kept going. They might have been swept away eventually, but something caused Alvis pull back on the reins and the horse to stop.

It was the voices again. They were still far off, vague, but eerie, even to Alvis. With his mind muddled by the alcohol he wasn't certain if he was actually hearing them, or just imagining they were there. He decided it wasn't the O'Learys, not the husband or the wife or the four filthy kids, at least not in any way he heard them before.

Alvis twisted in the saddle to look all around him trying to locate where they came from. He thought they were in the hills above him. He stared up in the trees wondering what it was, who it was, and what could be wrong, by now thinking something *was* wrong. "What the hell is goin on?" he whispered. "Ain't nothin up there. This is stupid." Now feeling nervous, he thought better of trying to get through the flood, got the gelding turned around, and headed down the road toward home. It was then that Luke Putt floated by.

Alvis caught only a glimpse of him out of the corner of his eye, but it made his head snap around. "Jesus!" he exclaimed. Luke Putt was about thirty yards away and slightly downstream from where Alvis was on the road. He seemed to be alive — one arm and his legs were thrashing as if he were trying to swim. His head turned from side to side as he struggled to breathe, but he was losing the battle with the current. Alvis just sat there and watched as if it were something he didn't want to get involved in, but urged him on, wished him well.

When that seemed to do no good, without thinking about it, without planning what he might do, Alvis vaulted from his horse onto dry ground and began to run down the road and toward the creek, reaching the edge of it just as Luke Putt slammed into a rock and managed to grab hold and keep himself in place.

Alvis knew what Stony Creek was like; he lived next to it all his life. He had seen it rampaging and angry, seen it tear the gate to the millrace apart as if it were paper, pull down trees and carry them along, knew that a few years before he was born it moved the mill a quarter of a mile downstream, and had seen several bodies pulled out after floods like this. No one but Stephan knew Alvis had been drinking that day, and he never told, so all who heard about this, and everyone soon did, wondered where his courage came from. Without hesitation, without a whimper, Alvis threw himself into the raging creek, and somehow, staying afloat and moving forward like a dog, reached Luke Putt's side and grabbed his arm to tow him back to shore.

"Ow!" Luke screamed. "My arm! My arm is broken, Alvis! *That* arm!"

Alvis let go. All he could do to hold himself there was to grab Luke Putt's shirt and hope the minister could keep them both attached to the rock long enough for something good to happen. He doubted that would be the case. He swung his head around best he could hoping to find some solution to their plight, but there was nothing but roaring, debris-filled water all around them, and seventy-five feet between them and good land. Unable to come up with another plan he managed to get himself around next to Luke, yelled, "Hold on to me," and with his right foot pushed them away from the rock.

They had no chance. With a man on his back Alvis wasn't strong enough to go where he wished. Even with four legs and Alvis' two arms trying to propel them to the side, the current pushed them downstream like just another log. Keeping their heads above water was a task, which didn't matter as much to Alvis since Luke had his good arm around his throat so tightly he could barely breathe as it was.

It was never known how far that they went. After ten minutes their energy was spent. Alvis' arms stopped moving, his legs stopped kicking, as did Luke's. They just floated, were turned and twisted, sent downstream and side to side and scraped against rocks as muddy water washed over them, got in their noses and their mouths, and broken tree limbs smacked their faces.

When he realized there was nothing they could do, Alvis thought the last thing he would see in this world was his family's mill as he floated by. The idea of dying calmed him. He seemed to realize that only in death was he finally achieving the stature he always sought in life.

The light was dimming. The hills hid the low sun in the southwest sky. The fields on the right bank and the forest beyond there were barely visible through the foam. Alvis turned his head to look one last time, his legs began to drop, he felt his torso fall as well, and then his feet hit bottom.

"Oh," he muttered as he stood, the creek water gushing around him, but not knocking him down. He wondered where his strength came from all of the sudden, then turned and saw that they had been swept into an obstruction — tree trunks and branches formed a dam. Water poured through the cracks as with a sieve, but Alvis, and, as he discovered when he turned all of the way around, Reverend Putt were safe, and only ten easy steps from land. Yet this was not done.

"My wife and daughters are in here somewhere!" Luke Putt shouted, gasping in breathes as he trudged toward the road. "We've got to find them!"

"What?" Alvis just stared at him as the minister stumbled over the last of the rocks that lined the creek. "Yer...What the hell are *they* doin here?"

Luke didn't answer. He was running up the road, best he could with his right hand cradling his fractured left arm. He was a young man, not yet thirty, but was short and bottom heavy, so he seemed to waddle from side to side as he ran. Alvis quickly caught up to him. "What are they doin here?" he repeated as if the question mattered.

"We were crossing the ford, and the wagon was knocked over. Oh, Lord, we've got to find them."

It would be dark in an hour; it was nearly dark now. They were a half a mile below the ford; there was a half mile of raging water they would have to search, and even then there was the chance his wife and daughters had already floated by. Alvis had enough of this. He wanted to go home. He thought he knew how it was going to turn out, and didn't want to be haunted by the memory of this night for the rest of his life. It was horrible, too horrible; he didn't need to be reminded that the world was so brutal. Then he heard the voices that made him stop fifteen minutes before.

It was upstream, far upstream, no clearer than it was before, but he didn't hesitate this time, didn't wonder where it came from or what was wrong. He ran as fast as he could, then realized that the clatter from his footsteps was drowning out the sounds. He stopped to listen, was about to start up again when he saw a sight that made him jolt and gasp.

She came out of the flood waters that Alvis started to ride through fifteen minutes before, seemingly rising up from them like a ghost in the gray light, ambling as if she had no purpose to her walk down the road. As she came closer Alvis could see that her whole body heaved with grief; her arms flapped in helplessness, her mouth was formed by a scream that made no sound. The creek water soaked her clothes; her hair was matted down. Luke ran passed Alvis and pulled his wife to him. It was as if she had used up all of her energy to get there. She collapsed to her knees towing Luke down with her. With a long look into her eyes Alvis knew that it was hopeless. The sorrow made his head drop. But then he heard those voices again.

Alvis started up the road again, feeling Luke watch him as he went by. He knew he was going to have to do this alone. He could feel the burden, and it terrified him. His life hadn't been designed for this, for having the responsibility of others' lives. He could barely account for himself most of the time, and now there were two little girls who would die if he weren't strong enough or smart enough, if his fear made him hesitate or stop. It swelled up in him and brought tears to his eyes, then made him sob as he trudged through the water and up the road.

He was about halfway to the ford when he saw them. His head went back as he muttered, "Oh, God." Both were clinging to a sapling trunk that had been rooted on dry land two hours before, their tiny hands and arms somehow holding on as the current pushed the rest of them downstream. Their faces were cringed in terror; their tears were washed away by the water that splashed onto their faces.

Rachel and Sarah? No, Rachel and Mary were their names. One was probably about eight by now, the other four or five. They were a hundred feet away; there was nothing but surging water in between Alvis and them. The other bank was closer, if he could get across maybe he could... He would have to go all the way to the ford at Columbia Furnace to do that, but it was probably flooded and unpassable. There wasn't enough time. They couldn't hold on much longer. It was a miracle they had lasted this long. He couldn't go home and get some rope, or find someone to help, and he knew Reverend Putt wouldn't be much good with just one good arm and a wife in shock. He was on his own.

Alvis kept going up the road, never taking his eyes off of the girls. The fact that he survived being in the creek earlier didn't make him confident, it just meant that his ruination was probably guaranteed this time. God was not going to let him get away with doing that well twice in a row, regardless that it was a minister's daughters he was trying to save.

To his credit he didn't think about it, didn't hesitate, didn't even pray as if believing it would do no good. Alvis ran into the creek as far as he could, still struggling to stand with the water up to his waist, then finally gave in to it. He took one last look downstream at the girls at the tree, tried to judge the distance and direction, and began to swim, or what passed for swimming — his legs and feet thrashing more than kicking, his hands moving as if digging in dirt.

Once in the water he realized how little power he had, how much God would control what happened here. The thought caused dread to run through him. He hated to go out this way — just minutes after becoming a hero. He would have liked to have been around to enjoy the acclaim, to have people actually be nice to him, to respect him, for a change.

With Alvis propelling himself across the creek, and the current sending him downstream, he moved at a diagonal as he thought he would, but figured he was probably not heading toward the girls. That would never happen. He felt badly knowing he was failing. He hoped Rachel and Mary could hold on long enough for someone else to reach them, someone who had led a better life. He was sure they could. He lifted his head to shout to them to be strong, to hang on, and for the first time in three minutes saw where he was. His right arm suddenly lifted and looped; he swung it around Mary's waist and pulled her close as the current sent him by. She struggled at first, her fingers reached back as if only she felt safe only at the rock, but quickly realized that she was being rescued. With a quick shout of, "Rachel!" she hugged Alvis' arm with both of hers and let him take her downstream.

This was a shame, Alvis was thinking. She would have been better off where she was. He was probably on his way to his death, and now he was taking a five year old girl along with him. It was just a reaction, just a reflex, him grabbing her like that. He felt badly, but there was nothing he could do now except to try to defy the odds and get them to shore. He raised his head up to see where they were and... Alvis noticed the rock a second before they slammed into it. He didn't have time to avoid it or soften the collision. The back of his neck hit first and something like an electric shock ran through his body, then his limbs went numb and weak.

Mary was jolted by the crash, as well. Her arms came loose from Alvis; she was propelled over his right shoulder, floating downstream on her own. Although stunned and in pain, Alvis realized she was gone. He twisted around one way, then the other before he saw her gliding away. In an instant he shot his left arm out, his hand just barely reaching her foot, but three fingers on her shoe was enough for him to hold her in place, and a better grip pulled her back.

The trek to the right bank was an easy one. Just five feet toward it the water was only at Alvis' chest. He held Mary high above the surge like a trophy, and set her gently down on the grass.

"Are you okay?" he asked as a courtesy, before running back upstream for Rachel. By then he had no doubt she would be saved as well. He sprinted into the water until his feet no longer touched, dove toward her, let the water carry him, and came up by her side. "Where's my mommy and my daddy?" Rachel pleaded.

"They're fine, sweetheart," Alvis said tenderly. "They're

over on the road. You'll be with them in a little while."

Alvis was smarter this time; he had done it before. He judged where he wanted to go, and how he was going to get there. He had Rachel on his back with her arms around his neck, took a look at how the current ran, saw where the rocks were so he wouldn't be surprised, and pushed himself off. Rachel would later tell her parents that Alvis was laughing as they floated down the stream, but it wasn't something he would remember. He aimed them toward the bank, managed to bounce them gently off of a rock in the right direction, then another, then used the last of his strength to get them to land. He let Rachel stay on his back as he waded the last few feet to the field, then crouched so she could climb down. When he saw the Reverend and Mrs. Putt come up the road on the other side of the creek he let out with a howl so loud it was probably heard in Woodstock.

CHAPTER 11

"You are late!" Hessie got up off the pile of hay, brushing the back of her dress as she strode toward him. The late evening orange light outside of the open doorway made the pasture grass seem to shimmer.

"I had trouble finding a place to get across the creek; it is so flooded. Then I got confused. Are we still on your property?" Peter Metzger turned and pulled the heavy barn door closed with both hands.

Hessie nodded to show she accepted that excuse. "This used to be the Cummings' dairy barn before my father bought their place. He was going to turn it into apartments for the servants, but figured it would be too easy for them to wander off this far from the house. He uses it to store hay in now. We are just waiting for it to fall down."

Peter nervously looked at the walls and the ceiling as if concerned with that happening then. Satisfied the barn would stand until they left, he walked in a few more steps. "I guess you know why I am here."

"All your note said was that you wanted to talk to me. I am assuming that it is not because you have an interest in courting me."

Peter had to think fast to keep from insulting someone he needed as an ally. "It has crossed my mind at times, but I am afraid that my affection is being commanded by another these days."

"Oh, how sweet. Did they teach you to talk like that in

Charlottesville?"

Peter was relieved that he wasn't going to have to continue with the pretense. He did find Hessie attractive, but even if that was what drove him, he sensed her to be manipulative, deceitful — hard to control. His concern over her behavior would be too much of a distraction. He didn't want a wife he had to constantly tend to. Besides, from what he understood, Richard Faraday had more debts than assets. Anyone who married Hessie might spend years paying off her father's creditors. "I need to know how Anna feels about me. I want to marry her, and, and I cannot court her in public, as one usually does."

Hessie felt as if she had just been given a gift. She had unwrapped it, looked at it, had no idea what it was or whether or not it would do her any good, but was grateful anyway. "Why not?" She showed an attitude of sweet innocence. She hoped there was enough light for Peter to appreciate her sincere expression.

"There, uh, um, was a problem with the determination of the value of her father's interest in the foundry after he died. It was a misunderstanding more than anything else, but I am afraid that it has caused bad blood between her mother and my father. Unfortunately, it has kept Anna and me apart." Peter hoped there was enough light for Hessie to appreciate his sincere expression.

"I guess that explains that," she said after a few seconds of thought. "Once, I mentioned your name, and Anna seemed to get, get, what is the word — weak, queasy, as if she were about to swoon. She begged me not to ask her about you again, and to please never mention your name in front of her mother or grandmother."

"Then she does care for me."

"Yes, Peter she does. She seems to care a great deal about you. But tell me, was that you up in one of Maggie's bedrooms wearing a dress?"

Peter hoped there was too little light for Hessie to see him turn red. He managed to get a grin on his face right away.

"I do not know how many people have asked me about that." His voice was an octave too high. He brought it down. "All I can figure is that Alvis Clapp somehow knows of my affection for Anna, or hers for me, and tried to discredit me. He might have some intentions as far as she is concerned. The idea that she would have anything to do with the likes of him is baffling, but perhaps Alvis has some fantasies that he thinks are real. It is the only way I can explain it. No, that was not me up there."

Hessie nodded. Anna already told her about the dress and the bonnet on the floor, the fact that Peter was seen crawling across the pasture to get to the house, and everything else. "I did not think so. It *is* more likely that Alvis is a liar and a fool. And yes, he may have some designs on Anna. As beautiful as she is, I imagine many men do."

"Yes, I am concerned about that. But, since, as you said, she does care for me, maybe I can win her before anyone else gets a chance. I want to meet with her, to talk to her. I want us to spend some time together so we can get to know one another. Do you think that you could go to her with my request?"

"You do know that I will be defying my stepmother and my father by helping you."

Peter wished there was enough light so he could see better. He didn't know if Hessie was joking, being serious, or trying to mislead him. If he could look into her eyes maybe he could tell. Two weeks before he might have trusted her, but since the party he did not know what to believe. His grasp of the world had slipped there for a few minutes. He could not escape the fear that it might happen again. But he was desperate, had no choice; he had to trust Hessie. "It would be for her benefit as well as mine."

Hessie had to make a quarter turn to hide the grin that was on her face. She put a hand to her mouth to stifle a laugh, and bow her head as if she was thinking. When she was certain she could control herself, she came back around. "Yes, Peter, that is probably true. You know, with some luck, with God's help, we will all get what we deserve."

◆ ◆ ◆

"You do know that once I start this letter there is no turning back."

"Yes, unless we crumple it up and toss it away." Sonny was leaning back so that the front legs of the chair were off the floor. He held himself in place with the fingertips of one hand on the kitchen table.

"I am not talking about that, Sonny," Marion Lutz said sternly. "What I mean is that you are taking a big risk here. You —"

"I know." Sonny leaned forward causing the feet of the chair to thump unevenly on the floor. He didn't look directly at his sister-in-law. When she got that look in her eyes and that tone in her voice she was too scary to face head on. Even his brother Charlie seemed to cower from her then. He was nervous enough about this; she was going to get him terrified.

"I don't want what happened with Clarisa to happen to you again."

"Eh, that was okay. I got over that right away." Sonny waved his hand as if dismissing the idea.

"You did? You moped around for a year after that. You—"

"I was fine," Sonny said defiantly. "I got my work done; I did not start drinking or anything. I was fine after a few weeks."

"A few weeks? A few weeks? You didn't have anything to do with anybody for over a year. You stopped going to church for a while—"

"I went back."

"You wouldn't go on picnics, or to dances. There were several girls who were interested in you, and you wouldn't have anything to do with them."

"Who?"

"Molly Shufflebarger, for one."

Sonny shrugged. Molly was Marion's second cousin. He had to be careful what he said. "She was okay, she was just —"

"What, too short? She's a sweet girl, Sonny. You would have been lucky to have her, and now it's too late. How about Ivy? Were her eyes the wrong color?"

Sonny started to laugh. Yes, to be honest he had been despondent for a long time after Clarisa rejected him for Forest Lee. She was his only joy for the ten months she was in his life, the only thing that made his existence unpredictable and interesting. He never told her that, never really told her anything about how he felt. He always assumed she knew. Why else would he have come around so much? The day he heard she was marrying Forest Lee he galloped to her farm in a panic, vaulted from the horse and ran up the steps to the front door. Her father answered his heavy, persistent pounding. The look of sympathy on his face almost knocked Sonny to the ground. It made him realize what he was feeling and how he looked. By the time Clarisa came into the parlor he had composed his appearance, but nothing else. His voice shook as he asked her if it was true; the life drained out of him when she admitted that it was. He said something to her, he couldn't remember what, and had no idea how he got home.

"Do you want to go through all of that again?" Marion asked

Sonny frowned. "What are you saying — that I shouldn't have anything to do with another girl again because of what happened with Clarisa?"

"No. You know I'm not saying that. I am just wondering if you should have anything to do with this girl."

"You are saying that I'm not good enough for her."

There was that look of sympathy again. Marion started to say something; she moved her lips, but couldn't get the words out. It took her a few seconds to figure out how to put it. "Sonny, she's a princess. She is as close to being royalty as we have in this county. She — "

"And I am just ordinary?"

Marion was getting annoyed. She was trying hard not to insult Sonny, but ... "You are a fine man, Sonny. All you Lutz men are. You're handsome and strong and hardworking and decent. You're everything a girl wants in a man. But this is Maggie's girl. Who knows what's she's really like, or what she wants? To her the ideal man could be, um, could be, I don't know, Alvis Clapp."

Sonny burst into laughter. "I think," he said when he had calmed down, "we can pretty much forget that."

"Oh, you haven't heard what he did, have you?"

"What, finally went crazy from being such a dwarf?" Sonny seemed to back away from the words as if trying to deny that they came out of his mouth.

"Sonny, I've never heard you say something like that about anyone."

Sonny shrugged. "I dunno, he's just, I dunno, I guess I just don't like people who don't do any work. So, what did he do?"

"He rescued Reverend Putt and his family from Stony Creek the night of that bad storm last week."

"He what?" Sonny looked at Marion as if she were making it up. "Who's Reverend Putt?"

"He lives on the road from Clapps' Mill to Bedford. He's a Baptist preacher, I think."

Sonny nodded to show that he was following the conversation, but paused to think about what she said. "Um. How did he and his family end up in Stony Creek?"

"Their wagon turned over going across some ford up there. They said that Alvis jumped in and pulled them out one by one."

Sonny stared straight ahead as if he were shocked that the universe was different than he imagined. He looked at Marion to confirm that she was telling him the truth, and did not detect a wrinkle in her story. Gradually it became apparent that there was something about it that was upsetting him. It was a half a minute before he spoke. "Well, do you think, I mean, now's that he's a hero, that Anna would like him?"

Marion tilted her head to look at Sonny. Her lips pursed. "This is just what I'm talking about, Sonny. This will drive you crazy. You are going to worry about every boy that she knows, or might know, or could know someday."

"I thought what you were talking about was her marrying someone else and making me miserable."

"What I am saying is that this is too much, uh, too much emotion for you. Your life is, is..."

"Boring?"

"Steady. Like I said, you Lutzs are fine men, but none of you have ever been known for your passion."

"Charlie was never all that excited about you, is that what you're saying?"

"I've known your brother since we were eight. I knew I wanted to marry him by the time we were ten. He knew it when we were twelve. He didn't have to work too hard at it. I don't think he ever lost any sleep worrying about me."

"So I should find someone easier, instead of someone who makes me feel, feel happy?"

"Passion is a vice, Sonny."

The words came out so strong, so composed, that Sonny felt as if he had been chastised. "I am just asking her if she wants to go on an outing to the Springs with me and some people from church." He said it like a child insisting on his innocence. "This isn't going to be a love letter, or anything."

"And if she turns you down?"

"I will just go on with my life as usual, I guess."

"You know you can't ask her again."

Sonny shrugged. For some reason his face burned bright red. "Why not?"

"It wouldn't be gentlemanly. Actually, it depends on how she turns you down. If she seems to be encouraging you to ask her again, then of course, you can."

Sonny shook his head. "I don't know anything about this stuff. That's why I need you." Sonny looked at her with pleading eyes.

"I hope Charlie and your folks don't blame me for what happens."

"We will name our first girl after you."

Marion's head went back with a chuckle. "I have a feeling her first daughter is going to be named Maggie, but thanks anyway."

"You *will* help me."

Marion dipped the pen into the ink with one hand and slid the paper over to in front of her with the other. She took one last look at Sonny, frowned, waited for him to stop her, then said as she started to write. "Dear Miss Sigler."

"Wait. Is it Miss Sigler? It might be Miss Faraday."

CHAPTER 12

"Oh, nooo!" Hessie exclaimed as her hands went flying up to the top of her head. She paused at the window just long enough to make certain of what she was seeing, then scurried out of her bedroom into the hallway, lifting the skirt of her dress slightly as she pranced down the stairs. She darted left then right to avoid a servant girl who was mopping the foyer floor, yanked open the front door, did not bother to close it, ran across the porch, down four steps to the yard, then down the lane, not stopping until she was just in front of the horseman who was approaching the house. She reached up, grabbed the bridle and yanked the gelding's head around. "Alvis," she hissed as she started leading horse and rider back toward the road, "this is stupid. What are you doing here?"

Alvis wasn't sure if he should protest Hessie's interference. She was certainly disrupting his plans, but maybe she was right; maybe this was stupid. Wait a second — she didn't know why he was there, so how could she tell if this was stupid? He jerked back on the reins, making Hessie stumble forward and almost fall.

"What are you doing?" she wailed, turning to face him. "Get out of here! Get out of sight! If you want to talk to me go down there somewhere."

"I didn't come to see *you*," Alvis said. "I came to pay a visit on Anna."

Hessie's head flew back. She muttered something, then glared at Alvis as if thinking that would make him obey, but the

would think..." Hessie sighed. "Alvis, to win a girl like Anna you cannot be too forward, too bold. You have to act aloof. Do you know what 'aloof' means?" Alvis shook his head meekly. "'Indifferent'? It means that you have to act as if you do not like her very much. Of course, you have to let her know that you are available, but you have to show her that you do not really care if she wants you or not. Do you understand?"

"Okay, yeah, but how will she, I mean — "

"Leave it to me. I will let her know that you came by. That will tell her that you are interested. But if you do not come back right away she will start to believe she has lost her chance with you, and that will start to haunt her. She will feel as if she has done something wrong. I can see it now — after a few days she will look out the window every hour hoping to see you riding up the lane. She will ask me when you are coming back. She will ask about this visit and make me repeat everything all over again, ask me how you looked, what the expression on your face was, what your tone of voice was. Do you see what I am saying?"

"Yeah, I have ta make her want me."

"No, Alvis. You have to make her *need* you."

"Anna, will you come here, dear?" Rebecca asked as she stood in the hallway outside of Anna's bedroom. If her mind hadn't been on something else she might have noted the significance of Anna's door being open while Anna was inside.

"Yes, ma'am?" Anna said, putting the book down, getting up off the bed and walking to the doorway.

"I want you to see something." Rebecca walked up the hall into Hessie's room and to the window. Anna followed. "Hessie is talking to someone in the lane. She ran outside like the house was on fire when he rode up. I.... Oh, he is not there anymore."

Anna leaned toward the glass next to her mother. All she saw was Hessie coming back to the house with her lips locked hard together and her eyes cold. "Who was it?" Anna asked.

"That is what I wanted to know. It was a young man, I think. It wasn't Peter Metzger; I am certain of that." Anna's back stiffened. It was the first time anyone mentioned him in almost four weeks. She thought that she was well over him, but just her mother saying his name caused a surge of conflicting emotions to run through her again as if she were about to have a relapse. She was annoyed at herself for having any feeling left as far as he was concerned. She hoped it didn't show. "And I do not think that it was Ian Froth," her mother said.

"He has left the county, from what I hear," Anna replied, glad the subject had been changed.

"Yes, I heard that as well. You do not know anyone that Hessie is seeing, do you?"

"No, ma'am," Anna answered. "I do not know who she likes. She has not told me about anyone."

"Well, it is very improper for her to see someone without introducing him to us first."

"Yes, ma'am. Maybe that is why she sent him away. Maybe she was concerned with what was proper."

They backed away from the window as Hessie came close to the house. Rebecca followed Anna out of Hessie's room and into hers. When Anna realized that her mother wasn't going downstairs right away she turned to face her. "Yes, ma'am?"

Rebecca reached behind her and closed the door. Her expression showed that a lecture was coming. "I was just wondering if you have decided about the picnic yet? You have had the letter for several days. It is rude not to reply promptly."

Anna plopped down on the bed. "Oh, I don't know," she whined. "I don't know those people; I don't know *him.* I don't think that it would be that much fun."

"Dear, you know that you really should get out and do something. You have hardly left this room in a month. I am sorry that you are heartbroken about..." She stopped when Anna turned away. "The Lutzs are fine people. Your stepfather has known them for years. Sonny is certainly a handsome boy. It is just a picnic. If you do not have a good time or do not like him, then you do not have to see him again."

"Yes, ma'am."

"The way that your stepfather and I feel about this now, if being here makes you feel this badly, then perhaps you should accept Melanie's invitation and go spend a few weeks in Fauquier County. I hear Upperville is a pretty little town. The change of scenery might do you some good."

"And Melanie can remind me that she is married and I am not," Anna turned away and muttered.

"What, dear?"

"Nothing, Mother. Yes, it would be fun to be with Melanie and her husband."

"John."

"Yes. John."

"Good. Decide if you want to go. We can talk about it later. But please, do go on that picnic. I think you will enjoy it."

"Yes, ma'am. I will write him a note this evening."

Rebecca nodded, smiled, went out the door and closed it as Anna lay back on her bed and grimaced. Anna could hear Hessie's footsteps coming up the stairs on her way back to her room. She wanted to wait until she was certain her mother was gone before going to tell Hessie the latest developments, and to ask her who the visitor was. Anna got up, walked to the door and put her ear against the wood to listen for her mother's steps going away. Instead, she heard her mother's voice — a soft whisper, and Hessie's reply in the same tone. She stopped breathing, but still had trouble making out the words. She wasn't aware that her mother said, "I am afraid that she is still not over him. We may have to send her away for a while."

CHAPTER 13

"Meem's Bottom? Why there?" Peter asked.

"I don't know, Peter," Hessie replied. "That is just what she told me." She stood in the open doorway staring to the east as the rays of the early evening sun made the western slope of Massanutten Mountain glow with an orange haze. "Have you ever been on the other side?"

Peter glanced impatiently at where Hessie looked. His words came out rapidly and without much inflection. "Yes, yes, plenty of times. Page County? Yes. We ship our iron to the South Fork. I have to ride over there once in a while to deal with the barge company."

"What is it like?"

"Oh, I don't know," Peter said, trying not to sound annoyed. "A lot like here, except that their iron is not as good as ours. You have never been there?" He was instantly sorry he asked that question and kept this discussion going.

"No, I have been north and south of here, to Winchester and as far as Staunton. I always wanted to see what was to the east. Where is Fauquier County?"

"Uh, on the other side of the Blue Ridge, and a little north. Why?"

"I was just wondering. Anna has a cousin there. They are about the same age. She talks about her a lot."

"Oh."

Hessie walked back into the barn. "Meem's Bottom was all that she said. I did ask her where, specifically, you all were to meet. She just said, 'He will know.'"

"I will know? That *is* strange. There is the Otterbein's farm, the Higgins' house, the Hebner's, the ford, Screamersville..." Peter examined Hessie as he mentioned each place, and the only one she seemed to react to was Screamersville.

"At dusk."

"Dusk."

"She thought that it would give you enough light to find your way, but it will be dark when you are together."

Peter nodded. He did not show any excitement, any enthusiasm, just confusion. He had been given his instructions, but felt there had to be more. He did not want the conversation to end until he was certain Hessie told him everything. "How is she getting there? How is she able to sneak out of the house? Are you going to be with her?" Peter uttered the questions so fast they seemed to be one sentence.

"None of that is your concern. I have told you everything. If you care for her, if you want the two of you to be together, then be at Meem's Bottom tomorrow at dusk."

◆ ◆ ◆

"Why won't you tell me?" Anna was in Hessie's room leaning against the wall next to the closed door. Her face was bright with a look of laughter. "Who was he?"

Hessie tried to appear spirited as well, but was so nervous about the conversation that each sentence was making her stop to wonder what Anna knew. "I told you — it will be a surprise."

"Was it —"

"You have already mentioned every boy that we know, and I have denied all of them?"

"Yes, you did, but you seemed to react when I asked you if it was David Hertz."

Oh, thank goodness, Hessie thought. Maybe she can relax now. "Did I?" She was smiling, almost giddy.

"It *was* him," Anna said slowly and softly, as if talking to herself. "And when you went out to the Cummings' barn last night, it was to see him again, wasn't it?" Anna had the look of someone who was reading the final chapter of a good mystery.

Hessie went into shock, but quickly realized that would not do. "When, what, last night?" she said as soon as she recovered. "You saw me?" That was the wrong response.

"My room faces the back fields, remember?"

Yes, it does, doesn't it? Can she see the barn from there? Hessie's mind and eyes went off to the side as she pictured the view was from Anna's window. "No, I was just going out to get Porcupine to bring him in. I am surprised that you even noticed."

It was Anna's turn to be dazed and questioning. "Oh," she said, a little disappointed. "But didn't I see Porcupine over in... Oh, it doesn't matter." Anna said. "David Hertz, huh?"

"I did not say that. It could have been someone else, anybody."

"Well, why do you have to see him, whoever it is, in secret?"

"I told you—I went out to get Porcupine."

Anna stared at Hessie the way her mother would hoping that she would break down and confess. Hessie stared straight back, making Anna feel as if she were prying into something that was none of her business. Her guilt make her shift positions and fold her arms across her stomach. "I have told *you* everything about who I like."

"Yes, and I do appreciate that."

"Well, why won't you tell me?"

"Like I said, I want it to be a surprise."

Peter Metzger sat on his horse at the northern edge of

Rude's Hill looking north. It was still an hour before dusk, but he felt he had to be there early to try to figure out where he and Anna were supposed to meet. He contemplated the mystery for most of the day, was so distracted by it that he barely got any work done at all. Twice his father came into his office and caught him staring out the window thinking about it, and at two o'clock had to remind him that he was supposed to be down at the furnace for the next smelting. He spent an entire day pondering it, and he understood it less than he had the evening before.

To his left, the Valley Turnpike wound down a cleft in the hill to Meem's Bottom. He was about ten feet from the road and about that far above it, his horse standing in grass and weeds about a foot high. Occasionally a horseman or a wagon would pass; he could feel them turn to look at him, and probably wonder what he was up to. It was his concern about their suspicions that was keeping him from pulling out his telescope and examining riders coming toward him from the north, or spying on the few farmhouses that were scattered throughout the more than a thousand acre, level plain fifty feet below him.

A half of a mile to his left the North Fork of the Shenandoah River snaked through the woods before swinging east a little more than a mile in front. There it was forded by the turnpike in the suburbs of the town of Mount Jackson. To his right, Smith Creek ran near the base of Short Mountain in the Massanutten Range. About a half a mile away, where the mountain rose in a series of steps, Screamersville occupied the opposite bank of the creek for five hundred yards or more. It was a community of cabins, huts and shanties built on both sides of two muddy or dusty streets, out of the way and protected from casual visitors. His foundry occasionally hired temporary laborers from there, but only when they were desperate for help, since it was hard to keep them working for more than a few hours at a time, or sober for two days in a row, or prevent them from stealing anything that would fit into their pockets or under their shirts. It did not make any sense that Anna would be there. He turned his gaze back to the flat, lush fields in front of him.

"He will know," is what Hessie told him that Anna said. He spent nine hours thinking about it, and still had no idea what she meant. He reviewed everything he knew of the place, of the people who lived on the farms there, tried to remember if anything happened there that might be significant, anything that might involve Maggie or the Siglers or the Faradays, and could not think of a thing. There were no miracles, no notable achievements, no infamous crimes or strange deaths that occurred there that he was aware of. But maybe the clue wasn't there yet. Maybe that was it.

He should be on the other side, Peter told himself. Anna would arrive from the north, at least that made sense logically, but then, he was starting to believe, logic had very little to do with this tonight. Maybe he was better off where he was, he decided. If she saw him waiting by the side of the turnpike for her to show up she would know he hadn't understood where they were supposed to meet, and probably be hurt. He knew enough about women to understand they get upset if men cannot read their minds.

He didn't care what the travelers on the road thought, it had now become necessary for him to spy on them. Even though he could see riders as they descended to the North Fork, crossed the ford and headed toward him, he could tell nothing more about them. While he hadn't ruled out that she would come here alone, he thought that it was unlikely, especially with Screamersville so close-by. People had been known to have been robbed on this stretch of road at night. Every once in a while the sheriff and his men would roust the inhabitants there, find someone who matched the description of the thieves, and cart them down to the Rockingham County line and make certain they kept on going.

So it would be two people on horses, or in a wagon, or a carriage. They would turn off somewhere, onto a lane to one of the farms, or onto the road that ran up to Mount Airy, a small church-centered community to the north of Screamersville and up Short Mountain a mile and half.

It wasn't Mount Airy, he was thinking as he pulled the telescope out of the case and rested it in his lap. Technically Mount Airy wasn't in Meem's Bottom, just nearby. It had to be one of the farms. But which one? There was a small place west of the turnpike, up near the ford. It was called the Higgins' place. Richard Higgins had been the farm manager at Solway Court from the twenties into the forties, but had retired to that house and about ten acres to be closer to a son and his grandchildren in Mount Jackson. He had died three years before. His widow was still alive, and still occupied that house, Peter thought. He had considered that Anna might have meant there, but that seemed too ordinary. Other than the fact that Mr. Higgins had worked for Maggie, there was no connection, nothing that would mean anything to him, or to Anna, unless she had had a special fondness for the old man, but then how would he know that, and why would Anna think that he would know that. True, Mrs. Higgins was a widow, Rebecca Sigler had been a widow, and his father... He had ruled out that Anna had sent him to Meem's Bottom as punishment, to force him to perform penance — if he started believing that she knew of his sins, and had the power to force him to atone for them he would surely go mad. He spent all day thinking about that, worrying about it; he didn't want to go over it again. Another farm — the Hebners', the Otterbeins', that one over there or the one just below him? There was no connection to any of them, nothing that meant anything. He brought the telescope up. In a little while Anna Rose Sigler was going to be somewhere in front of him. He had to figure out where.

For the next half an hour Peter sat on his horse on Rude's Hill and examined every rider, every wagon driver and passenger, and stared inside of each coach or carriage. He, of course, received glares in return from everybody who went by, and comments and oaths from a few. While some seemed to be slowing down to begin a turn at a drive or a road, all continued toward him and soon climbed the hill, or descended to the bottom next to him and went on into Mount Jackson.

It was getting dark. The day had been cloudy; the evening was as well, so dusk came early. There was no moonlight or starlight to ease the darkness. She said he should get there while he could still find his way, if only she said to where.

Peter put the telescope back in the case. He leaned forward with his hands on his knees and stared to the north. Maybe it was magic that he was missing, he was thinking. Maybe it was God that was keeping him from knowing what he should do, or Maggie. He muttered a curse. He would have to do without either. If Anna was at Meem's Bottom, he was going to find her if he had to search every inch of the place. He pulled his horse around and spurred it onto the turnpike and down the hill. It was then that the rain began to fall.

It was a sprinkle at first, something to cool him down and wash the dust off, but before he reached the beginning of the lane to the nearest farm, it began to fall harder. By the time he reached the farmhouse his clothes were wet and his face was dripping. He stopped for a few minutes and looked into the darkness all around him, but it was impossible to tell what was there, even though for an hour before he had looked over the place, measured each barn and outbuilding, stared at the fences, evaluated the hay, investigated....

Peter wasn't aware a door had been opened. The rectangle of light that escaped as the farmer came out of his kitchen was behind him. The first words made him jolt; the sentence made him panic. "I saw you watchin my house, boy."

"Oh, Jesus," Peter whispered. He was hoping if he sat still the man would think he just imagined the intrusion and go back inside. At least he had learned that he hadn't been expected, that Anna wasn't there. That should save him the trouble of looking around the place or peering in the windows. He stopped breathing, he hoped his horse would be quiet as well. The rain masked sight and sound so this shouldn't take long. At least that was how he saw it. Which is why the shotgun blast surprised him.

Peter wasn't sure if the gun was aimed and the farmer missed, or if it was just fired into the air to scare him, but once his body and his hearing were back to normal, he decided he didn't want to take the time to ask, didn't want to wait around for him to reload, and in fact, probably had no business being there in the first place. Grateful to still be alive, with renewed spirit, he kicked in his heels, got his mount going, pulled on the reins to guide it north, and slapped it in the flank to get it to go quickly. They might have reached a gallop, but in a half a minute they were up against a fence with no apparent way through. "Oh, no!" Peter screamed as the horse skidded to a stop, turned and smacked up against the rails, pinning his leg in between.

Peter's exclamation was a perfect target. The trigger was pulled again; the balls clinked off the rails just two feet away, making Peter change his mind about heading back to the turnpike. He yanked the horse's head around again, and went east, but the vibrations of the hooves gave him away this time. A third explosion from the gun made him wonder if he were surrounded. He considered stopping, calling out, asking for a chance to explain, but had no idea what he would say. He shook that idea from his head. This was serious, he realized, desperately serious. Even in the darkness and the rain that gun could be aimed in the right direction. "Oh, God, just let me get out of here alive," he prayed, and then it hit him. In a flash like a bolt of lightning he realized why he was there.

He wasn't going to meet Anna, at least not that night. She was nowhere around. This was an ordeal he had to go through, a test of his devotion for her. She had to be certain he was sincere, was willing to endure pain, suffering, fear of death, or worse, humiliation, in order to be with her. No, it was more than that. It was also a trial, a determination by God, by Maggie of his worthiness. If he survived, if he evaded this murderous farmer, if he escaped all the dangers he might face that night, then she would know, he would, they all would, that his motives were just and his love sincere.

◆ ◆ ◆

Alvis thought that the guy would never quit working and go inside. What kind of fool tries to build a house in the dark while it's raining? "Jeez," he whispered as he crouched in the bushes along the road, tired and wet. He hated to see what those angles were like. It wasn't going to be much of a place if this was when he worked on it. Even the idea of believing Anna would want to marry him just because he knew how to build a house was ridiculous. There were a thousand men in the county who could do what he was doing. At least that many. He had seen it done a hundred times. If he wanted to, he could do it as well. It was not a big deal. Sonny Lutz was more of a fool than he imagined. As it turns out he probably didn't need to be here, but he had to see it for himself. He was feeling a whole lot better than he had earlier in the day after someone told him about this.

Alvis stayed where he was for a few more minutes just in case Sonny returned. When he heard a horseman approaching from his right, he ducked back in, waited until he went by, then pushed his way out onto the road. He stopped for a few seconds, listened, looked both ways, then walked over to a rail fence, bent to slide through it, glanced in the direction of Sonny's cabin on the other side of a log barn, and headed up to the house.

Alvis had no idea what he was going to do there, but just being able to walk around the place, to look at it as he pleased, gave him a feeling of superiority. He could burn the house down if he wanted. Okay, the outside walls were stone, but he could go home and get a hammer and a bar and pull down the wood framing. Sonny Lutz was at his mercy. "What a fool," he whispered.

Alvis was just about to leave, believing the man he imagined to be his rival wasn't as much of a threat as he feared, when he remembered the horseman who rode by about ten minutes after Sonny finished working. The thought stopped him, made him think. He tried to remember where he came from, whether he rode over the low ridge that was west of the house, or if he came down the lane from Sonny's cabin. He had a haunting feeling that it was Sonny who left. Alvis thought he knew where he was going. Depression quickly covered him like a blanket. The feeling of power he felt by being able to creep around the place undetected was gone, replaced by feebleness, and a rage, and a need to retrieve the belief that he was the predominant man in Anna's life. God put him on the road that evening three weeks before to save the Putts so Anna would think more highly of him, just as He sent that storm at the Fricks in 1771 so Maggie and Thomas Bledsoe could meet. There was no other way of looking at it. Sonny Lutz was not only getting in his way, he was defying the Lord, and there should be a punishment for that.

Alvis looked around wondering what he could do, what he could break. There were no windows in the openings yet, no glass he could shatter. There didn't seem to be any tools around; like the good farmboy he was Sonny had put everything away. He knew he probably couldn't keep the house from being built, but didn't want to leave without doing something to keep his rival from feeling secure. Sonny Lutz had to know he was in a war, and battle could take place at any time and take any form. Alvis wanted him to have to pay attention to that for a while. Let *him* lie awake at night wondering if he were about to lose, and his life soon to be ruined. Let's see how much work he gets done then, he thought.

Alvis stepped through the doorway down into the yard, stumbling over the pile of dirt that came from Sonny and Johnny Crouse digging the foundation footing. He looked around trying to see what was in the yard, barely able to make out shapes in the darkness. There was a pile of stones that had been unloaded from a wagon to his left, and framing timbers beyond it. Scattering them around the yard wouldn't do much good. Sonny would just pick them up and put them back, probably cursing about kids coming around late at night. He had to do something more serious, something that would give Sonny a message. If only he could think of...

◆ ◆ ◆

Peter Metzger could not be killed, he kept telling himself. He thought about heading home after the farmer gave up and went back inside. He spent ten minutes weighing it all, deciding if he could get away with it, if his cause was honorable enough for him to survive. He had to work hard to convince himself that it was, had to change some beliefs, revise some history, but eventually created a truth that allowed him to continue to search for Anna Rose secure in the thought that he would be safe.

Over the next several hours he rode into the yards of each of the farms in Meem's Bottom even though he was certain she wasn't around. Feeling as if he were performing a sacrament, he peered into windows at families eating dinner, at a widow sitting alone in a chair reading a book, at a man who kissed and fondled his wife. He opened barn doors, and sneaked into dark sheds whispering her name like an obsessed lover.

It was only when he walked into the church at Mount Airy that he expected her to be there. For some reason, for a few seconds before he pulled open the door, there was a sensation that ran through him, a rush of affection he believed could have been caused only by her waiting inside. But once in the sanctuary, lit by just the dim glow of lamps coming through windows of houses nearby, he knew she wasn't there, not seated on the first step to the altar as he expected, and would not stand, smile and whisper "Hello, Peter."

That was the only time that night he became angry, not at her, not at himself, but at the world, the heavens, God, and at any other force that might be controlling the events of the night and of his life. It was then that he was ready to be done with this, thinking he had accomplished enough, had spent three hours in pouring rain, had been consumed by a nervous fear of being caught, and the demoralizing effect of possible failure, yet kept on going. He would have turned and headed for home then, but there was one more place he had to go.

The only way to get to Screamersville from where Peter was on the Mount Airy road was to go back to the turnpike. When he reached the intersection he pulled his horse to a halt. To the right was the route home. He stared into the darkness up the turnpike like a man yearning for a long lost friend. It was now close to midnight. The rain had eased about an hour before, but was starting to pick up again, this time accompanied by thunder and lightning. He could see the sky light up just to the west, somewhere near Third Hill. The thunder was loud and belligerent like advancing marauders, the clouds, when they showed, were ugly and threatening.

Anna wasn't around. She wouldn't know if he left without searching everywhere for her, but *he* would. If he left now he might start to wonder about her affection for him, become insecure, perhaps even desperate. It would show, and she would realize why. This was Maggie's girl. Keeping a secret from her would be like trying to hide from God. Reluctantly, Peter turned his horse to the left, headed south on the Valley Turnpike, then ten minutes later took the road that ran to Screamersville.

Peter had never been as afraid as he was that night taking what was called the Hiden Springs Road. For the first half of a mile or so its route was through pasture; there was no place for the rogues to hide, but later, where it paralleled Smith Creek on its way to the ford, anyone could be down the embankment waiting for him, and get to him before he could react. Fortunately the storm was now right above him; the lightning not only illuminated the path, but everything else as well. That, and their fear of God's wrath, might be enough to scare any bandits away. It was his plan to ride down one street, then up the next, get back to the turnpike as quickly as possible, then trot all of the way home. Logically, with some luck, everyone would be in bed as he rode through the town. They wouldn't even know he had been there.

But, as in all of the Screamersvilles of the world, the inhabitants never seemed to sleep. Just as he crossed the line into town with a shanty on one side and a shack on the other, the lightning flashed. In that burst of brightness he saw at least five dirty faces with blank stares and wide eyes looking straight at him like the dead come to life. He gasped in a breath, wrapped the reins tightly around his hands in preparation to flee, but continued down the bog they called a street. There were no other sounds he could hear, just the storm as the rain pelted wood roofs and paper windows, or splashed into puddles that were already full. There seemed to be no movement but his, as if his presence had made the people there stop what they were doing like felons caught in the act. They sat or stood, just watched him go by as if it were the Fourth of July and he was on parade. Peter reached the end of the street and took a breath for the first time in five minutes.

This was almost over. He had done everything Anna could have expected of him. All he had to do was make it up the second street without his mind and his heart wavering, without him starting to resent her for making him do this, or wondering what this really was. If he could keep the faith for another two hundred yards, then he should be...

"Hey, mister, at's a nice horse you ave there."

Peter wasn't sure were the voice came from. The sound was shrouded by the rain. He thought it was from the side, from a spectator, but the lightning blazed, and he saw him standing in the muddy street just in front. In his right hand he held what seemed to be a gun. Peter considered just swatting his horse and galloping home, but he saw this as a challenge to his ability to scare his enemies away.

"Well, thank you," Peter replied in a friendly voice. "Say, what do you have there? Is that a pistol?"

"Why yes, it is. It was quick of ya ta see that."

"Thanks. But, you know, the trouble with pistols is that they are no good when it rains. Your powder gets wet, and you can't fire the durn thing. What you really need is one of these." Peter quickly reached into his inside coat pocket. "You probably can't see it. It's a revolver. It's sort of new. It fires cartridges. You don't have to worry about the powder getting wet with one of these."

"Yeah, I've eard of em. Fact, ere's a good chance I might be gittin one soon, damn soon."

"Well, if you work hard and save your money, then yes, maybe you will."

"Well, shoot, I thought ere might be an easier way. Like, maybe ya could give me yers."

"I would like to, I really would, but I am afraid that that is not in the best interest of society. You see we have a system that rewards initiative and hard work. It is what makes our culture strong. If I let you have something for nothing, then I undermine the whole process and our civilization crumbles. Do you see what I am saying?"

"An yer horse, too."

"Well, that falls along the same lines as what I said before. Where would the incentive be in working hard?"

"You kin purty much climb down anytime."

Peter had never shot a man; he never even considered it. Shenandoah County was no longer on the frontier; it wasn't the kind of place where a man needed a gun everyday. He brought one with him just in case this happened, and was glad he did, but he wasn't sure what he was going to do with it. If he fired where he thought the boy was and missed, he might have a mob on him before he could get away. If he hit him, then there was the sheriff he would have to face. How was he going to explain being in Screamersville late at night? He certainly couldn't tell the truth, that some girl wanted him there so he could prove his love for her. That was almost as pitiful as being up in one of Maggie's bedrooms wearing a dress.

"Whatta doin, thinkin bout it? If ya think about it much longer, then ya better git ready ta duck."

"Duck? Why?"

CHAPTER 14

"Good morning."

"Mornin," Johnny replied as he hiked slowly up from the road. His eyelids were heavy, his face puffy. When he reached Sonny just outside the doorway of the house he let out a massive yawn like a fish taking in water.

"Got a pot of coffee on the stove in the cabin if you want some."

"Nah, that's okay. Might wake me up, an I'd realize where I am. Jist as soon believe I'm still sleepin, an this is a dream."

Sonny smiled at that. He walked over, picked up a board that was about two inches thick, six inches wide and about six feet long. He laid it across two wooden sawhorses as Johnny took a step back. "Speaking of sleeping, you didn't come around here last night by any chance, did you?" Sonny said.

"Last night? Uh, uh. You know me, I generally don't like ta hang around any place where there's work ta be done if I don't hafta. Why?"

Sonny shrugged. His head shook in short, quick tremors.

"Why? What happened? Somethin git taken?"

"Nah, not that. At least nothing that I have noticed. It is just, just something somebody did. Kind of a joke, I guess."

Johnny could tell Sonny was a little upset by what happened, whatever it was. "What?"

"Ah, they just made an arrow over there for some reason.

Took one of those two- by- fours, laid it on the ground, took some rocks, and made a point like an arrow."

"Aw, gee."

"A bunch of kids, probably, was all it was."

"Yeah... Probly." Johnny glanced over at the ground where Sonny pointed. "Where was it, zactly?" he asked. "Which way was it pointin?"

"I don't know." Sonny was holding a four foot long measuring stick in both hands, so he just nodded over toward the rail fence. "There somewhere."

Johnny wandered around until he found where the pasture grass was still flattened. He circled the impression several times, then stopped and gazed out at the countryside to the east. "It was pointin that way." He had an expression of sorrow on his face as if his favorite tavern just closed.

Sonny looked over and nodded. He marked the board with a pencil.

"Ain't that the direction the Faradays live. Her."

Sonny stopped with the saw poised in the air."Yeah, I suppose. What are you saying, that somebody did that because I'm taking her on that picnic tomorrow?"

"Well, sure would be one way ta look at it. I mean, nobody's bin round here fore now. An it did point right toward her."

"Ah. Could have been anyone. Doesn't have to mean that."

"Yeah, it coulda bin made ta look like an Indian's arrow, which sorta makes me think of Maggie."

"Yes, it could have."

"Ya sure ya wanna go through with this?"

"I am getting a little tired of people asking me that. It was just some kids, okay?"

"Yeah. Actually, it was probably some other boy that likes her tryin ta scare ya away." Johnny walked over and leaned down on the board Sonny was about to cut to hold it in place.

"I suppose. That is a pretty feeble way to court a girl if you ask me," Sonny said as he began to saw. "Who might have done it, do you think?"

"Oh, I dunno."

"What about that blacksmith?" Sonny said loudly to be heard over the grinding of the saw. "Ian, whatshisname? He is not back, is he?"

"Uh, uh, still gone, an it's gittin some people talkin, I'll tell ya. Woulda thought he mighta turned up somewhere by now, Winchester or someplace. Day after he was at Maggie's with her, he vanishes off the face of the earth. Least his body shoulda floated to the top."

"I thought you said that his stuff was gone, too."

"Yeah, well, she mighta sunk it all with him. Smith's anvil be real good fer that."

Sonny stopped sawing halfway through the board. He was grinning. "Do people really think she might do something like that? It is a little farfetched, isn't it?"

"She shot her own husband, Sonny! Yeah, she might do something like that. I mean, this is Ian Froth we're talkin bout. He come around my daughter, I might wanna do him harm, too. Well, cept, uh, we'd, uh, be purty much thrilled if any boy would show her some attention. Have a feelin I'm gonna be workin ta feed her til I drop dead from exhaustion."

"Yeah. Nah, it probably was not because of Maggie that he is gone. From what you said about the way he is, he might have just met some other real pretty girl and run off with her."

"Cept there ain't no pretty girls missin. I keep count."

"Yesh, well, it does not mean that Maggie had anything to do with it. Shoot, I was over at Anna's house last night, and I am still here." Sonny put his arms out as if to demonstrate that he was still alive. The blade of the saw in his right hand flexed and boomed like thunder.

"You went to her house?"

"Yes, it was Marion's idea. I mean, sending her a letter was fine, but Marion said I ought to go over in person and introduce myself to her and her parents before Sunday."

"Last night?"

"Yes. Last night."

"You were over at her house last night an somebody puts that arrow there. What more do ya need, boy? My God, if I were you, I'd find me another girl real quick."

❖ ❖ ❖

"Lord forgive me for what I am about to do," Hessie whispered. She paused for a few seconds to wait for her heart to slow and her breathing to calm, then rapped three times on Anna's bedroom door. She heard the bedstead creak, then footsteps coming toward her. When Anna opened the door she had an expression of annoyance on her face as if the intrusion had interrupted something momentous she was doing. When she saw it was Hessie her expression softened, but not by much. She left the door open and walked back over to the bed, allowing Hessie to enter into the room.

"What's wrong?"

"I thought you were my mother." The words came out almost as a whine.

Hessie sat down in a chair a few feet from the bed. "What has she done this time?"

"Oh, just this matter about me going on the picnic tomorrow. I don't know those people; I don't know how much fun it would be."

Hessie nodded in sympathy. She was a little concerned about it herself, but as long as Anna kept this attitude she felt there was no danger there. It was a fine line, she realized. If Anna refused to have anything to do with another boy, then her mother was going to assume she still had some affection for Peter, and send her away to Fauquier County where she would be out of Hessie's control. Anna could fall in love there and be married by the end of the summer. Hessie had considered asking if she could go with her, but figured her father wouldn't allow her to go off practically on her own like that. His idea of raising a daughter was to keep her locked in her bedroom until she died of terminal virginity. Her only hope was to drive out any feeling Anna might still have for Peter. She wasn't sure if it would perk her up enough for her mother to stop being so concerned, but she had to try. She would deal with Sonny Lutz later if he became a problem. She hesitated a few seconds before she spoke to compose herself again. She wanted to make it sound spontaneous even though she had spent most of the morning and the hour since lunch running it through her mind. "Do I have something to tell you," she said with a look of rehearsed excitement on her face.

"What?" Anna acted as if there was nothing Hessie could say that would have any effect on her mood.

Hessie glanced toward the open door, got up, walked over, stuck her head out, looked up and down the hallway, closed the door, went back and sat down. She leaned forward with her hands on her knees. "Guess who they found lying in the road in his underwear near Screamersville this morning?" she whispered.

Anna seemed to shake her head and shrug with indifference at the same time. That was enough of a response for Hessie.

"Peter Metzger."

"What?"

"They found Peter lying in the road in just his underwear this morning near Screamersville."

"Wait a minute. Who found him? What…"

"Um, I don't know. 'They.' That is what they said; 'They found him.'"

"Dead? Was he dead?"

"No, no, he was just sleeping, or knocked unconscious, or drunk, or something." Thank goodness, it was just that, Hessie thought. Peter getting beaten up made her feel awful as it was. She always felt she was the moral one, that the others were selfish and evil. She spent the morning trying to dislodge the fear she may have crossed the line with this, but eventually convinced herself she had no way of knowing how it would turn out. She only wanted Anna to never, ever be interested in Peter again. Just him being seen around Screamersville at night would have been enough.

"Who told you this? When? This morning? Last night?"

"I went to Palotti's Mill with my father this morning. It was all they were talking about."

"Screamersville? What was Peter doing near Screamersville?"

Hessie showed Anna a mask of disbelief. She wondered if she was going to have to explain everything to her.

"What?" Anna said in reaction to Hessie's expression. "What is in Screamersville?"

Hessie turned away as if it were a question she did not want to answer. She paused before she spoke, not out of reluctance, but from a fear that her enthusiasm might be obvious. "Whores."

"What?"

"Whores. Prostitutes. They have whores in Screamersville, Anna. And from what I understand, not very expensive ones. You do know what — "

"Yes, I know what whores are," Anna said quickly. "Is that why Peter was there?"

"Can you think of any other reason why he would be in Screamersville late at night?"

Anna had the look of a young child trying hard to think of the answer to an adult's question. Her eyes squinted, wrinkling the skin on her forehead; her mouth seemed to be poised in readiness to speak as soon as her mind figured out the correct response. The rest of her wasn't moving as if she was using all of her energy to process the information. "Peter does that?" She didn't wait for Hessie to answer. "Is that why he wanted Granna's money? For them?" She knew she wasn't really asking a question. She didn't expect Hessie to answer. Her gaze seemed to be to the inside of herself. "Are all men that weak?" This time she did turn to Hessie for the answer.

Hessie shrugged. This was working better than she

thought. This might turn Anna against men for months, for years even. She had to be careful with that, or Anna was going to figure it out. "It is what we count on, isn't it? Them being so weak."

Anna went from a blank, dull expression to a smile, then a giggle. "Yes, I suppose it does help. But can we trust any of them? I always thought that falling in love would be easy. It's, it's like being outside during a thunderstorm. You never know if you are going to get hit by lightning."

"Yes, it can be. That is a very good way to put it. You never know, do you? I mean, a man can seem to be perfectly all right, decent and kind, but he might be hiding some dark secret that you will not find out until it is too late." Oh, thank you, thank you, thank you. "What is Sonny Lutz like?"

"Oh, I don't know." Anna slumped down on the bed. "You know that he came by last night?"

"Yes, I heard."

"He just showed up without letting me know that he was coming. He didn't even change out of his work clothes. He rode his horse, instead of coming in a carriage so he was soaking wet by the time he got here. I mean, he seems nice enough, but he asked about my school, and I asked about his farm, so now we have nothing to talk about tomorrow."

CHAPTER 15

"Hey, Sonny, which way ya gonna go?"

Sonny couldn't help but hear the question, as loud as Jerome Miller shouted it, but the words didn't register right away since he was in a state of shock and panic caused by Anna's reaction to having to travel to the Springs in a farm wagon. *A farm wagon*? She didn't say anything, but that seemed to be an expression of repulsion on her face when she first saw it sitting in front of the house with Jerome and Elizabeth in back. They noticed it as well, he was sure of that. Elizabeth seemed to be annoyed and disgusted at Anna's response, as if she thought Anna felt she was too good to ride in a mere farm wagon, a princess like her. He immediately wanted to apologize, to explain, but there was really nothing he could say. He, of course, did not own a carriage. That came with wealth at a later age, and there wasn't one he could have borrowed, except his parents' two person gig, and since he had to bring Jerome and Elizabeth with them, that wouldn't have done. This was a disaster already, and they hadn't even made it down to the road. Maybe Marion was right — it was going to be too much for him. Somehow he was feeling despondent and frenzied at the same time. What was it Jerome asked?

"Um, I thought we would just go straight down the Middle Road here," Sonny heard himself call back. "It's the easiest way."

"Why don't we cut over to the Back Road. It's a real purty drive."

"Oh, I don't know." Sonny tried to sound cheerful, friendly, but just thinking about having to make a decision was getting him irritated. Some of those hills over there were steep. With the rain two nights before it might be muddy — two horses, four people and a wagon, they might have to get out and walk up. That would just about do it, making Anna walk in the mud. He couldn't make Elizabeth walk, she just realized she was pregnant about a week before, and they were there just as a favor to him, the only young married couple he knew well enough to bring along as chaperones. Jerome was probably going to do this the whole way down there.

He was like that. He should have tried harder to get Charlie and Marion to come. He was thinking this, right? He wasn't actually talking to himself, was he? Not yet, anyway.

"Nah, this will be okay. Besides, if we go by your place, you might decide to jump out, and go in and take a nap." Sonny instantly wondered if he should have said that, making Jerome look lazy like that.

But she laughed. Oh, thank God. Sonny looked over at her to confirm he wasn't hearing things that weren't there. She was still smiling. He twisted to grin at Jerome and Elizabeth. They grinned back. Yeah. This might be okay.

"I am sorry to make you ride in a wagon," he said, as the words flashed from his mind to his tongue. "It is — "

"Oh, no, this is *fine.*" Anna said, sounding sincere, protesting Sonny's apology. " I ride in ours all of the time. Usually in back with the others. It is nice to be able to sit up here."

Orkney Springs, for those who do not know, occupies the southwestern corner of Shenandoah County, up hard against the sheer wooded slopes of Great North Mountain in the Allegheny Range. It was mostly a local resort since the turn of the century with various owners, but by the early 50's more people were willing to make the long journey over bad roads in coaches, carriages or on horseback from other parts of Virginia.

Originally called "Yellow Springs" from the golden residue the water left on the rocks, it was said the minerals there cured or prevented a number of ailments. For the people of Shenandoah County it was someplace that wasn't home, just a short trip to get them off the farm and away from work for a few hours. There were meadows where they could lounge on blankets and the children could play, and woods to hide lovers as they strolled along the headwaters of Stony Creek.

The trip from the Faraday farm took about two hours over roads that were rutted and rocky. The wheels would slide from side to side, threatening to get them stuck. The wagon would bounce up and down sometimes so severely that Sonny felt a need to apologize as if it were his fault. They talked some at first, quick comments that required no response, followed by an awkward, deathly silence, until Sonny asked Anna if she had gone to church that morning, then wished he hadn't, feeling it might be too personal and perhaps a little judgmental, but Anna cheerfully replied that she, her mother, and her grandmother had gone to services at the Lutheran church, then had to repeat it when Elizabeth asked again.

There followed a discussion of several people they both knew, stories about women and their babies, about the elderly and their ailments, that sort of thing. Sonny appeared to be interested in the gossip, said, "Huh," several times, but was soon lost in the array of names and relationships.

Elizabeth asked Anna about her seminary, what it was like, what she had studied, and for fifteen minutes there was gap between her and the other three in education and status that they all seemed to be aware of, even though Anna was reluctant to say much more than she had to in order to answer Elizabeth's questions. Sonny tried not to let it bother him, but couldn't find a way around the fact that they lived in different worlds, that he might seem ordinary and inferior compared to her and her life. His mind rushed to find something he could say to make him look educated, some comment about the world, about art or music or politics or philosophy, something to show he did have some interest in the things that interested her, but his life was farming, his family, church, and little more. The discussion ended without him adding a thing.

It was only when Anna asked Elizabeth about the baby and whether they had chosen a name that the conversation involved all four of them, and soon became lively. For the next hour they made up names, and variations on them. Sonny and Jerome irrepressibly threw out any names they could think of, each more absurd than the next. By the time they climbed Supin Lick Ridge and were descending toward the Stony Creek valley they had unanimously decided on George Washington Jefferson Matthew Mark Charlemagne Plato Jerome Miller if it were a boy, and Mary Maggie Betsy Ross Maggie Annette Elizabeth Barrett Elizabeth Miller for a girl. If by chance Elizabeth gave birth to a pony, they would call it Thunder.

Members of Sonny's church were already at the Springs when they arrived. Although the congregation at the Conicville United Brethren Church numbered no more than a hundred, and the regular attendees usually about half of that, there were at least 60 people down at the Springs that day. They laid claim to a lawn behind a whitewashed log building that was one of the three rooming houses at the resort. Almost directly across the street from it was the first floor framing of a new hotel, one that would have twelve guest rooms when it was done, someone said. As Sonny walked from the wagon toward the gathering he examined the construction, compared it to what he could do, then nodded to indicate to himself that they weren't any better at it than he was.

When he turned back around he saw that all eyes were on him and Anna as they approached, although a few of the women and most of the men pretended they were taking food out of baskets or carrying on conversations while they looked sideways at them. "She's so pretty," a young girl exclaimed so loudly that Anna heard it and began to blush.

For the next half an hour Sonny felt as if he had only

been her driver. There wasn't a person there who did not have some connection to the Fricks, the Bledsoes, the Siglers or the Faradays. At least seven of them were related to Anna somehow, and told her so, which reminded Sonny that he too was one of her distant cousins. He wanted to tell her this, but she was surrounded and being talked to by so many people he couldn't get close enough to speak to her. So, at the urging of some of the men, he left her there and wandered off with them across the street to look at the new hotel and to talk about things that men talk about when the women have more important things to do.

Anna felt trapped at first, so many people, so many questions and comments. She wouldn't be finished responding to one woman when another would ask her a question. She had no choice but to be brief to someone. They didn't care. She began to feel the elevation of unconditional admiration. It no longer mattered to her that she didn't feel very pretty that day; hadn't done a good job of brushing her hair, did not like her dress, or that she was feuding with her mother, and still a little broken-hearted about Peter Metzger, or sore from being bounced up and down on the ride there, or that the gnats were swarming all around her. She smiled sincerely, giggled and laughed, and when a two year old girl offered her a pine cone as a gift, she graciously accepted it, then reached down and lifted the child and held her in her arms for the next half an hour.

"Okay, who's the next batter?"

"Have you ever seen this played?" Elizabeth asked Anna as they walked over and sat on a blanket on the edge of the field after the meal was done and the woman had washed the dishes in the creek, and put them back in baskets.

"No, what is it? I..."

"It is called baseball."

"Oh, *this* is baseball. I have heard of it. What do they do?"

"Well, the pitcher, that's John there, throws the ball at the batter. That stick thing that Wallace is holding is called a bat, and he tries to hit the ball with the bat, then run to first base over there before anyone catches the ball and touches him with it or hits him with it."

"Hits him with it? Doesn't that hurt?"

"Probably. But men aren't happy if they aren't hurting themselves one way or another, are they?"

Anna shrugged as she wondered if that was true. Maybe Elizabeth was right; she had never thought about that. She realized there were quite a few things she didn't know about men, or understand.

"They can be strange creatures, can't they?" Elizabeth said, as if she knew what Anna was thinking.

Anna was taken by surprise. She giggled. "Yes, I know. I mean, why can't they be more, uh, more..."

"More like us?"

"Yes!"

"Would we have any need for them then? They would just be hideous women. I like the fact that Jerome works until he is too tired to move. I like the fact that he is strong and protective so I don't have to be. If he has to do strange things like play baseball then that is fine. I just think..."

Anna looked out into the field just as Sonny ran after a ball that was hit over his head. She had never seen a grown man run like that. Her brothers were always chasing each other playing tag or another child's game, but to see a man do this seemed odd, out of place, almost undignified, yet ... There *was* something appealing about it. He moved the way an animal might in the forest or on the plains, chasing prey or to escape being it, a warrior charging into battle; long, graceful strides, perfect balance. There was a power the actions displayed, something not ordinary, as if within him, within all of them, there slept the prowess of beasts, unused and hidden by day to day tasks. When he caught up to the ball he spun and threw it with such a force that a soft whelp escaped her throat and her heart began to race as if being a spectator was enough to transform her as well.

This was a disaster, Sonny was thinking as he trotted up the field. Why did she have to look over then, just as he let a ball go over his head. It was as if he had never played baseball before, as foolish as that was. He must have looked ridiculous running after it. What a bad idea this was, bringing her here, making her ride in a wagon, then being set upon by all those people from church — now him looking as if he could not do a simple thing like play baseball. He should have come up with something else for them to do. Like what? They could sit on her porch while she talked about Greek philosophers or French poets, and he described what his sheep did that day? Maybe he could invite her over to watch him plow a field. Wouldn't that be fun? If he were lucky Elizabeth was telling her what a fine person he was, decent, hardworking, things like that. Maybe that would be enough for her to want to see him again.

"Jerome is a farmer?" Anna asked, disappointed the players seemed to be standing around while the batter swung the bat and missed several pitches.

"That's three strikes! One more an yer out."

"No, he's a blacksmith. He and his father have a shop in Conicville. They are always busy."

"Oh."

"I hear you are friends with that blacksmith in Stony Creek. Ian Froth." The name hung in the air like the distant rumble of thunder.

That seemed so long ago now, Anna was thinking, as if it had happened in another life. "Yes," she said, casually. "He was at my great-grandmother's birthday party. I spoke with him there for some time."

Elizabeth had no response to that, not that it required one. She stared at Anna for a few seconds, perhaps waiting for her to continue, or maybe trying to read her mind. She turned back to the field and watched a batter hit a ball high into the air that another player ran over and caught. "If they catch the ball before it hits the ground, then that is an out."

The game might have gone on forever. It did last almost two hours. By then many of the men were bent over trying to catch their breathes in between pitches, or moving slowly going after batted balls, but no one dared admit they had enough. What stopped them was the mother of one of the players walking over and calling out, "Hey, whatta ya say ya all come on over, an we start singin now?"

There were expressions of protests on some faces, resignation on others, but none said anything to object. Even before they left the field they begun the second most important part of the game — talking about it. Plays were recalled and discussed, someone pointed toward the woods where a ball had landed, one story contradicted another, and the friendly arguments started that would last until the next time they got together on the field. When they reached the spectators the talking abruptly stopped as if it were a ritual men performed only in secret.

Sonny felt and looked meek as he and Jerome walked over to where Anna and Elizabeth lounged on the blanket. He wasn't sure what she thought of the whole thing, but he was embarrassed by the way he played, perhaps even by the fact that he *had* played, as if thinking he seemed unrestrained and brutal during the game, showed a side of him that might have frightened her. He was feeling he now had to appear to be civilized and unthreatening, so he smiled, hung his head slightly and was careful not to look right at her.

"Who won?" Elizabeth asked.

"That doesn't matter," Jerome replied. "We were just havin fun."

"Oh, I'm so sorry."

Sonny cackled at that. Anna did not seem to understand the joke, so she just smiled while gazing up at Sonny, who continued to look off to the side. He still hadn't spoken to her since they walked over. She wasn't sure if he was being shy, was tired from playing, or if there was something wrong. She still had a vague gnawing of insecurity caused by Elizabeth's icy stare when she mentioned she talked to Ian Froth at Maggie's birthday party. While she watched Sonny play she went from embarrassment to fear to panic, and, after working hard to justify it, acceptance that she had done nothing wrong, and if anyone was at fault it was Elizabeth for being so strict and judgmental. There weren't that many people in Shenandoah County; one couldn't help but associate with someone who's life they might not approve of. It was really none of Elizabeth's... "That was fun to watch," Anna finally said, afraid Sonny might never speak to her again.

"Aww," Sonny dared to look over at her. He had to tell if she was being sincere. He smiled at her smile, raised his head up some. Now if he only could think of something to say so he wouldn't be just standing there with that silly grin on his face. "Um, yeah, it was." That was smart. "I mean, it was fun to play, too. I am not very good at it. I don't play as much as some of the others. There is a team at the church that play teams from other churches, but I usually do not have time." That's enough.

Anna nodded. "That was fun to watch," she said again.

"Come on, you all, get over here. Tom has a new song that he wants to teach us."

❖ ❖ ❖

"Oww! Damnit!" Alvis muttered. "Damnit all to hell! Jesus!" Reaching up he grabbed hold of a branch above his head, and using all the strength in his scrawny arms, pulled himself up far enough so he was almost standing. He wiggled his body left and right, twisted his torso, tried to lift his leg, but his foot still wouldn't budge from the fork of the tree. He leaned left, then right, pushed himself away, but the ground fifteen feet below seemed further than that, so he got nervous and pulled himself back in. It was about then the singing started. He snapped his head around to look over his shoulder. "Ain't that sweet," he said, seeing part of the congregation through the leaves. "Farmboy sings, does he? He must be a sissy."

Peter Metzger was thinking pretty much the same thing nine trees down. The baseball game scared him. It took him most of an hour to convince himself that no girl would be impressed with a man just because he could run fast and throw a ball. In fact, there was something childish about the whole thing, as if Sonny Lutz had nothing better to do than to play some foolish game. Most men were concerned with making themselves better, elevating themselves, and here was Sonny Lutz running around a field like a headless chicken. He watched Anna while the game was going on, through the telescope and without it, and she did not seem very interested. She chatted with the woman she sat with, and even that did not seem to go well. There were long pauses in the conversation; she seemed to be uncomfortable at times.

So he came to the conclusion she was there just to convince her family that she liked someone else, so they wouldn't get suspicious about the two of them. But it still bothered him to see her with Sonny. Accidents happen. She might inexplicably fall for the guy. He really needed to see her, or at least to give her a sign he was around and cared, and he needed to get a sign from her. He started getting annoyed again that Hessie didn't show up at the barn the night before, the night after he was at Meem's Bottom. He assumed she would be there; he thought Anna might be there as well. After all he went through that evening — the humiliation of being beaten, robbed and left by the road, there wasn't much more he could have done to prove his devotion to her. Somehow Anna should have showed that she appreciated it all.

But now they were singing like school children, so maybe this would be okay. If that wasn't ridiculous. She was probably bored to death by it all. That was the trouble with people like them; there was never any excitement in their lives. They fought no wars, tried to conquer no worlds, didn't really do much except work and raise children and die. This was probably thrilling for them, the most fun they've had in years. Where was the exhilaration of hard fought victory and the terror of possible defeat. Why bother getting up in the morning if not to keep your life from being ruined? What about the demons one has to destroy, the dragons that have to be slain? Where is the passion? Was that thunder?

The first clap didn't stop the singing. It fit in like a bass drum accompaniment. The second was louder, closer and got everyone's attention. Being next to the mountains they hadn't noticed the black clouds that were coming their way, couldn't see them with the trees on the slope hiding the western sky. With the third boom they didn't need to see what was there. It got them to stand, to yank blankets off the ground, then start to move in so many directions so quickly they ran into each other, impeded each others' progress, stepped one way then another trying to work their way out of the crowd and get to shelter.

Sonny offered a hand to help Anna up. He was surprised at how soft her skin was. Once she was on her feet he let go, but with the throng pushing them one way and another, he took her hand again and began to lead her away. The thunder no longer mattered to him. The rain, when it started, was not really there. All that existed in the world was the sensation of his hand cupping hers, and hers his. No sight, no sound, no other people. Not just tactile, not that simple or ordinary, but not sensual, not at first, nor was it a fusion of beings, a merger of souls, at least not yet. For just a few moments it was an unthreatening world for Sonny, nothing more than that, just the feeling of having a person on his side who did not have to be there. He didn't know where he was taking her, and didn't care. He could have weathered the storm with her holding onto his hand like that. Somehow he vaguely, unconsciously followed everyone else around to the front porch of the log rooming house. He let her hand go. The sensation was gone. She wiped the water off her face as he watched, unaware his face was dripping as well. He started to say something, but more people came onto the porch, and they had to step back, then further as more crowded in, moving to the back wall as sixty people squeezed into a space barely large enough for thirty.

The lightening sliced and flashed to the ground about every minute; the thunder cracked; the wind picked up and howled, driving the rain sideways, so those at the edges of the porch pushed in to avoid it. Anna felt pressure on her back and moved closer to Sonny. He had to inch his way toward her as well. Soon there was no space in between. His chest pressed against her breasts; his thigh touched hers. He wasn't sure what to do with his hands so he kept them at his side. Her head was slightly to the side of his, her left cheek was just off of his.

Anna had never been this close to a man in the six years since her father died. Richard Faraday was not a man for hugs. She knew it was improper; she understood that well. Sonny was practically a stranger, but there wasn' much she could do. She had no thoughts about what Sonny might be feeling. Her knowledge of men and their responses was not that deep. But she was aware of her need for security with the storm raging just a few feet away, and in a desire to further escape it, she nestled her face onto Sonny's shoulder, her cheek brushing his, the skin of her neck rubbing the collar of his shirt. Sonny finally did what he had wanted to do for the last few minutes; he brought his hands up and placed them on her back, not pressing her toward him, the crowd had already done that, but gently, softly touching her, letting her know he was there. She embraced him as well; her arms running under his as if holding him in place.

CHAPTER 16

"Books?" Johnny asked. "Yeah, Sloane's in Woodstock. Think Wilhelm's got some, too."

"Wilhelm's does?"

"Yeah. Used ones. Way in the back, if ya kin git through all that junk."

Sonny nodded. He didn't seem to be in much of a talkative mood that day, so Johnny let him get by with that little bit of a response. He had yet to ask him about the picnic, whether he had a good time, or if he thought Anna did. He hadn't been there on Monday. Elias Meyer, Sonny's grandfather, needed some rotted barnboards replaced. When he got there on Tuesday the look on Sonny's face was so vague, so undecipherable he thought he best not bring it up. He figured maybe Sonny had come to his senses, realized there really was too much danger in courting Maggie's girl. That was fine with him. He didn't want to have to worry about standing too close to him in case Maggie missed. He was going to sleep a whole lot better if he weren't involved in a plot that had something to do with Anna Rose.

Still, he was curious about what happened. Sonny asking about books made him think maybe he was wrong assuming the day went badly, and that Sonny wasn't going to see her again. "Plannin on doin some readin?" he asked after nearly a minute of silence.

The look Sonny gave him seemed to show he was annoyed as if it was a foolish question. It made Johnny decide not pursue it. He turned his back on Sonny immediately, but realized he forgot how long the board was he was getting ready to cut. He was afraid to ask again, so he walked toward the window with a measuring stick in his hand. He could feel Sonny's eyes on him as he checked it again.

"Forty-three and a quarter, isn't it?"

It sounded like a complaint. Johnny felt as if he had been chastised. He wasn't used to that from Sonny. They always got along fine. Johnny knew what he was doing, seldom made a mistake, but when did, Sonny usually shrugged it off or joked about it. He didn't want to snap back at him, that wouldn't do any good, but he couldn't leave things the way they were. "Oh, yeah," he said as he picked up the saw, "How'd things go Sunday with Anna Rose?" He spun around to be able to gauge Sonny's reaction.

Sonny seemed to be working hard to appear nonchalant, like a felon insisting on his innocence. "Fine, fine," he said with a shrug of his shoulders, but with a look of apprehension in his eyes. "It went fine," he said a little too quickly, and with a voice that was a little too high. "I had a good time. I think she did, too. It was not of much importance, actually. It was just a picnic."

Johnny was aware he was staring, but couldn't help it. There was something wrong here. He thought looking at him hard would give him a clue as to what it was, but Sonny turned away without another word, and went back to nailing the piece of window jamb that was in the opening.

But in between the blows of the hammer Sonny realized he wasn't hearing the saw cutting wood. His hammer paused at the top of the swing as he figured Johnny was expecting more. The barrier came down gradually, like a mountain eroding over centuries. "Actually," he said, allowing himself to lean against the wall like a man too weak to stand, "I think it was one of the best times, the, uh, best, I don't know, the best feeling I have ever had in my life."

Johnny nodded slowly as his eyes went back in thought. His brow wrinkled. "Well, I guess I kin see why yer bein so fretful then. A good time like that would be enough ta torment any man."

"And if it never happens again?"

"Is that what yer so worried bout? What, you think that what happened with Clarisa is gonna happen here?"

That thought made Sonny stand upright. His eyes grew wide with recognition. "Yeah, maybe."

"You learned somethin from that, didn't ya?"

"Yes, that what follows feeling good and being happy, is misery."

"Ah, yer worryin too much."

"Shouldn't I?" Sonny took a step toward Johnny. "I've been thinking about this. I know what it is like now. If she had not wanted to go with me in the first place, that would have been fine; I would have been disappointed, but gotten over it. Now, if she does not want to see me again, then, well, maybe there is something wrong with me. I mean, she has gotten to know me some now. Do you see what I am saying?"

"What yer sayin is that you've thought about this way too much. You sound like a philosopher, or somethin."

"Oh, yeah, which one? Which philosopher?"

"Uh, I, uh..."

"She would know. She could probably name a half a dozen, and, and I am like you, I would just stand there with my mouth wide open looking stupid. Uh, no offense."

"Yeah, okay."

"So you can see I have a problem."

"Well, what'd *she* say? I mean, did she —"

"She did not complain about anything, but maybe she was just being nice. I don't know."

"You couldn't tell? How come you can't tell when a girl is havin a good time? Did she smile, laugh, that sort of thing? Did she want to go home early?"

"I don't know. No, she —"

"Think, boy. Try to remember."

Sonny started at the beginning, when he picked her up in the wagon. He told Johnny about Jerome and Elizabeth, about the ride down there, what Anna said about her school. He recalled every bump in the road, every time they raced downhill so fast that Anna was probably scared they were going to turn over, and probably wondered if Sonny knew how to handle a wagon. He talked about the throng that descended on her when they first got there, how he was embarrassed, afraid they wouldn't leave her alone, about the baseball game, which baffled Johnny since he knew nothing of the sport and had no idea what Sonny was talking about. Then Sonny told him about the storm, and their flight to the shelter of the porch. His speech slowed, he hemmed and hawed, turned bright red, but kept on going, telling him how they were pushed further and further back, and closer and closer together.

"Ya hugged her right there in front of everyone? My God, boy, yer gonna hafta marry the girl."

A smile burst through Sonny's embarrassed expression, but didn't fit. He turned serious right away. "Yes, well, I am not sure she is going to see it that way."

"Was it a close hug, I mean, was it jist you all putting yer arms on each others' backs, or did ya like press..." Sonny's look was so harsh Johnny had to stop. "I, uh, guess that's a little personal."

"Yes, a little."

"She hugged ya. Ya gotta figure it means somethin."

"Yes, well, it may be she was just afraid because of the storm."

"Maybe, but..."

"Look it, we have to get back to work. We're so far behind... I did not get anything done on Monday; yesterday wasn't very good, either. I can't let all of this get to me like this."

Peter stopped pacing as the barn door opened. "You are late!" he complained. "I have been waiting for nearly an hour."

"Who cares?" Hessie whispered under her breath as she

walked in. She knew Peter was going to be angry, but that was fine. She had no need for him anymore. Anna wasn't going to Fauquier County. She didn't see any way Peter could help her get rid of Sonny, which is what was commanding her attention at the time. Besides, him wanting to meet with her after what happened at Meem's Bottom showed he was foolish and desperate. He might be as clumsy as Alvis. He might even somehow expose her, and she didn't know how she was going to get around that. Okay, yes, she thought, she did have to be there; she still had to manage Peter, and probably would for some time. She frowned as she pulled the door closed with both hands, but had a smile on her face as she turned to face him. It was too dark for Peter to notice, but he did detect the lilt in her voice. "Now why are you so mad, Peter?" she said. "Everything is going according to plan."

"It is? Is it?"

"Yes, it is. Everything is perfect."

"She knows that I looked all over for her at Meem's Bottom?"

"Of course she does. That was so sweet."

"And that I got attacked in Screamersville?"

"Yes. She was *very* concerned. Are you all right?"

Peter nodded, then realized Hessie probably couldn't see that in the dark. "Yes, except my head still hurts sometimes. But it was worth it if she now appreciates how much I care for her? Is *was* a test of my devotion, wasn't it?"

So that's why he came back, Hessie thought. "Yes, Peter, it was. I am sorry to have deceived you, but Anna insisted you had to go through that so she could trust you."

"And her and Sonny Lutz?" His concern showed as annoyance. "Going down to the Springs with him?"

"Peter, Peter." Hessie sounded like a mother treating a sick child. "Guess who everybody thinks she likes now?"

Peter's anger drained from him like water running off a mountain slope. "That *was* it."

"Yes. You should have known that."

"Why didn't you tell me before? Fortunately I have friends in Conicville or I would not have known at all. I was very concerned. That is why I rode down there."

"You did? You went down to the Springs?" He *is* as bad as Alvis, Hessie thought. Anna is going to marry Sonny just to get away from these foolish boys.

"It did not seem as if she had a very good time."

Hessie knew she had to be careful now. She wasn't sure what Peter saw. If she said the wrong thing he would realize she was lying. "No, she did not. She did not have a good time at all. She thought the baseball game was boring, and the singing childish."

Peter nodded.

The thought came into Hessie's mind so fast she didn't have time to judge it, to analyze it, to decide if it would do any good, but in an instant she realized that Peter *could* be of some help. "But," she said quickly, "after what Sonny did she is not sure if she wants to see him again, so we may still have a problem. I tried to talk her into — "

"After what he did! What did he do to her?"

"Oh, you didn't see that? He wouldn't keep his hands off of her. There was a thunderstorm?"

"Yes, yes, a bad one, believe me."

"She said they all crowded onto the porch of some house there."

"Yes, the rooming house. From where I was I couldn't see them."

"Well, evidently they were all pushed together, and he took advantage of her. She said she whispered to him to stop, but... She couldn't get away from him without making a scene, so she just had to let him do what he wanted."

"That... That! I am going to kill him! That son of a — "

"Peter, you cannot do anything. Think, if you attack Sonny it will give it all away. It will ruin everything. She can take care of herself."

"Evidently she cannot."

"Look, be calm for now. Don't worry. It will all work out the way we want it to. After that we can both take care of Sonny Lutz." Hessie was starting to feel better. Perhaps some bad public opinion might make Sonny back off. She was so scared after talking to Anna, after seeing the expression on her face when she talked about Sonny, after she described the hug with a giggle and beaming, fiery eyes, that Hessie thought she might have to shoot her to keep her away from Sonny. This might be better. It was good start, anyway. She told herself to work on it later.

Peter would not calm down, but did begin to realize his anger might get him into trouble. He let out a long breath, pursed his lips to keep him from saying what was on his mind. "I want to see her," he said.

"Oh, I don't know, Peter. It is taking quite a risk. I don't think her mother is convinced there is not anything going on between you two. She watches her all the time. It is hard enough for me to get away like this. I think it would be impossible for Anna to sneak out. Don't worry. You two will be together soon."

"Who was that?" Alvis asked.

"Who was who?" Hessie looked through the barn door out at the dark pasture, but really did not see anyone.

"I swear I jist saw somebody ridin away from here."

"It was probably someone cutting through. The Godfreys are always doing that."

Alvis nodded to show he accepted that as he hobbled in, leaning on a cane.

"What happened to you?" Hessie figured he was going to tell her anyway.

"I hurt my ankle, okay? Down at the Springs."

"Good, God, Alvis, have you been drinking? You smell as if a still exploded all over you."

"Gotta do somethin. It hurts like hell. Excuse my French.

What I meant to say, is..."

"Oh, forget it, Alvis. You can read all you want and learn to talk better, but you will always be Alvis Clapp. Okay?"

"Why are you bein so mean ta me, agin? I thought ya wanted me an Anna ta — "

"Alvis." Hessie let out in breath, "I have things to worry about. And actually so do you, if you are serious about marrying Anna. She had a wonderful time down at the Springs. She likes Sonny very much and plans on seeing him again. She did not say anything about it, but there is certainly a chance she could marry him, and right now I cannot figure out what I can do about it. Okay? I am sorry, but I do not see you being any help here. I asked you to find Ian Froth, for example, and you barely looked for him."

"I, uh..."

"'I, uh.' That's good, Alvis. That is how much help you have been. Whenever I need someone to stand there and say, 'I, uh,' I will let you know. As far as anything else — "

"Damnit, Hessie, shut up! I'm tired of puttin up with yer abuse." Alvis swung the cane in the air like a club, making Hessie take a step back as her face tightened with alarm. "You were supposed ta be helpin me, but ya haven't done a damned thing. So ya know what I figured out, I don't need ya. I kin take care of Sonny Lutz myself. In fact, tomorrow, I'm goin down there, an I'm gonna tell him ta stay the hell away from Anna. I might even do it tonight."

"You are going to do what?" Hessie couldn't control her grin. She didn't care if Alvis noticed it. "You are completely out your mind."

"Oh, yeah? Well, I'm not fraid of him. You'll see." Alvis set the tip of the cane on the ground, turned to go out the door, but the bottom didn't hit level, so when he put his weight on it, it slid, causing him to lean, then tumble onto the dirt, hittting face first. "Sonabitch," he muttered.

"Alvis, forget it," Hessie said laughing. "Give up. You are falling apart here. In another week there will not be any of you left. I hate to say this, Alvis, but I think you have taken on more than you can handle. I mean, even if you beat Sonny Lutz, keep in mind that this is Maggie's girl you are going after. If she does not want it to happen, it won't. And trust me, Alvis, you are probably the last boy Maggie would want for Anna.."

CHAPTER 17

The girl was whimpering and sobbing as she ran up the road in the late evening light. She stumbled, as if forcing her legs to take her faster than they could. She was in her late teens or early twenties. It was hard to tell the way her face was crunched up with what seemed to be panic and distress. She was plump, not fat, with large breasts that were partially exposed even though she was using both hands to hold up her torn dress. Her brown skin showed dust that might have come from her lying on the ground, and her tears and sweat streaked it. When she reached the top of the rise and saw a carriage approaching she stopped, stood in the middle of the road so it couldn't pass, her chest heaving, her breaths shallow and fast. She took a quick, impatient glance back at the way she had come.

"Oh, Lord, oh, Lord," she wailed when the driver and his passenger, his wife, were close enough to hear. "Help me," she pleaded. "Help *him.*"

"Help who?" the man asked. He seemed to be in his late fifties, with a full gray beard, and thin gray hair showing under a black slouch. His gaze went from her breasts to down the road, but there was nothing there he could see, no one who needed help, but then the hill hid his view, so he stood, but still couldn't see anyone. "Help who?" he repeated as he slowly climbed down, warily looking left and right at the fields on either side, and over at her with suspicion, causing her to let go with a whimper, then a sob. "Oh, Lord, help him," she repeated. "Help that brave boy."

The man glanced back at his wife as if asking for advice, but the expression of bewilderment on her face showed she could provide no guidance, so he walked slowly to the crest of the hill by himself and looked down the road.

"What happened, dear?" he heard his wife ask the girl. "Did some boys bother you?"

"Oh, yes, ma'am, yes, ma'am, they did."

But they were gone now, the man saw. Except for one who was still in the road, trying to get to his feet. There was blood on his face; his shirt was torn. Is this who she wanted him to help?

"But that brave boy saved me. He rode up an started fightin em. He chased em away. That brave boy saved me."

"Who were they? Did you know them?"

"It's Alvis Clapp," the man called back.

"Who?"

"Alvis Clapp," the man said more slowly and louder. "From the mill. He seems ta be hurt." He walked down the slope.

"No, I didn't know them at all. I was just walkin home. Why would those boys try to do that to me? I'm a *good* girl."

Alvis was struggling to get to his feet. With each maneuver he let out a loud moan. The man approached cautiously as if he wasn't sure what he was seeing. The road ramped down to ford Swover Creek; there were woods on either side, good places for someone to hide, so he worried he might be walking into a trap, but the rustle of leaves came only from Alvis' horse as it drank from the stream twenty feet into the underbrush.

"There were three of them," the man heard the girl say from behind him. "The meanest boys I ever saw. I hope he's okay."

"My cane. I need my cane, please," Alvis said, once he managed to stand. He kept his right foot suspended an inch off of the ground, balanced himself with his arms out to the side like a circus performer as he turned his head in search of it.

The man walked to the other side of the road. He bent to pick up the two pieces of the cane that were laying in the dust covered weeds. He held them out to show Alvis. "I"m afraid it's broken, son."

"It must have happened when I thumped one of them over the head with it. Oh, well," Alvis sighed. "I'll jist hafta do my best, I guess. Kin ya help me git ta my horse?"

"Ya know yer bleedin, don't ya?"

Alvis started to wipe the blood off his face, but felt himself teeter, so he put his hand back out. "It's nothin. I'll jist wash it off when I git home."

The man stood in the road, looked one way, then another, at Alvis and at his horse, then back and forth, and came to the conclusion that it would be easier to bring the horse over to Alvis than to take Alvis to his horse. "Uh, why don't ya jist sit down there fer now, an I'll go git yer mare."

"Yes, thank you, kind sir."

"How could that skinny thing chase anyone away," the man muttered as he walked into the woods. "I guess it ain't really none of my business."

"That brave boy's a hero. He's a real hero."

"That went well, didn't it," Hessie said, as she followed Anna into Anna's room.

"I guess so," Anna said as she kneeled on the bed, then twisted to sit.

Hessie waited just inside the doorway for Anna to respond before she reached back to close the door. She walked over to a high-back cushioned armchair that was by the bed, and plopped down onto it. "He certainly is handsome. A big rugged farmer. That's about every girl's dream."

"He *is* handsome, isn't he?" Anna grinned at the thought.

"And bringing you flowers. That was so sweet."

"It was, wasn't it?" Anna nodded.

"It is a shame he did not know the name of them. I guess that really doesn't mean anything. Not everyone knows the names of flowers."

"I suppose. It isn't really important, is it? I really wish you hadn't asked him. It seemed to make him uncomfortable."

"Yes, I *am* sorry." Hessie seemed sincerely apologetic. "I did not mean to. I just thought, I was just curious what they were. It did seem to affect him though, didn't it? He did seem to be uncomfortable at dinner."

"Did he? I really didn't notice." Anna looked at Hessie with some curiosity, the way she tried to watch her during the meal, but with the conversation moving around the table she hadn't been able to concentrate on her step-sister, or think about what she was doing, or why. "You certainly asked him a lot of questions," Anna finally said. "He probably thought we had him here for a job interview."

Hessie showed a look of sweet innocence. "I was just trying to help. I mean, we have to make sure he is the right one for you."

"*We* do?" Anna said. "Since when is it..." She had to be careful. She didn't want her resentment to show. "I would think it would be my choice," she said with a display of mock defiance. "After all, I am the one who might be marrying him."

"Well, perhaps I should not bring this up, but it seems that you do need some help in that regard. Weren't you in love with Peter Metzger at one time."

All the muscles in Anna's face seemed to droop at once. "How was I supposed to know what he was like?" she said loudly.

"That is just what I am saying. We have to be sure. Who knows? Sonny might have some deep, dark secret. Many people do." Hessie hid her grin with her right hand.

"Well, I doubt that he is the type to go looking for prostitutes in Screamersville."

"Maybe, maybe not. Men do strange things, don't they? Who knows what being rejected by Clarisa Mott did to him?"

"That was several years ago, wasn't it? I am sure that he has had the time to recover since then."

"That is just what I am saying. What did he do to to get over something that humiliating. As far as I know he did not court any other women."

"How would you know? You barely know him. You don't know everything he has done."

Hessie had an expression of mild disgust as if that were a foolish idea. "This county is not that big, Anna. Next to farming and making iron, gossip is probably the most important activity."

Anna nodded to show she agreed with that. "So what do they say about me? What have you heard?"

The question surprised Hessie. She never thought she would get this lucky. She wished she knew it was going to come up so she could have been prepared. She was deep in thought, and paused for so long that it got Anna worried.

"What? What is it?"

Hessie still couldn't think of what might best suit her needs.

"They say I am a spoiled princess, don't they?"

"Uh, they do?" This might work. This might work just fine. "Is that why you are seeing someone like Sonny? So you won't seem snobbish, so people will think that you are just an ordinary girl?"

"No, of course not," Anna protested. "I am seeing Sonny because I like him. He is hardworking and decent. He is a kind man. That is all there is to it. It would not matter if he were rich or the King of England. I would feel the same way about him."

"But there is a big difference in you two. You heard him, he has not had very much education. You can speak German and French, and know some Latin. You read all of the time. I doubt that he has read even one book. What would you two have to talk about?"

Anna just stared at Hessie, not with hostility, but to examine her. For some reason this seemed to matter more to

Hessie than it should. Maybe Sonny had offended her somehow a long time ago, maybe his family had, but she knew Mr. Faraday liked Sonny; her mother had said so, and it was evident that afternoon at dinner. So there was really only one thing it could be. "You are jealous of Sonny and I, aren't you?"

"What?"

"You are jealous that I might get married before you. That is it, isn't it? Or you want him for yourself."

"That is ridiculous." This could ruin everything. "How can you not trust me? How can you accuse me of that?" Hessie closed her eyes as if she were about to cry. Somehow she forced her voice to come out paltry and shaking. "You are my best and dearest friend. I am only concerned with what makes you happy. I do not want you to make a mistake and choose the wrong man. Please believe me." Please. Please.

Anna frowned at first, then a sense of surprise came over her as she realized what she had done. The shock caused her to let herself fall to the bed. Her strength seemed to drain out of her like the sun going down. "I am sorry," she said softly. "I didn't mean to hurt you. It is just, just... This is so hard. I never thought that it would be. I just want to be happy."

"And I want you to be happy, too." Hessie began to feel bolder. "I just thought that maybe you might be happier with someone else, someone more like you."

"Like who?" Anna sat up.

"Oh, I don't know. Someone from our, uh, our class, with money and education."

"Like who?

"There must be somebody. Maybe somebody will come along someday who is perfect for you. It will be like a fairy tale. A handsome prince who will rescue you from ..."

The look Anna gave Hessie told her she shouldn't continue. "I thought that is what I have now."

CHAPTER 18

It rained most of Monday. It was a steady, although not a hard rain. There was no thunder, no lightning. It stopped in the late afternoon, then the sky gradually cleared. By the time Sonny stopped reading and came out of his cabin, the sun was shining in between scattered, low hanging, dark clouds. When he reached the house he saw Johnny waiting for him with his hands on his hips as if he had been standing there too long and was annoyed by it. "What'd ya do yesterday?" was the first thing Johnny said.

"What do you mean? You know what I did yesterday. I went to Anna's for Sunday dinner."

"Uh, huh. Remember right fore ya took her on that picnic ta the Springs?"

"Yes, I do remember last week pretty well."

"Remember what happened the day before?"

"What — the arrow that somebody made out of a board and the stones? I had just about forgotten about that. Glad you reminded me."

"Well, come here an take a look at this."

Johnny was standing ten yards off the southeast corner of the new house, between it and a pasture that held about seventy sheep. He was looking down at the grass that Sonny hadn't had the time to cut for several weeks. As Sonny approached he pushed the long, wet blades aside with his foot.

"What is it?"

"What the hell does it look like?"

"It looks like a dead robin. Is it supposed to be something else?"

Johnny swung his head around as if his neck hurt. His mouth was tight with a grimace. "It's *supposed* ta be a dead robin. That's what it is. How ya think it got here? An why now?"

"It is a dead bird, Johnny. Birds die. It happens all the time."

"Yeah, cept there ain't no windows round here fer it ta fly inta." Johnny motioned to the glassless openings in the house. "Didn't fall outa the nest, a bird that big, even if there were any trees round."

"Maybe it was flying overhead, and, and all the sudden died of old age. It might have had heart troubles, or something."

"Ya really don't git it, do ya, boy?"

"What — you think Maggie did this?"

Johnny clucked. "Ya don't know bout Bart Bowers, do ya?"

"Never heard of him. But I suppose you are going to tell me who he is. Did Maggie have something to do with him?"

"Not much, cept she killed him."

"That wasn't her husband she shot, was it?"

"Nooo, this was someone else she killed. Bart Bowers worked fer her. This was back, I dunno, twenty years ago, back fore I got here. He was stealin from her, from what they say. Every once in a while he'd take a cow, lead it off inta the woods an butcher it, take the meat down ta Rockingham an sell it."

"Yeah, a cow or two now and then. She killed him for that?"

"That's what they say. He was ridin back in his wagon late one night, a storm comes up, branch breaks off a tree right above him, hits him smack in the head."

"And you think Maggie did that?"

"Well, hell, what are the odds that limb would fall right then an right there? Ain't jist somethin that happened."

"A coincidence." Sonny nodded several times for emphasis.

"Lancelot Bourbon."

"Who's he?"

"Old man Higgins caught him foolin round with some servant girl. Two weeks later he gits drunk an drowns in Narrow Passage Creek."

"That's ridiculous."

"Ain't it? Little bit of water in that creek."

"No, I mean, that is ridiculous that anyone would think Maggie had anything to do with that, or the other one either."

"There's bin *more*. An don't fergit Ian Froth still ain't turned up."

Sonny's face twitched, but he showed no other sign of alarm. He got a grin on his face right away, but his voice was too high. "From what you said, I imagine there were quite a few men who wanted him gone."

"Yeah, ya might think that, cept now yer seein her, an this happens. The way I figure it, Ian Froth didn't pay no attention to the signs, an might still be alive today."

"That's..." Sonny was so nervous about the conversation that his thoughts were interrupting his speech

"It's a sign, Sonny."

"It's a dead bird, Johnny."

"Sorry to bother you, Charlie, but I got word Marion wanted to see me." Sonny came in the door with a rap on the wood. His older brother was sitting in a heavy stuffed armchair with tattered and stained upholstery. Even after Sonny walked in he continued to stare mindlessly toward the window. From the look on his face that seemed to take all his energy. His clothes were still wet with sweat; his hair matted down. "How'd the thinning go today?" Sonny asked.

"Oh, are you still alive?" Charlie said, turning to look at him. "Been so long since I've seen you, thought maybe you had gone to the great hereafter." Charlie was heavier than Sonny by about twenty-five pounds. That came from their mother's side, as did his nose that was slightly longer and larger. "I hear from Johnny you are making good progress on the house. Soon as I get some time, I'll get over to see it."

Sonny nodded. "Yes, it is going okay. A month, maybe more."

"Great. Sorry I haven't been able to help you. I've been meaning to, but…"

"You have your own place to run. Didn't expect you to help. This is my… You have three children to feed. Any idea why Marion wants to see me?"

"Didn't even know she did until you showed up. Guess she heard some gossip she figures you ought to know. Shoot, most the gossip she hears she figures *I* ought to know, but sometimes it gets real hard to listen."

Sonny was smiling at that as he walked into the kitchen. Marion had potatoes boiling on the wood stove next to a frying pan of pork chops. The room was twenty degrees hotter than anyplace else in the house even though the door was open to let in what little breeze there was. The sounds of children playing came from the backyard. "You should get him to build you a nice summer kitchen. You could die in all this heat."

Marion forced a smile onto her face. "Maybe in his spare time."

"My mother said you wanted to see me."

"Yes, she came over this morning and watched the children while I took care of a few things here. She is so good with her grandchildren." Marion knew that wasn't what Sonny came to hear, but she couldn't help it. She had to stall until she thought this out some more. She walked over and watched the pork chops cook, lifted the cover on the potatoes, then examined the chops one more time.

"What was it you wanted to tell me?"

"You're going to stay for dinner, aren't you?"

"Yes, sure." Sonny was beginning to realize something was wrong. His mind started to rush as he wondered what the bad news could be. He knew it didn't have anything to do with family; his mother would have told him that herself. It had to be about Anna.

"How did things go on Sunday at dinner there?"

What could she know that he did not? "It went fine, I think. I had a good time." At least he thought he had. "It was a little, I don't know, awkward. Having to face her mother and her step-father, and her grandmother. I was a little nervous. I do not know if she noticed. What do you know about Hessie Faraday?"

The question made Marion stop to think. "I, uh, not very much. Why?"

"She seemed to be –- she did not seem to like me very much. She kept asking me questions I could not answer. Heck, they were questions a college professor probably could not answer." Sonny forced out a chuckle. "But I think it went okay. Anna and I sat on the front porch after dinner. We must have talked for over two hours. She likes to hear about history, so I told her all of the stories Grandpop told me. She told me a lot of things about Maggie I did not know. It was pretty interesting. Did you know that Maggie married a third husband, sometime after the one she killed?"

"Yes, of course. You didn't know that?" Marion said. Sonny shook his head. "He wrote a book, a history book, didn't he?"

"Yes, that is what Anna said. I am going to see if I can find it."

"Peter Wirtz."

"Yes. So what was it that you wanted to talk to me about? That?" He hoped. He pulled a chair out from the table and sat down.

Marion had an expression of tremendous grief when she turned to face Sonny. It made him gasp. He couldn't imagine what it could be. He thought things were going well between him and Anna. It had to be something else. In an instant he thought of Johnny and the dead bird, and wondered if Marion heard that someone was making threats, if he should be more afraid than he was. Having mentioned Maggie and the husband she shot made him consider her, but that didn't make sense. His intentions were honorable; his actions reflected that. Why would she... The hug? Was that it? Had someone from his church, someone on the porch that afternoon told Maggie what he did there in front of everyone, accused him of being improper with her great-granddaughter? But he had been at church since then. No one seemed to treat him differently. Several even asked when he was going to bring Anna to a service. It shouldn't be that.

"How well do you know Peter Metzger?"

"Who?" Sonny heard, but it was such a shock that his mind didn't work right for a few seconds.

"Peter Metzger."

"Well enough to wave to him on the road if I see him. Why?"

Marion pursed her lips, opened them, closed them again, said, "Well..." She took in a deep breath. "I have heard Anna has, has some affection for him. Evidently it is something that has been going on for some time."

"She has never mentioned him."

"Well, that's just it — she can't, because his father tried to cheat her mother when he bought her father's interest in the foundry. But — "

"But what?" How could this get worse?

"He was seen riding away from her farm last week. Going across the back fields."

"By who?"

"I don't know. It is just what I heard."

If it were true he was going to feel worse than he ever had. He couldn't let that happen. "Were they sure it was him? It could have been someone else. They could be wrong."

"Oh, I don't know, Sonny." Marion was starting to be sorry she said anything. Maybe Sonny was right. No one knew for certain it was Peter. She just didn't want Sonny to be taken by surprise again. She thought she was doing the right thing, but seeing the expression on his face — he looked like a puppy that had just been scolded. She had gone this far; she might as well finish it. "Somebody wonders if Anna is seeing you so her mother will not get suspicious of her and Peter."

She might as well have beaten Sonny on the head with a club. After he was finished being stunned he realized it all looked different to him now. And the bad part was that it all made sense. He never would have thought Anna was that evil, but one never knows. "Are you sure?" he managed to say.

"No, no, I am not sure. That is the thing — not all gossip is true. It might not have been Peter riding away from the house, for one thing. And for another, it might be Hessie he is seeing. I probably shouldn't told you at all, but I thought you should be prepared for the worst "

"When was it? Exactly?"

Marion's head shook with short, quick tremors. "Last week sometime. I don't know which day. I could ask again."

"Who told you all this?"

"I can't tell you that. She got the information second hand. It is hard to find where something like this starts."

"I could ask Anna about it."

"No, you can't. If it is true — "

"Then she will deny it. And if it isn't true — "

"She will be hurt you would think that."

"And probably think I am crazy for bringing it up."

Sonny didn't stay for dinner. He went out the front door with a quick "good-bye" to Charlie. He headed over to his place, wandered around the outside of the new house, then through the inside, climbed up the ladder where the stairs were going to be, and stared out a second floor window opening as the sun went down behind him. His mind was busy going over everything — his conversations with Anna word by word, the expressions on her face, the inflections of her voice, everything he knew about her, everything Johnny said.

Without realizing it, Sonny had lost the feeling that everything was right with the world In his weakness he remembered the dead robin lying in the yard. He practically jumped back down and ran out the door. He paced everywhere off of the southeast corner of the house looking for it in the near darkness, as if the corpse might give him a clue about what was going on, but the dead bird was no longer there.

Once the idea was in his head, he couldn't shake it — he was making enemies with his courtship of Anna, somebody desperate enough to go to some effort to try to stop it, and somebody with enough power to think they could get away with it. He hoped that was what the gossip was, just another attempt to get in his way, a lie to make him forget it all. He wasn't about to, but did realize they stole the greatest joy that he could have, that faith in another's affection, the heartening belief that someone cares.

◆ ◆ ◆

"What do you mean that you can't work for me anymore? What is the problem?"

Johnny had a hard time getting it out. His whole body seemed to be quivering as he figured out what he should say. The bags under his eyes showed he hadn't slept well the night before. He looked even more disheveled than usual as if he had trouble getting dressed that morning. The jar of moonshine he usually kept hidden in a pocket was in his right hand. He took a quick swig. "It's jist too dangerous, Sonny," he blurted out after he swallowed. "I think the world of ya, I really do, an I wish ya all the best, but I jist don't see no reason ta die ta help ya git this house finished."

"Johnny, that's ridic..." Sonny knew it wouldn't do any good. Johnny's fear was too deep; there weren't any words Sonny could come up with that could dislodge it.

"I'm goin home."

"I thought you were going to help Charlie today?"

"Not *that* home. My Pa's, if he's still alive. Got ta thinkin last night. Sorta thought it made sense ta set things straight there jist in case, ya know, jist oughta be ready ta meet my maker."

Sonny stood there. He could only shake his head. "I do not know why you think God is going to punish us for building a house, and me for courting a girl."

"It ain't God I'm concerned with."

"Maggie?"

Johnny nodded with several quick thrusts of his head.

"You do not think she wants Anna to marry me? That is what you think this is all about?"

"If she don't want it ta happen, it ain't gonna happen. An I think we've seen a purty good sign that that's what happenin."

"She is in her nineties, Johnny. I am not sure she has a whole lot of power left."

"Yeah, well, God's a little older, an I'm scared of Him, too. I think you oughta take a hint an start bein concerned with what they want, ya know?"

Sonny went to see Anna two days later. He just showed up shortly after dinner, about an hour before sunset. It was unplanned and unannounced, but she seemed happy to see him, greeted him with a smile, as did her mother. They spent the time out on the porch. She talked about a book she just started reading about a ship captain who was obsessed with killing a white whale. "It is so beautifully written," she said. "So much detail. I think that I might want to be a writer someday. I know it is unusual for a woman to want to do that, but I cannot imagine anything that would be more interesting."

Sonny heard only part of what she said that night, and spoke very little himself. When he did his voice shook, he mispronounced words, stammered, could not come up with ideas or thoughts that were needed to keep the conversation going. Several times she asked him questions, but he was so lost in thought he didn't hear, made her repeat, then replied with only a single word. He wasn't hostile, felt no anger, just confusion, wanting himself to want her, but knowing it might lead to his ruin. He really wanted to ask her about Peter Metzger, thought he was ready for the truth, whatever it might be, but could never get up the nerve.

Anna went to Sonny's parents' house for Sunday dinner several days later. It was a date they made the week before. Charlie, Marion and their three children were there. Sonny's older sister Julia, her husband John and their four children came up from near Harrisonburg for the afternoon. The other sister Helen lived near Luray, was seven months pregnant and decided not to make the trip. Anna helped with the cooking, the serving and the cleaning, chased the children around the yard in a game of tag, and later, as they sat on blankets in the coolness of the evening nestled up against Sonny and held his hand.

She was relieved that they all seemed to like her. Sonny's mother was especially gracious; Julia was sincere and sweet. Only Marion kept her distance, never laughing with the others, not asking Anna a question or replying to a comment. As far as Anna knew that was the way she was all the time, and with the others warm and welcoming she didn't pay it much mind. On the ride back Sonny barely spoke at all, seemed tense, nervous, ill at ease. She wanted to question him, ask him what was wrong, but decided that it was simply the common ailment of getting to know another person.

Sonny rode over three days after that. He was aware of how he was acting and what she must be thinking, had considered waiting until he was more confident, more comfortable, but doubted that would ever happen until he found out the truth. He was determined to ask her about it this time, stood at the edge of the porch with his back to her as he watched the sun go down, realizing that as soon as it was dark he would have to leave, but still couldn't bring himself to do it. He left a few minutes later, leaving her despondent and confused, and wondering what was wrong.

Sonny rode home thinking it was probably over. She

wasn't going to put up with much more, the way he was act-ing. He didn't know what Peter Metzger was like, but knew he was educated, had some money, was a member of her group, her class. Competing with him wasn't an option, he decided. He couldn't see anyway he could make her like him more than she did Peter, and knew if he tried he would end it looking desperate and foolish.

As Sonny reached his farm he was wondering if the dread would ever go away. He removed the tack from his horse, put the mare in the paddock without thinking much about what he was doing, then wandered over to the new house just to keep from being trapped inside with his thoughts and fears. As soon as he walked in the door he saw it in the moonlight — hanging from a second floor joist, a piece of rope, probably taken from his barn, and tied into the shape of noose.

CHAPTER 19

The carriage moved down the lane tossing gravel in its wake. A brown-white-tan beagle ran from the southside yard barking furiously at it, followed by a smaller black dog which added to the clamor. As the carriage swung around to the front and stopped, the two remained ten feet away still protesting the intrusion.

Anna stepped down slowly, cautiously, as if she felt she had to make a special effort to keep from being injured. When the two dogs saw her they stopped barking and wagged their tails as they moved within two feet of her. Kip, the smaller one, leaped off the ground trying to get close. "Marble, Kip," Anna said without much inflection, or affection, "you two certainly are loud."

Rebecca looked at the dogs, then at Anna as she offered a hand to help her mother down. When Anna ignored the dogs and walked toward the front door she watched her and wondered. The door opened before the three reached it. Emily, the servant girl with curly red hair, stood in the foyer holding onto the latch.

"Good morning, Emily," Rebecca said as she walked in.

"Good mornin, ma'am," Emily replied.

"How is she today?" Martha whispered as Emily closed the door.

Emily glanced toward the open doorway of the parlor to her left. "I'm afraid she hasn't been doin very well, ma'am. She hasn't eaten much the passed few days, and didn't want to get out of bed this mornin. Only when I reminded her you all were comin did she decide ta get up an get dressed."

"Oh, my," Martha whispered. "Have you sent for a doctor?"

"No, ma'am, she wouldn't let me. She said a doctor couldn't do nothin about her bein so old."

Rebecca and Martha exchanged frowns as Anna looked at both of them and was alarmed by their reactions. What had been bothering her the last few days was immediately replaced with her concern for Maggie.

"She's in here." Emily walked to the parlor entry and put her left hand out.

Maggie was sitting on the sofa wearing a dark gray dress. Her long white hair covered her shoulders and ran down her onto her back. The two large windows were open to let in the breeze, and the room was comfortable, but sweat covered Maggie's face and moistened the cloth of her dress at the collar. She was wiping her face with a handkerchief when the three walked toward her. "Here to pay your last respects?" she said loudly before Martha bent down to kiss her.

"Oh, Momma, don't say such things." Martha protested. "You are just not feeling well today. There is no reason to believe —"

"Dear, I am ninety-eight years old. There is every reason to believe. But not yet. I plan on staying alive long enough to see this one get married."

But when Anna stepped forward, Maggie held her away with both hands and examined her. She didn't say anything when Anna placed a kiss on her cheek, but continued to watch her as she slid a chair closer to the sofa.

"Momma, don't you think we should get Doctor Willis? He might be able to do something for you."

"Do you think that he has any pills that will help *her*?" She nodded toward Anna, who seemed surprised at Maggie's attention.

"Me?" she said.

"I thought you were in the midst of falling in love. That is what I have been told. You should be beaming and radiant. You are acting as if you have eaten something that disagrees with you."

Anna didn't want to talk about this. For several days she had been feeling like a failure as a woman as if what was causing Sonny to be uncomfortable was somehow her fault. Even though it was constantly on her mind, she still had no idea why he had suddenly become distant. She was getting tired of thinking about it, and now Maggie wanted to discuss it. "No, ma'am, I am not falling in love. I thought that I was, but it turns out I am not. He is disinterested I think. He is very ill at ease around me now."

"Dear," Rebecca said, "I didn't know that."

Anna shrugged.

"It is the Lutz boy who you are seeing?" Maggie turned her head slightly to the side to present an ear toward Anna.

"Yes, ma'am. Sonny Lutz is who I *was* seeing. I do not think that I will see him again. He did not even ask me to go to the 4th of July parade in Stony Creek this afternoon."

Maggie nodded to show she heard. "They are fine people. You do know that we are related to them, don't you?"

"Yes, ma'am. He told me. His grandfather married your cousin."

"Second cousin. That poor girl. Johanna was so healthy and beautiful when she was young. For some reason once she got sick, she stayed sick."

"Yes, ma'am. Sonny said he didn't know her. She died before he was born."

"And I knew Gott Lutz well, Sonny's great-grandfather. He was a few years older than me. We called him 'Vinnie,' because he was so 'winzig,' uh, so tiny. Strong as an ox, though, and a good farmer."

"Yes, ma'am."

"And you say this boy is uncomfortable around you?"

"Yes, ma'am. He did not used to be, but lately he seems

to have trouble finding something to talk about, doesn't smile very much. I think maybe he does not like me very much anymore, but is afraid to tell me." A look of sadness took over Anna's face.

Maggie smiled in sympathy. "It may be, dear, that he does not feel that he deserves you. If a man *feels* that he does not deserve a woman, he usually does not. And to show you affection is to take a risk of rejection. Do you see what I am saying?"

"Yes, ma'am — maybe he does not think he is good enough for me and does not want to be hurt?"

Maggie nodded.

"But I have tried to show him that I care. How could he not realize that? He is the best man I ever met. Every man should be as decent and honest and hardworking as he is. And he is certainly handsome and strong."

"Dear, falling in love is very much like going to war, and I am afraid that the Lutzs are not used to fighting wars. They go up against nature and themselves, but they do not have the, uh, the ruthlessness they need to conquer new worlds. And I imagine that courting you is like having to conquer a new world for him. He has never had to face such an undertaking before."

At first Anna was bewildered by what Maggie said, but then remembered her thoughts the day of Maggie's birthday party when she was having to fend off Frederick Rutherwood in the food tent. It wasn't just gossip she should fear, she thought then, but the ebb and flow of people's emotions, and the deeds that will be caused by them. Is that what Sonny was going through? Was he having to fight a war caused by that, battles she wasn't aware of? Was he having to contend with how people around him were reacting to their relationship, with the envy, and the gossip, and, perhaps even conspiracy? It could be nothing else, she realized. That is why she had not been able to figure out why he had suddenly changed. Within her surged a need to see him, to comfort him, to help him understand how she really, sincerely felt about him.

"It is," Maggie said, as if reading Anna's mind, "*his* fight.

You really cannot do anything about it."

Anna was stunned. "Why not?" she asked with her eyes squinting like Maggie's.

"Because it is something he has to do alone. Until he decides that he is the best man for you, until he truly believes he suits you more than any other man does, he will not be willing to take the chance that you will reject him."

"So if that never happens, then I guess that it will not be Sonny. Oh, I will never get married."

"Of course you will, dear. Perhaps to this boy. Or it maybe to another, someone who you have yet to meet, or maybe someone you already know, someone you never thought you would want. It will work out, you'll see. God has a way of providing."

The staccato thumps on the outside wall weren't loud enough to wake Anna up, nor was the creak of the ladder wood as the intruder made his way up, rung by rung. He slid the the partially open sash higher without it making a sound, and dropped his legs inside. Fortunately for him, there wasn't a dresser or a table beneath the window. The floorboards squeaked as he crept toward the bed; he was certain she might hear, but she remained asleep on her stomach with her hands haloing her head. Slowly he reached over and gently grasped her shoulder to turn her over. When she started to move he covered her mouth with his palm and whispered, "Anna, don't scream. It's me, Peter."

Anna's eyes flew wide open with shock. She twisted her head one way then another as if suffering from convulsions. She clenched his fingers to try to pry his hand away; her legs kicked beneath the covers; her scream was muffled.

"Anna, it's *me*, Peter Metzger."

The words did not make her stop struggling.

"An-na." The name came out slowly, dripping with

desperation. Into Peter's mind flashed all of his beliefs, all of his assumptions about the two of them, and they started to crumble like sand castles battered by a wave. In his terror he could do nothing but lie. "Hessie said that you wanted to see me, and this was all that... Hessie told me to do this. She..."

Those words did make it through Anna's panic. Her brow wrinkled; she stopped kicking and swatting at him, reached up and gently peeled his hand off her mouth. "What...did...you... say?"

"Hessie told me that you wanted me to do this." The words seemed to sprint out of his mouth. "You do know that I have been meeting with Hessie to arrange for us to be together, don't you? She told me you cared for me. Why are you acting this way?"

Anna stared up at canopy, pursed her lips, twisted her head to look over to where she thought Peter was, stared at the canopy again, started to say something, stopped, then finally spoke. But, "Hessie said what?" was all she could manage to whisper through her confusion.

"She told me that you care very much for me and want us to be together."

"When?"

"Forever."

"No. When did she tell you this?"

"Last week, the week before, and the week before that." Or something like that.

Anna still couldn't figure it out. It made no sense that Hessie would be encouraging her to be with Peter, unless she really did think so little of Sonny that she thought even Peter might be better. But then it had been Hessie who told her about Peter looking for prostitutes in Screamersville. It was that that finally got her over him. The only thing that seemed logical to her then was that Peter was lying. But why was he doing this? Had he gone insane and blamed her for all of the humiliations of the passed few weeks. She could hear him breathing and knew where he was. She thought about it for a few seconds, ran each motion through her mind, and decided it would probably work. She said, "Peter," sweetly to keep him in place, then quickly rolled to the other side of the bed, pulling her legs out from beneath the sheet, but as she tried to stand her right foot caught in a fold, and she stumbled forward and clumsily down, hitting the floor on her right forearm and elbow, her right leg still stuck in the bedding.

"Are you okay?" she heard from just above her. "Boy, you took quite a tumble. Here let me help you up."

Anna only whimpered as Peter lifted her and she shook her foot loose from the sheet. She was too terrified to scream, to escape, to do anything. She hoped she didn't die then, but knew there was nothing she could do about it if it were to happen. She could feel Peter's hands on her biceps. A month before that would have been the fulfilment of a dream, but now it just made her back to stiffen, and her throat to convulse. When Peter leaned his head in closer as if to kiss her, she managed to break free and take two steps away, suddenly feeling as if she were not in the danger she imagined. "Please leave," she whispered, still in a state of shock and confusion.

"Anna, we need to talk. It is ridiculous that we cannot see each other. I know you care for me."

Is that what this is — Peter suffering from delusions? She knew she had to be careful. "I used to, Peter, but that was before I knew what you were really like."

"I can explain that, Anna. You should have asked me about that a long time ago. I had no idea anyone would believe Alvis Clapp about that?"

"What?"

"Yes, yes, that *was* me in that room wearing a dress. I did it for you. You must believe that. I had to be certain there was not another man in your life, and the only way I could do that and not be caught was..." Peter couldn't finish. The memory of it was making him feel weaker than he had in a long time. He was starting to wonder how he had been bold enough to climb through Anna's window, like a drunk waking up and remembering what he had done the night before.

"I heard you tried to find out if Granna was leaving her money to me."

"What? I, uh…" Damn that Charles Miller. "When? I don't remember ever asking anyone about that. Why would I care about Maggie's will? Who told you that?"

"Don't deny it, Peter. I know you spend money on prostitutes. Please just leave."

What was that about? "Anna, I have never been with a prostitute in my life." Telling the truth made Peter sound sincere this time.

It made Anna hesitate. "I, uh, know about you being found on the road near Screamersville one morning."

"I wasn't looking for prostitutes; I was looking for you. Don't you remember? You said…"

"Oh, thank you. You thought I would be in Screamersville like one of your whores? Do you think that little of me?"

"I wasn't looking for you in Screamersville." Okay, he was, but that was just a technical point. "Hessie said that you…wanted…to…meet…"

"Hessie said what?"

Peter felt his muscles lose their tone. Anna could have pushed him over with a feather. He could no longer deny that he had been conned. He knew by who, but had yet to figure out why. "You never told her I was supposed to meet you at Meem's Bottom, did you?"

"No, Peter, you are the last person I would want to meet anywhere."

"You don't care for me and want us to be together, do you?"

"No, I definitely do not."

Great. He had just climbed into a young woman's bedroom window, and decidedly without her permission. It wouldn't take long for word of that to get around. He was going to have to leave the county, there was no doubt about that. He wondered where Ian Froth was hiding. Maybe he could join him there. His life was ruined and all because... "Why did Hessie do that to me? I swear, she was the one who told me that we were to meet at Meem's Bottom. I looked all over for you, including Screamersville. I thought it was a just a test of my love for you. Don't you see, this is all her doing."

"And she told you to climb in my window and scare me half to death?"

Peter paused to think this one out. If he lied now she wouldn't believe any of it. "No," he said meekly like a young child caught misbehaving, "this was my idea. I just had to see you, and knew how hard it was for you to go anywhere without your mother getting suspicious. At least that is what Hessie told me. I was just worried about you. After what Sonny Lutz did to you, I thought you might need me."

"After what Sonny did?" Anna had trouble keeping her voice down to a whisper. She waited to make certain she didn't hear a door opening and footsteps in the hallway. "I didn't realize Sonny did anything to me. He has been a perfect gentleman every time we have been together."

The poor girl was so frightened that she was afraid to talk about it. But then, who had he heard it from? He had to be sure. "On the porch, down at the Springs, during the thunderstorm?"

Anna was relieved that it was dark and Peter couldn't see her blush. "Who told you about that?"

"Then it *is* true. He did take advantage of you."

"It was a hug, Peter, nothing more." She had told just one person about that. Without a word she spun around and took several quick steps toward the door, opened it and went into the hallway. In a minute she was back in the room with Hessie in tow.

"What are you doing?" Hessie protested for the third time.

"I want you to hear something. Tell her what you told me." There was nothing but silence. "Where are you?"

"Down here. Under the bed." Peter wiggled out and stood. "I wasn't sure who you were going to get."

"Peter?" Hessie breathed. Realizing who stood before her, she made a dash for the door, but Anna's right hand on her forearm brought her back. Anna's left hand covered her mouth in case she were planning on screaming. She struggled to break free, but Anna just tightened her grip. "You don't want the others to hear this, do you?" Anna asked. She felt Hessie relax, so she did. Anna let go of her arm and took her hand off Hessies's mouth.

"I don't know what you are talking about," Hessie insisted.

"Did you tell Peter that I wanted to see him, that I cared for him?"

"Is that what he told you? Of course not. Why would I do that? I dislike him as much as you do. I have not talked to Peter in, I don't know, five years, maybe longer."

"Then how did he know about the hug?"

Whoops. Hessie knew she was going to win or lose here. Fortunately her mind was rushing, so she came up with the idea immediately. "Because he was down there spying on you that day."

The only sound in the room was a whimper that came from Peter. He knew he should deny it, but it did sound like something he would do.

"How would you know that, if you hadn't talked to him?"

Hessie was ready this time. This was perfect. "Because Alvis Clapp was down there too, and he saw him."

"Alvis Clapp? What was he doing there?"

Hessie felt as if she now had control of the whole thing. "He was spying on you, as well. He wants to marry you."

Anna had to walk away from that. Hessie certainly sounded convincing. But Alvis Clapp? How in the world could he ever believe he would have a chance with her? But then, everything else was so strange, that might fit as well.

"Do you remember," Hessie whispered, "that day someone rode up the lane and I went out to talk to him?"

"Yes, you would not tell me who it was."

"It was Alvis. He came to pay you a visit. Wasn't that sweet? I figured that I'd better get rid of him. That's why I ran out of the house so fast. There have been other times. I was just concerned with your well-being. Which is more than I can say for some people."

"That's not true. Anna, I do care for you."

"You just care for her money."

"Why…" It was a flaw in his argument and he knew it. He had to make it go away. "I do not know why anyone would think that. Okay, I know what my father tried to do; that was wrong. But I am not like that."

"You asked Granna's attorney about her will."

"Who told you that?"

"Granna did."

It was doomed, Peter knew. To win this he was going to have to turn Anna against Maggie, and that could never happen. Maybe if he… "Of course I know Charles Miller, her attorney. We have been friends for years. Occasionally we have a drink together. Maybe, maybe, one of those times I might have mentioned the will. It is the sort of things men talk about when they are drinking. I certainly did not ask because I wondered how much of her inheritance you were going to get. Anna, you are the most beautiful, the most wonderful girl in the world. Why would any man be concerned with how much money you might have someday?"

"He's lying, Anna. You know what he is like."

Anna walked over and sat on the end of her bed. She lowered her head and cradled it with her right hand. All that was on her mind was the misery she had felt getting over Peter a few weeks before, and now she was wondering if it were necessary. She wasn't sure what to believe, or who, but after the way Hessie acted around Sonny, it was possible to believe that she might do this to Peter as well. She was jealous. That was all there was to it. She was trying to keep Anna from marrying anyone. Another lesson learned. So now she might have two suitors, assuming Sonny ever gets over what it is that is bothering him, and comes to see her again. She wasn't going to figure this out now, she needed some time. She stood, realizing she was getting more and more annoyed. She hoped it showed. Even at a whisper her voice was so strong it backed the two of them off. "Hessie, go to your room. I will talk to you in the morning. And if you ever say anything to anyone about tonight I will tell them what you did, even if you didn't do anything." Hessie waited as if there was more. "*Go*, Hessie"

"And Peter, I do not know if I should appreciate your devotion to me, or be concerned about your sanity. Perhaps both. You took a big risk just to be with me, but do not ever do this again. If I want to see you, I will let you know. Please, just leave, and let us both hope a servant doesn't see you climbing back down and shoots you."

◆ ◆ ◆

The staccato thumps on the outside wall were loud enough to wake Anna up. It had taken her more than an hour after Peter left to finally get to sleep, and even that was fitful, so just a slight noise was sufficient to reach her brain. As she swung out of bed and walked to the window she could hear the creak of the ladder wood as the intruder made his way up rung by rung. She slid the partially open sash higher without a sound, put both hands on the ladder and pushed as hard as she could. "Go away, Peter," she whispered.

In a drunken haze Alvis wasn't sure what had happened, why the ladder seemed to be swaying. He let out a surprised whelp when he realized he was about to fall, tried to jump free, but his foot caught on a rung, and he hit the ground with a belly flop, his right arm beneath him, the bone of his forearm snapping in half.

"They really should put that ladder under lock and key," Anna muttered, "before someone gets hurt."

CHAPTER 20

Sonny was so relieved to see that noose hanging from one of the joists that he started laughing. The sight shocked him at first, repulsed him, perhaps even frightened him, but that lasted for just a few seconds before he realized it was a sign the rumor wasn't true. Anna wasn't seeing him just to cover for her affection for Peter. He was still a threat to someone, to someone who wanted him away from her, and the way he figured it, someone who knew what she was doing and who she liked. It took only a minute or so to convince himself that he had it right The idea of that made him feel better than he had in a long time. He considered getting on his horse right away, and going back to her house, but it was late, she would never understand his jubilance, and he knew he was treading on soft ground as it was. It was that that finally sobered him, the thought that he may have ruined everything with his suspicions, his aloofness the last few weeks and his brooding, pondering mood.

He decided he would go there the next day, the next evening, after he finished working. He would apologize to her, but knew he couldn't explain, couldn't tell her the truth, couldn't let her know he hadn't trusted her. He hoped by then he could come up with some explanation for it all — too much work, too little sleep, that kind of thing. He would have all day to think it out. For now he just wanted to go to his cabin and sleep better than he had in three weeks.

◆ ◆ ◆

"What are you doing over here?" Sonny asked, looking at Marion closely to try to interpret the expression on her face. It wasn't sorrow, although it seemed as if it weren't far from it. There was some anger there; she was definitely annoyed about something. She was stiff, not smiling, her eyes were hard and penetrating. "Hi, there, Lizzie," he said to his four year old niece as he crouched. "How ya doin?"

"It's not Lizzie." She huffed out a breath. "How many times do I have to tell you, Uncle Sonny? It's E-lis-a-beth." She had her hands on her hips in mock disgust.

"Okay, Lizzie, if you say so."

"Okay, Uncle Elias."

"Dear, why don't you run over at look at the sheep. There is something that I want to talk to your Uncle Sonny about?"

They both watched as Elizabeth sauntered away.

Sonny felt a dread take over him, but he couldn't figure out why. He couldn't think of a reason for Marion to be angry; as far as he knew he had done nothing wrong. If she heard some gossip that might upset him she would have had that look of sympathy on her face. Once Elizabeth was out of hearing range he turned toward her. "What?" he said.

Marion just stood there shaking her head, not saying a word as if trying to make him confess. When he didn't, she finally said, "Sonny, what happened between you and Anna down at the Springs last month?"

What was this about? "I told you — we had a picnic, played baseball, there was a thunderstorm..." The hug? Was that it? When were people going to stop bothering him about that? Okay, no one had actually mentioned it yet, but...

"There are rumors going around that you took advantage of her on the porch during the storm."

"Took advantage of her?" Sonny looked and sounded as guilty as a felon. "In what way?"

"They said you..." Marion's voice cracked, she had to turn away. "They said that you put your hands all over her."

"What?" He knew that it was now time to protest his innocence. "I had my hands on her back. She had her hands on my back. It was a hug, nothing more. Even if I were that way, do you think that I would do anything like that with all of those people there, people from church? Who said this?"

Marion seemed to relax some, but she wasn't looking apologetic yet. "I, uh..."

"I have seen Anna several times since then. Do you think that she would want to be with me if I had done something improper with her?"

Sonny figured it was an easy question, but Marion seemed to need to think about it. "Who knows what she is really like, Sonny? She was with that blacksmith at Maggie's party, wasn't she? And since you asked me about it, I have done some checking about Hessie Faraday, and there are things in that family that are not quite right. She has a cousin in Stony Creek I have heard some stories about."

"That doesn't mean Anna is like that. You have met her? Did she seem — "

"Sonny, you don't know what you're getting into. These people, those people, are different from us. We don't know what they are like?"

"What are you saying — that I should forget about her because of some gossip? What you have told me today is that gossip isn't true, or it isn't true all of the time. I did nothing wrong with Anna, and now I have to worry about a bunch of lies about us. I guess the only way to escape it is to go back into my cabin and never come out, never do anything, never see anyone, certainly not court another woman. Is that what you think I should do?"

Marion's demeanor didn't change. She looked at him as if she disapproved of everything about him, the way one would view a beggar on the street or a prostitute leaning in an alley. "I just don't want you disgracing this family, Sonny."

"What are you doing over here?" Sonny asked, staring at Johnny as if he weren't certain if he were real.

"Jist lookin fer work, is all." Johnny kept his head down in apology. "Rumor is yer buildin a house."

Sonny stood there with his mouth open as if he didn't understand what Johnny was saying.

"I mean, if ya need the help," Johnny seemed to get even meeker as if the next step would be dropping to his knees and begging.

"I thought you were too nervous about Maggie to work for me," Sonny said, once he recovered.

"Yeah, well, guess I came ta my senses. What I mean is, I found out somethin, an it made me sorta wonder bout all that."

Sonny was still having some trouble following the conversation. He had spent the hour since Marion left fuming about whoever it was that was trying to ruin his reputation, and Marion's suspicions about Anna. Now Johnny showing up was something else he had to deal with; he really wasn't prepared. He wondered when his life was going to get back to normal, when what he had to contend with didn't surprise him, didn't make him have to examine his view of the world. He had spent a lot of time the last two weeks standing still in contemplation, or muttering to himself trying to figure it all out. Just when he thought it was all behind him ... What was it Johnny said?

"What? What was it you found out?" That seemed like the right question.

"I found Ian Froth." Johnny seemed to gain some strength. "You won't believe this, but he got the hell outa the county cause he was scared of Maggie, an ended up at my Pa's." Johnny was grinning as if the joke was obvious. "From the fryin pan... " It was a few seconds before Sonny understood what Johnny had said.

"Ian Froth was at your Pa's?"

"Yeah, don't know if that was some sort of divine punishment, or what? He didn't make a whole lot of sense, but he seems happy. Go figure, ya know."

This might have been amusing, but Sonny really didn't need to be entertained, so the words didn't have much effect on him. True, it did show Johnny was wrong about Maggie doing away with Ian Froth, but he had already decided Maggie wasn't the enemy who was trying to drive him away. He still hadn't figured who it might be, and it was keeping from getting much work done that day. Maybe he did need Johnny. While he stood around trying to understand how the world worked, somebody should be putting the lathe on the studs so they could get the walls plastered.

"Are you ready to do something?" he asked.

"Whatever it takes."

Sonny spent part of that day dealing with a sick cow, trying to get her to stand, then feed her calf. She had been ailing for days, hadn't stayed with the rest of the herd of sixteen cows and calves as they wandered throughout the east pasture, but he hadn't been able to get himself to do anything about it until then. Even that day he didn't feel that taking care of the farm was what he should be doing; there were things that were bothering him more than his work. He did manage to get the cow and her calf penned together, but it took more yelling and pushing and pulling and being annoyed than what he was used to. After that he didn't feel like doing much, even though he hadn't finished thinning the corn plants, and in a week was going to have to start harvesting the winter wheat, and had chores to do to get ready for that. He could hear the pounding of Johnny's hammer as he nailed the lathe, so he headed over to the new house to check on his progress. Johnny noticed Sonny's shadow in the open doorway and turned to face him.

"Going okay?" Sonny said.

"Piece of cake," Johnny replied. "What ya bin doin?"

"I, uh,..." He started to tell him about the cow and calf,

but that didn't seem very important, so he said, "Getting mad, mostly."

Johnny felt an instant need to defend himself, but realized he hadn't done anything wrong. "Bout what?"

Sonny walked over and leaned against a side wall next to a window. The glare coming through the opening kept Johnny from being able to see him. Just Sonny's voice came through the shadows. "Oh, things are not going very well between Anna and me."

Johnny felt a twinge of guilt hearing that. He figured it had something to do with him suggesting Sonny might be making the gods angry with his courtship of her. It didn't matter; the more he thought about it he realized those two should not be together. Sonny was one of the best men in the county, but she really was a princess, and should probably marry another member of the royalty.

"What do you know about Peter Metzger?" Sonny asked.

"Oh."

"What?" Sonny stood straight up and walked into the room far enough to be seen. The expression on his face made Johnny nervous and consider if he should say more. "What is it you know that you didn't tell me?"

Okay, you asked for it. "Well, there was some talk bout those two a coupla months ago. You know bout Alvis Clapp sayin he saw Peter Metzger up in one of Maggie's bedrooms wearin a dress durin the party, don't ya?"

"No. Peter Metzger wearing a dress? What...?"

"You don't git out much, do ya? That was purty much it. Alvis was outside, near one of the tents, looks up an says, 'Ain't that Peter Metzger up there in a dress,' or somethin like that. A buncha boys went in ta find him, but didn't, sos nobody knows if it was him or not."

"What does that have to do with Anna?"

"Well." Johnny drew out the word. "Some of em figger he was up there ta keep an eye on her, that's there's somethin goin on tween him, an he couldn't show up at the party causa what his father tried ta do when he bought Charles Sigler's part of the foundry. You know bout that, right?"

"Yes, I have heard about that."

"Well, that's purty much it. It may be that Peter has a hankerin fer her, is all it could be. I mean, likin a woman who don't like you kin make ya do some strange things sometimes."

Which would explain Peter Metzger being seen riding away from her house through the back fields. "Where do you hear all this gossip?"

"Oh, buncha us git together in the woods next ta Steenburgen's in the evenin. Somebody calls it a, a, uh, yeah, a 'literary society.' We jist talk bout anything that comes ta mind, ya know?"

"Peter Metzger in a dress?"

"Yeah, some of em thinks it was Maggie what caused it."

Sonny was starting to relax so much that he smiled. "You all really believe she has that much power?"

Johnny shrugged. "I dunno. Don't really wanna talk bout it. I guess, I dunno, I kinda feel badly gittin you all nervous bout it."

"You didn't."

"Then that ain't why you all ain't gittin long."

Sonny told him what Marion had said about Anna and Peter Metzger. It seemed logical to Johnny, didn't surprise him that a woman might be that cruel, but he tried not to let it show. Then Sonny told him about the noose.

"A noose?"

"Hanging right above where you are standing."

Johnny scurried to the side and looked up at the joists as if it were still there. "What the hell was that all bout, ya think?"

"I guess someone is trying to scare me away from her."

"Don't make no sense if she was jist usin ya."

"That's the way I feel. I just hope she will forgive me for the way I have been acting."

"Well, hell, there's one thing bout women." Johnny stopped. He bit the inside of his cheek. "Aw, fergit it. I'm the last person that oughta be givin ya advice bout anything."

It was poorly constructed, although Sonny wasn't aware of that. The foundation was good, but from there up it was rickety. It seemed strong, felt strong when he tried to shake it, but it wouldn't take much to bring it down. Sonny had been working on it all day, trying to keep the logic right, the pieces interlocking the way they should. By the time he was on his way to Anna's, his reality was in place, built in such a way that suited him, gave him confidence. He did have some concern about how she would receive him, but every time it came to mind he dismissed it with the belief that a big smile and a strong voice would make her forget everything that happened the passed two weeks.

He was surprised he was nervous as he turned up the lane. He stopped at the beginning of it, there where the slope of the land hid him from the house. He took a deep breath, spent a half a minute running it through his mind once more, like an actor being certain he knows his lines before making his entrance on stage. Satisfied he was confident and happy for good reason, he spurred his horse up the lane and to the house.

It was Anna who opened the door. The sight of her surprised him, made his muscles twitch and his mind to go blank. He recovered quickly though. "Good evening, Anna," he said with a smile. "Sorry. I hope you don't mind me dropping by."

Anna was making excuses as she watched him ride toward the house, then decided she really didn't need one. Not wanting to see him again should suffice. It had been a while since they had a decent conversation, a while since he smiled at her. When he brought her home after dinner at his parents' house the week before she had kissed him on the cheek, but he didn't pause after that, didn't look into her eyes, didn't move his mouth toward hers to take it further, just tramped off the porch and to his horse without a look back. The next time he was there, she hadn't even bothered. At first he seemed to be offering a caress as if it were just a polite gesture, but she held back, and he turned and left without another word.

It simply didn't work out, she had told herself for several days. Sometimes it does, sometimes it doesn't. It didn't mean she would never meet anyone who was right for her, it was just that Sonny wasn't. That was all it was, by her way of looking at it. It was best to end it as soon as they realized it would never work, rather than prolonging it. There should be no guilt in saying that. She hoped she didn't hurt him, but if she did, the pain wouldn't last forever.

She greeted him with a cold expression as she pulled open the door, and didn't take a step further out the way one usually does. But his smile seemed so sincere, his manner so warm... She realized she smiled back, realized in just that instant she felt better than she had in weeks. She couldn't help it; joy is hard to fight. "No, I'm glad you are here," she said in response to his apology. "Let's sit outside."

"I am sorry," was the first thing Sonny said, "about the way that I have been acting. I have been working so hard, on the farm and to get the house finished, that I have been very tired." The words came out with emotion and inflection even though they had been rehearsed on the ride over. "I know that is not much of an excuse, but," Sonny was about to surprise himself, "it is so hard getting to know someone."

Anna sighed. She was beaming. "Yes," she said immediately. "Yes, it is so hard." The words galloped out of her mouth. "Maggie says that you take a chance. You reveal yourself to another person and take a risk that they might renounce you. I am sorry if you thought I might do that to you."

Thus the conversation went for nearly an hour. Anna told Sonny about many of the heroines from the books she had read, and they discussed their plights and perils with Sonny providing insights he didn't know he had in him. He talked about Clarisa Mott for the first time with Anna, and what happened with her, and why he thought it turned out as it did. She didn't bring up anything about any of the men and boys who had expressed an interest in her, and Sonny didn't ask. But later, as the conversation turned to Maggie, Sonny said, and he never knew why, "That was something about Peter Metzger being up in the bedroom wearing a dress."

Anna didn't hear the last three words. At the mention of Peter Metzger her mind began to rush, and the words, "up in the bedroom," caused it to panic. Thoughts began to fly around her consciousness like dead leaves in a storm. Her demeanor changed instantly; all of the muscles in her face drooped at once; her eyes darted, then became hard, but wouldn't focus, her shoulders slumped; her body stiffened. When she was finally able to compose herself all she had to face was the fear that Sonny somehow knew of Peter's visit two nights before, either from Hessie or from Peter himself. That idea caused her to focus on only that as she wondered if it was true, if it could be true, how that could happen. Once she considered the possibility that Sonny was spying on her as the others were, and saw Peter climb through her bedroom window, and was letting her know that, she became outraged, but caught herself before that emotion showed. With a whimper and a deep breath she turned to face Sonny with what she could do for a smile.

It was too late. Sonny was immediately sorry he said what he did. He didn't intend to, the words were out of his mouth before he could do anything about them like a stallion bolting through the gate. But once he saw her reaction, once he felt her tense, then diminish right before him, all of the fears he was holding back rushed through the flimsy walls of his imagination, and his house came tumbling down.

He left two minutes later with just a few words, with a face that flushed bright red, then tightened with despair. As he mounted his horse in a haze he knew he would never be back there, and doubted he would ever be the same.

Ian Froth heard the wagon before he could see it. He was on the downslope of the hill, away from the road, with a hoe in his hands. The creak of the wheels, the clop of the horses and the rattle of the frame caused him to pause in mid-swing and turn his head in that direction. His brow wrinkled when the sound suddenly stopped. He walked up the hill, reaching the crest in time to see a young woman climb through the rail fence and start toward him. The boy that stayed on the wagon's bench looked like a small-beaked bird under that ridingcap. Ian watched as the girl approached. "I know you." he called out when she was close.

"Yes, I am Hessie Faraday," she answered, continuing toward him. "Edina's cousin." Throwing both hands around his neck she flung herself against him with such force that they both tumbled to the ground, ending up with her on top.

"Mae corn plants!" Ian cried out.

Hessie began to rub herself against him, short, steady gyrations, that soon followed a rhythm.

"Mae tossel!"

"Shut up. Lie still."

"'Oh, Lod mae rock, be nae saelent onto me. If thou be saelent onto me, A become like them that goo doon intae the peet. Hair the vyce...'"

"Burns. Remember Robert Burns?"

"'Draa me not away wid the wicket, and' — 'Oh, oh, oh, 'A like the lassies — Gude forgie me!'"

"We need you in Stony Creek."

CHAPTER 21

Heads turned and comments were whispered one pew at a time as Maggie made her way down the aisle. Even with Richard holding onto her left arm, and the cane in her right hand, there was concern over whether she was would make it to her compartment at the front of the sanctuary.

This was the first time most of them had seen her. Some, regulars who belonged to the Episcopal church for many years, would comment uniformly later that they couldn't recall the date, much less the year Maggie last attended services there. They knew she had been at the Lutheran church on occasion, and each time they heard about it they assumed she was feeling close to death and had a need to return to the strength of her childhood religion. Why she was there that day would remain a mystery for a while, but no one in the congregation, and not one of the clergy would ever question whether she belonged. Even when Richard took his place beside her, instead of retreating to the stairs in back that led to the servants' loft, no one objected publicly or in private.

It was a different service. All eyes found Maggie most of the at time. Even the rector seemed to focus more on her than he did on anything else. There was a nervousness to his delivery that was never evident before. The prayers didn't start until she managed to kneel. The hymns weren't sung until she found the right page. At the end of the service the congregation didn't file out in its usual way. They tarried at their pews, stretched to look to the front, mindlessly talked to one another as they glanced in Maggie's direction. When she and Richard started up the aisle, everyone moved aside. There was a reverent silence usually reserved for royalty until a five year old girl called out, "I love you, Maggie."

The girl's mother immediately bent over to scold her daughter for being so informal, making the child grow bright red and cast her eyes to the floor, but then Maggie paused on her way to the front door, turned her head, and in a soft, affectionate voice, said, "Thank you, my dear."

Thus the gate was opened. From each pew as she passed there were greetings. Some called her Mrs. Frick, some Mrs. Bledsoe, some used her proper name of Mrs. Wirtz, and a few were bold enough to call her Maggie. She tried respond to each salutation, would turn her head in the direction of the voices, nod and smile, say, "Thank you."

Several times she stopped to talk with members of the congregation she knew, had known for many years, and hadn't seen for a while. She asked about children long since grown, lamented a widow's loss from years before, and told one elderly gentleman that the best was yet to come.

She was three pews from the doors to the vestibule, when, after saying a few sentences to a young lady who attended school with Anna, turned to Richard and said, "Oh, I have left my prayer book up there. Will you please get it for me?" Another man who was standing nearby offered to walk down the aisle to retrieve it, but Maggie thanked him politely and refused his gesture. She untangled her left arm from Richard's and balanced herself with both hands on the cane while she responded to a question from a woman who was standing a few feet away, and seemed to be close to bursting with what she had to say.

Maggie soon lost the strength to stand by herself; she swayed, her legs gave out and she began to fall. The nearest person to her was a tall young man with blond hair. She dropped toward him; he quickly reached out and caught her, lifted her so she was standing, then gently guided her to a pew. "Oh, thank you, young man," she said. "I guess if one lives long enough, one goes back to being a child again."

"Yes, ma'am," he said, still wondering who this woman was that created such a stir just by her presence.

"I do not believe I know you," Maggie said. "Are you new in the county?"

"Yes, ma'am," he replied, then when it appeared she was having trouble hearing, repeated louder, "Yes, ma'am. My name is Benjamin Tayloe. I have moved to Edinburg in the last two weeks from Westmoreland County."

"Edinburg? Edinburg, did you say? Oh, yes, what they are now calling Stony Creek. What brings you to the Valley?"

Benjamin leaned down so he was talking directly into her left ear. "I am afraid that I have the misfortune of being a younger son, and my father is not particularly Jeffersonian. It is my older brother who will inherit the plantation. He, in fact, runs it already. There are not many opportunities for young men in Westmoreland County anymore, so I thought I would see if I could make my fortune elsewhere. I have heard a great deal about the prosperity that this region produces."

When Richard returned with the prayer book Maggie took it from him, but showed no sign that she was ready to leave. "That is interesting," she said to Benjamin Tayloe. "Have you purchased a farm yet?"

"No, ma'am, I have not decided if farming is what I want to do." Benjamin felt as if he were intruding. Evidently this woman was a long time member of the church, perhaps had traveled a great distance to be there and see those people, and here he was dominating the conversation and her time. He scanned the crowd around them before he continued. "I am leasing a cottage in Edinburg for now, and plan to teach school for a year or two while I explore the best opportunities for my investments. I have taken a position at the Stony Creek Seminary. I am taking a Miss Lystra's place, I believe."

"Oh, yes. I have a great-granddaughter who just finished her studies there. Karen Lystra was one of her favorite teachers. She is getting married, from what I hear. Are you university educated?"

"Yes, ma'am. I spent three years in Charlottesville. I considered becoming an attorney, and may still, but for now business seems to be what suits me best."

"I think my great-granddaughter would like to continue her studies. It is a shame there are not more opportunities for young women in higher education."

"Yes, ma'am. They need to do something."

"I would imagine if she does not get married right away she will probably teach. She has talked of being a writer, but I am not sure that is a respectable occupation for a woman."

"Yes, ma'am."

Maggie began to stand, which was a journey onto itself. At first, Ben reached out to aid her, but Richard offered his hand, and, as she had done a thousand times before, Maggie grasped it and made her way to her feet. "It was very nice meeting you, Mr. Tayloe. I am sure you will be a fine addition to our county. If I were stronger, I might invite you to dinner, but I am afraid that I do not do much entertaining anymore."

Ben nodded. "Good-bye. Perhaps we shall meet again."

Anna didn't know what to do. It took her just a few minutes to figure what made Sonny leave so suddenly, and from that, what must have caused his melancholy the weeks before. She hadn't imagined he knew anything about Peter Metzger and the affection she once had for him, but now realized that Hessie, or somebody, was spreading gossip about her. She wanted to write Sonny a note explaining it all, but to deny something he never mentioned would look like the workings of a guilty mind. Besides, she couldn't escape the fear that he had been spying her, watching the house, and saw Peter climb through her bedroom window. She hadn't yet thought it out enough to realize that it would have been impossible, that Sonny never would have been able to see who the intruder was in the dark, and that she never lit a lamp.

She didn't know what to do. Maybe it was for the best. As Maggie said, if a man feels he doesn't deserve a woman, then he probably doesn't. If Sonny thought she wanted Peter more than she did him, then perhaps he wasn't the one for her.

It was that that made Anna spend the last several days in her room with a book by her side, occasionally reading it when she wasn't lost in thought, picking it up when her mother knocked on the door, and carrying it with her when she opened it. This wasn't the kind of thing she wanted to discuss with her mother; she wasn't speaking to Hessie, and since school was over there was nobody else she talked to on a regular basis. She thought Maggie would understand, would help *her* understand, but she knew if she asked if she could ride over there, her mother and probably her grandmother would want to go as well.

So she spent several days thinking about all the conversations she and Maggie had over the years, stories that interested her, and those times when she was so bored she barely listened. She searched for some clue in those tales, something in that lifetime of experience that would guide her, advise her, tell her what to do.

For a time, and it occupied most of one day, she thought about Peter, wondered if he was wronged by her mother and the others, tricked by Hessie, and was as sincere as he sounded that night in her room. If confidence is the determinant of who was worthy of her love, then Peter must certainly be the only one. She remembered he awoke her with the words, "Anna, it's me, Peter," as if he felt he should be there. Maybe it was just because Hessie put those thoughts into his head.

Anna didn't know what to do. She wanted to see Sonny so badly, to explain it all, to find out from him what he heard and what he knew, then drive any doubts and fears out of his heart and his mind. She knew Sonny wasn't used to this, this kind of war, the madness of having to contend with jealous, insane people. His life was simple, peaceful, pleasant, the way she wanted her life to be. This chaos wasn't a world she knew was there either. Even Maggie never prepared her for this, or if she had, Anna missed it. She was feeling inadequate to deal with it all, believing she somehow failed as a woman, that there were secrets she hadn't yet learned.

So there was nothing she could do, except maybe wait, go on with life, go to bed that night, get up in the morning, and hope that somehow things will have changed.

◆ ◆ ◆

"I wouldn't worry bout it too much. She ain't right for you."

Johnny's voice shocked Sonny back into consciousness. He was a little annoyed he was caught just standing there thinking. He told himself to be careful to not let anything show. If Marion and the others had any idea of how miserable he was those looks of sympathy would last a lifetime. Even though the agitation from his unhappiness kept him awake most of the whole night after getting back from Anna's, he was in his fields working hard as soon as the sun came up. Anyone who happened by, anyone who observed him from the road would see he was doing what he should be doing, that his life was going on as usual. He wasn't sure about his appearance — he imagined his eyes were drawn, his face permanently formed by unhappiness. He was hoping Marion didn't suddenly show up. If she did, if she noticed, he would tell her he was up late nailing lathe. When she asked how things were going with Anna, he would say, "Fine. Fine. Couldn't be better."

"What?" he said looking at Johnny, trying to remember if he knew he was coming that morning.

"I said, 'she ain't right fer you.' Least from what I heard."

Sonny shrugged. There was really no need to have this conversation now; there was certainly nothing else he needed to know. He didn't want to have to explain why to Johnny, so he acted as if he wanted to hear what he had to say.

"Somebody's sayin now she was with Ian Froth at Maggie's party."

"You already told me that."

"No, what I told ya was she was with Ian Froth at the party. What I'm sayin now is that she was *with* Ian Froth at the party. See what I'm sayin?" Johnny looked at him as if he were impatiently waiting for Sonny to get it. "Up in one of the bedrooms."

"Oh. Okay. Yeah."

"You don't care?"

"I'm not sure it matters much anymore."

"Well, maybe this'll make ya git over her. Peter Metzger climbed inta her bedroom window one night last week. He was up there bout an hour fore he climbed down."

"Oh, yeah, that makes me feel better. Guess that explains that."

"What?"

Sonny shook his head several times. "Where did you find out all this — that 'literary society' that you belong to?"

"Yeah. Shoot, if it weren't fer you an Anna Rose, I don't what we'd have ta talk about."

Sonny sent Johnny away that day, saying that he was no longer in a hurry to finish the house. It had become an bad omen, a sign of his foolishness, his inability to judge, to predict, to understand and control the vagaries of the world around him. He never wanted to be anything but a farmer with a good wife and children, but now he felt trapped there as if it was all he could do, that anything else would exceed his capabilities, and forever the Lutzs would be thought of as honest, hardworking, and nothing more.

The day was dull, boring. That was the trouble with this time of year — the work took so little of his mind it was hard to escape from anything that was bothering him. Two days before he had gone through his cornfield with a horse hoe to get the weeds in between the rows, so the day before and today he had to cultivate by hand. There was nothing interesting about it, nothing that challenged him or made him think, so his mind couldn't escape from thoughts of Anna Rose. It was causing a constant uproar, a commotion of ideas, visions and sounds as if he were under attack by everything around him.

He really should have done something else, something more distracting, something to keep him from thinking about her. He was almost done, one more row, then he would find a more compelling job. With the end in sight he worked a little harder, a little faster, didn't pause to run everything through his mind once more. Soon he got into a rhythm – a couple of swings deep enough to get the roots, then a step to his right, a couple of swings, then a step, just like a square dance. He frowned at that; the idea stopped him. That was something he had looked forward to doing with Anna. It would never happen now. It took him nearly a minute to get over that. "Ahh," he muttered to himself when he realized how much this was aggravating him, slowing him down, changing him. He hopped over a step and vanquished another few weeds, a step, two swings.... He had met Clarisa at a square dance. "Aw, jeez," he whispered, stopping again. He wanted to scream, at himself, the world, God, the universe, maybe even Anna, if only he could figure out who to blame for it all.

"Hello, Sonny."

The voice came from the end of the row, up near the house, and spun Sonny around. With the sun at his back and the rays on her face, he recognized her in an instant even though in four years her appearance had changed some. "Clarisa," he whispered. "My goodness," he exclaimed. "What are you doing here?" he said as he hurried toward her.

"I have moved back to the county," she said. "I am a widow now." She tried to smile as if that was somehow ironic, but couldn't hold it for more than a few seconds.

Sonny stopped two feet away. He heard what she said, but wondered if he should ask about it, if she would want to tell him what happened. Evidently she did not. "I have a little boy and a new baby girl. I guess you knew that."

Sonny didn't, even though some of his friends and several members of his church knew her parents had become grandparents. He stood there wondering why he hadn't heard the news. Thoughts of conspiracy came to mind. "That's nice," he managed to say. "I am sorry you are a widow."

She still didn't want to discuss it. "You have not gotten married yet?"

Sonny just shook his head at first. "I, uh..." He started to say something. He thought he should explain, but was afraid more talking would reveal the deficiency he saw in himself, and the dread he was feeling. "Not yet." He shrugged.

"I am surprised. I would have thought some girl would have won you by now."

There was that look of sympathy again as if she realized what she did to him. He wanted to deny it, but thought if he brought it up it would all come streaming back. "A widow?" he said, wanting to change the subject.

Clarisa's head shook with quick, short tremors. Grief took over her face making Sonny sorry he mentioned it. If he could have thought of anything to say he would have moved the conversation in another direction, but his life at the time was taking care of his corn plants and Anna, and he didn't want to discuss either.

"You knew Forest was a newspaper editor, didn't you?"

Sonny didn't. He shook his head.

"A small paper — The Richmond Intelligencer. He, uh, wrote an editorial calling Philip Hargrave, the editor of the Richmond Gazette, 'a cowardly clump of grandiloquent river flotsam' for his support of Winfield Scott for President." The words came out more slowly as her voice became softer; they trembled like a wagon on a bumpy road. "Mr. Hargrave challenged him to a duel. He was killed next to a cotton mill in Manchester, across the James River from the city. So I decided to come back home."

There is a God, Sonny was thinking. This was perfect. He could not have asked for anything better to have happened. He was sorry for Clarisa's unhappiness, he really was, but this was an answer to a prayer. True, she couldn't make up for the misery she caused him, but she would help him get through this. Now all he had to do was figure how he was going to arrange for Anna to see the two of them together.

CHAPTER 22

During the night of July 16, or early in the morning of July 17, Cecilia Margaret Frick Bledsoe Fornier Wirtz, known by everyone as Maggie Frick, died in her sleep at the age of 98. Her body was discovered at dawn by a servant girl who went to her room to see if she was awake and needing anything. A doctor was sent for, arrived only an hour later, and officially pronounced her dead from natural causes. One of the workers on the farm, a boy of nineteen, was sent on horseback to the Faraday farm with a note for Martha Boelt that said simply, "Come at once." Mrs. Boelt, Rebecca Faraday and Richard Faraday immediately traveled by carriage to Solway Court, entering the front door just as the doctor descended the stairs. From the look in his eyes they knew she was gone. Martha tried not to cry; she had spent several years in preparation for this day, but it took just a few seconds for her grief to overwhelm her. She sought comfort in her daughter's arms as the tears glistened on her cheeks. After a minute Rebecca looked over at her husband and said, "Please, go get the children."

"Shall I tell them?" Richard asked.

"They will know."

In accordance with Maggie's wishes, she would be buried in the family cemetery in the plot adjoining Thomas Bledsoe. Her mother, her father, and one brother were buried nearby, as were two of her children and their spouses and children. Henry Fornier's grave was elsewhere on the farm and unmarked, and Peter Wirtz's was next to the cabin he occupied for forty-six years. It was decided the service would be held at the farm since there wasn't a sanctuary or a hall large enough to accommodate the number of people who were likely to show up, even if it were requested that only family and close friends attend. And, again according to Maggie's instructions, food and beverages were to be served, and a festive atmosphere was to be encouraged.

◆ ◆ ◆

"Granna loved you very much," Rebecca whispered. "She was very proud of you."

Anna nodded, but didn't look at her mother; she didn't smile. Her hands were clenched around a handkerchief she held in her lap, using it on occasion to wipe the tears from her eyes while Frederick Schultz, the Lutheran minister, read verses from the Bible she barely heard. Even though she did appreciate her mother's words, it did little to relieve the resentment she had felt the passed week over her mother not allowing her to go with them to Solway Court when they received the note telling them to come at once. She was hysterical for an hour that morning, at times screaming, desperately fearing Maggie was dying, and she wouldn't be there to say good-bye. Finding out later that Maggie died during the night did little to lessen her anger toward her mother. They barely spoke during the week before. Rebecca was busy with arrangements for the funeral so she was only slightly aware of Anna's alienation, which, when she did notice it, she took to be the effects of her sorrow.

Other than the service that was being conducted just in front of her, Anna took little notice of the events of the day. She saw the crowds arrive in the hours she was there, was slightly aware there was about a thousand people standing behind her, but made no attempt to scan the masses, did not look for anyone, did not care who might be there or who was not. Although she was feeling alone and lonely, she was hoping she could get through the day without having to talk to anyone. She was absorbed only by her memories, and wanted to be able to look back on them in private. Her mind was busy with every image and word, every thought and emotion that came from her friendship with a woman eighty-one years her elder. For the first time she realized what an extraordinary gift she had been given, and she was beginning to measure herself by whether she was worthy of it

Anna spoke just once during the service. Near the end, after Maggie's life had been reviewed and praised, her soul sent on with prayers, Alexander Kerr from the Episcopal Church recited a Shakespearean sonnet he thought was appropriate.gie's life. Anna had not heard it before, not from Maggie, not at school, but halfway through she began listening for the first time in a half an hour, and was mesmerized by the words.

> "That time of year thou mayest in me behold
> When yellow leaves, or none, or few do hang
> Upon those boughs which shake against the cold,
> Bare ruin'd choirs, where late the seet birds sang.
> In me thou seest the twilight of such day
> As sunset fadeth in the west,
> Which by and by black night doth take away,
> Death's second self, that seals up all the rest.
> In me thou see'st the glowing of such fire
> That on ashes of his youth doth lie,
> As the death-bed whereon it must expire
> Consumed with that which it was nourish'd by.

This thou perceived, which makes thy love more strong,

> To love that well which thou must leave ere long."

"Yes," Anna whispered.

Alvis walked to the window for the third time in about thirty seconds. The dress he had stolen from Stephan's sister was about four sizes too big, so he had to gather it in to keep from stepping on it. The bonnet was a nuisance as well. Now matter how tight he tied the ribbon, it wouldn't stay in place, so he had to shift it off his face to be able to see. "What the hell's takin so long?" he muttered in between swigs from his flask.

He could hear the Reverend Kerr's voice as he closed the service, but couldn't make out the words, couldn't see much except the backs of those who were seated in the back rows, and a few who were standing behind them. The rest of the crowd was in the northside yard. He would be able to see them only by going into the nursery, the sitting room, or the master bedroom. Every time he thought about that his nose began to throb. This would have to do for now. He examined them for about the tenth time, trying to see who was there, trying to figure who might try to stop them, wondering who he might have to shoot as he and Anna made their getaway.

That thought made him snort. He limped over to the bed and picked up the revolver, clicked the hammer back once with his thumb, and spun the cylinder, seeing again that each chamber was loaded. "Okay," he whispered. He was hoping he wouldn't have to use it, but figured somebody was going to get in their way — Sonny Lutz, Peter Metzger, or members of Anna's family who disapproved of his love for her, and hers for him. At least now he didn't have to deal with Maggie.

He could hear the murmur of the congregation as the service ended and they made their way toward the other tents. It drew him to the window, but not too close. He scanned the crowd from three feet back. "Where is she?" he whispered.

"Where the hell is she?"

◆ ◆ ◆

Sonny hoped that the service wouldn't take very long. He was going to leave once it was done. It wasn't what he intended to do, not what he thought about doing ever since he heard about Maggie's death. While he didn't feel any joy about it, it suited his plans so well he couldn't help but be encouraged. For several days he imagined how Anna would feel seeing him and Clarisa together at the funeral. He figured she would began to wonder if he had been just biding his time with her, if he knew about Forest Lee's death and was waiting for Clarisa to decide to return. For all she knew they had been writing to each other the last two months, and he was only seeing Anna to make Clarisa jealous, to force her to make up her mind. Anna talked about the risk one takes in getting to know someone, the chance that the other person might reject them, and they would start to see themselves as unattractive and unworthy. It had been his intention to make her feel just that. Let *her* start to doubt herself, he decided, have her world come crashing down around her. Even Peter Metzger couldn't help her then.

But standing a hundred feet away in the midst of the crowd, looking at what he thought was the back of her bonneted head, Sonny knew he couldn't go through with it. It wasn't just that this was not the appropriate place or time, but that he finally recognized how evil it was making him feel, how brutal, and was even regretting that he was comfortable with the idea in the first place.

Once the poison drained from his soul he started to appreciate how Anna was feeling that day. He understood her grief, knew the smile that had enlivened and warmed him when times were good between them was not there. that day wasn't there that day. He remembered those times when they were together before Marion, and others scared him away with rumors, of Peter Metzger, was saddened by the realization that he might never feel that affection for anyone again.

The service ended. He could barely make out the words of the final prayer, but from the actions of the ministers and those in front realized it was over. He noticed the food in one of the tents in the yard when he got there, and knew everyone would stay for most of the day. He was in no mood to talk to anyone. He reached down and grasped Clarisa's hand, turned and began to weave through the crowd, nodding to casual acquaintances, moving left or right to avoid those he knew well, and would probably want to talk. He had just sidestepped a mother and a little girl when he found himself face to face with Peter Metzger, not more than three feet away. Sonny's face twitched with shock as if Peter had gotten off the first shot. Peter's eyes didn't move, didn't look away, didn't soften in friendship or in sympathy. Over five seconds a smile formed on his lips, then grew to a grin, then to a smirk. The duel was done. Sonny felt his legs grow weak, and a dread overtake him. In thirty seconds he and Clarisa were out of the crowd. In two minutes they were in the wagon and gone.

Anna didn't want to have to go through with this. For the next several hours she would have to greet half the citizens of the county as if they were close friends. She appreciated that Maggie was so well known, respected, and loved, but resented that her Granna seemed to belong to so many people. This should be a time that the family should be left alone, to grieve privately, to talk about Maggie and what she meant to them all, to remember and somehow find the cheerfulness to recognize how she enhanced their lives.

Now she was stuck in a tent, surrounded like a medieval castle under siege. Even if her mother allowed her to go home, she would still have to fight through them all, talk to many of them, smile through conversations she did not want to have. The chattering around her was annoying. It was much too cheerful for a funeral.

Anna stood and looked all around. She moved along the outside edge of the tent behind her brothers who were chatting with some of their friends. She could feel Hessie watching her from the other side, but ignored her as she had for the last two weeks. At the entrance she had to step around a woman who said, "Anna, my dear..." and something else, but Anna dismissed her with, "Excuse me," and nothing more. Even if she could remember the woman's name, she didn't want to take the time. She had to walk one way then another before she saw him sitting near the south wall of the house, by himself, his hands behind his back, gazing into the tent. Anna wove her way to David's side, whispered something to him, and together they walked out of the tent and through the crowd.

Once they reached the front yard Anna was able to relax. She heard voices as she went by, heard her name called out, but didn't raise her eyes to look at anyone, didn't feel a need to respond. The attention only made her walk faster, and be consoled that she was almost there. When she stepped onto the front portico she calmed, perhaps breathed for the first time in two minutes, and wasn't bothered by the presence of the six or seven people who occupied the chairs. As she neared the door she heard someone say, "It is very similar to another sonnet he wrote that begins, "Those hours, that with gentle work did frame, the lovely gaze where every eye doth dwell, will play the tyrants to the very same..." Her head turned quickly to the side, but she couldn't tell which of the three men she could see had spoken, until he added, "I think it shows that Shakespeare had a keen perception of ..."

Anna's stare caused Benjamin Tayloe to stare back. She smiled; he did. Anna gazed for a second or two, looked closely and felt a rush of affinity, as if he were a traveler she just met on the road, and discovered was going in the same direction, and had the same destination.

He rose out of his chair. The five other occupants of the porch — a young married couple from the Episcopal Church, a fourteen year old girl from a farm nearby, Anna's older cousin Andrew Bledsoe, and Maggie's servant girl Emily watched as spectators as the two seemed to measure each other.

Anna's life flashed into her mind, creating an immediate and compelling concern for her future. For the first time she felt she was on her own, without guide or advisor, and knew only she, and God, controlled her fate. She looked back at Benjamin Tayloe, smiled again at him, then walked through the door.

It didn't make any sense, Alvis was thinking. Why were people coming inside? He could hear doors opening and closing, footsteps on the wooden floors. Was that someone coming up the stairs. He hurried to the door, knelt on the rug, took the key out of the lock, and peered through the hole just in time to see Anna ascend the stairs to the second floor hallway. She was alone. "Oh, Jesus," he whispered. "Oh, God. This is it." He watched as she walked toward him. As she turned the knob he was scurrying back to get under the bed.

Anna opened the door a few inches; quickly closed it without going in. She looked around at the at the doors in the hallway. There had to be a better room, she thought. In that room she would have to put up with the noise from the party, constantly having to listen to the voices of people she was trying to avoid. But where else? She knew Melanie and John were staying in the center room on the east side again. The way they were, they probably couldn't go more than a couple of hours without coming upstairs. On the north side, the old nursery was filled with junk; there wasn't a bed in the sitting room, and no, she couldn't lie down on Maggie's bed. That didn't seem right. All of the rooms on the south side looked over the crowd. This would have to do, she thought as she opened the door for a second time, and walked in. She reached for the key to lock it as she closed it, wanting to make sure she wasn't disturbed, but it wasn't in the hole, so she opened the door again, and started to walk out when she saw the key on the floor. Closing the door again, and locking it, she sat on the bed to remove her shoes, and a minute after lying down, the sounds from outside faded away and she was fast asleep.

Under the bed, Alvis couldn't keep from trembling. This was perfect, God-sent. It was actually happening the way he thought it would. He wondered how she knew he was there, in the house and in that room. He would have welcomed her with a passionate kiss, but didn't want her to see him wearing a dress and a bonnet. Maybe that was a bad idea, but he hadn't wanted to take the chance of being seen there and somebody figuring it out.

Now all he had to do was come up with a plan to get the two of them out of there. First, he had to get the dress and bonnet off, and hide the flask and the gun. That should be easy. Waking her up would be the hard part. If she came to before she realized it was him she might start screaming. With all those people out there he could have a crowd at the door in a matter of seconds. He didn't want to leave a pile of bodies in the upstairs hallway. That was no way to start a marriage.

It was sound that woke Alvis up, made him realize he must have dozed off for a while. He whispered a curse at the whiskey. It took a few seconds for him to remember why he was under that bed, where that bed was, but he still couldn't figure out what the rustling was above him, why the slats were creaking, who was grunting and moaning, and whose voice was....

"Goddamnit!" he screamed from underneath when he realized what was happening above him. "Goddamnit!"he repeated as started to slither out. He rose before he should have, his rear end caught on the bed stead, lifted it a foot and a half into the air, spilling the occupants onto the floor. Turning around, he caught a flash of skin as they disappeared down the other side. "You son of a bitch!" he shouted, moving around the end of the bed.

This was a first, Ian was thinking, someone else hiding under the bed. If he hadn't been terrified he might have chuckled at the irony, but all he could figure was that Mr. Wainwright finally caught them. He flipped over to be ready to defend himself, not concerned that his trousers were still down around his knees. He wasn't sure what he would say, how he would explain even if he had a chance.

"Get off her!" Alvis demanded.

Who *was* this woman, Ian wondered. The way the bonnet had slid over her face, he couldn't tell if he knew her at all, but it must be someone he had ... My God, he thought. "Maggie's back!" he shouted. "So soon."

Trying to study her face, what he could see of it, he missed the gun. Now that Alvis raised it up to the level of his chest Ian felt that he was about to die. But with the bonnet blinding him Alvis couldn't see that it was aimed off to the side. That was all the chance Ian needed. He lunged from the floor up at Alvis, clenching Alvis' right wrist with his left hand. Alvis spun to the right, trying to get away. Ian followed, started to stand, but couldn't move his legs, tripped, and fell into Alvis, causing the two of them to flip over the footboard and onto the bed.

Ian, with his pants still down, lied on top, grabbed for the gun. Alvis, his dress billowing around him, his bonnet now completely covering his face, reached it above his head, trying to aim it and get his finger on the trigger.

Mary Wainwright sat up where she was on the floor, quickly fastening the buttons on her dress. As much as she wanted to get out of there, she watched the struggle on the bed, trying to make sense of it, wondering why some woman thought to interfere, and why she had hid under the bed. A thought of Maggie's ghost entered her mind as well, but she doubted she would have lost that much height in the afterlife. Mary decided she couldn't wait around to see who it was or how the fight turned out. With all that ruckus, there would soon be a crowd outside the door. As Ian and Alvis rolled off of the bed onto the floor, Mary bolted for the door. She just made it into the hallway when the gun went off.

Somehow nobody outside heard the shot. Perhaps the din of a thousand people talking drowned out all other noise. Maybe it was just a fluke of physics. Not even Mary heard Ian scream "Mae tossel!" as he believed his life was about to change forever.

But the bullet somehow passed between his legs, scraping off a bit of skin from his thigh, burrowed through the plaster ceiling, and died somewhere in the attic.

CHAPTER 23

"Anna, could you come down here, please?" Rebecca's voice came from the bottom of the stairs.

Anna frowned, didn't put the book down immediately, just looked off to the side somewhere as she thought about whether she should acknowledge her mother's request. She finally decided she had to. Her mother didn't like to be ignored. "Yes, ma'am," she said as she climbed off her bed, knowing it wasn't loud enough for her mother to hear.

"Anna!"

"Yes! I'm coming! Goodness," she muttered.

What was it this time? Crumbs on the kitchen floor that the servants couldn't sweep up? Or maybe her room still wasn't neat enough. In the week since Maggie's funeral, it was one thing after another. How could her mother not realize what she was doing to her, and how she was feeling? And her grandmother? A few days earlier her grandmother mentioned at dinner that it was a shame Maggie didn't live long enough to see Anna get married. Hadn't she said she was going to, her grandmother reminded them. "It really is a shame."

Anna had whimpered at first, then began to cry right there at the table. She excused herself with a incoherent, sobbing mumble, skidded her chair back, and rushed upstairs with her hand over her face. Her mother immediately went to Anna's room and tried to console her, insisting that it was unfortunate, but no one, especially Anna, was to blame. Her grandmother apologized, which made feel a little better, and even her stepfather stood in the doorway and grunted as if saying Anna shouldn't take it so hard.

Things got worse after that. A friend who came by to spend the afternoon with Anna a few days later told her about Sonny being with Clarisa at the funeral, and wondered how long *that* had been going on. Anna shrugged as if it didn't matter, but later it began to haunt her. She wondered if that was why Sonny had become so aloof, that it didn't have anything to do with his suspicions about Peter. Maybe he was just been biding his time with her, never really liked her, and was just using her to make Clarisa jealous in order to force her to make up her mind.

The friend also told her that Benjamin Tayloe asked about her, and she told Anna what she heard about him, which interested Anna, made her smile for the first time in days. But since she hadn't heard from him, no note or visit, maybe what he found out about her he didn't like. The way it was now, she was considering marrying Peter just to annoy her mother.

Anna stopped at the top of the stairs to compose herself. She wasn't sure what her mother wanted to do battle over this time, so she told herself to be ready for anything. She glanced down the stairs and could see the skirt of her mother's dress, and hear her whispering to someone. She wasn't in the mood to deal with her mother, much less with a visitor. She considered turning around and going back into her room, but it made her feel as if something was wrong with her. She managed to get a smile on her face as she started down the steps.

"Anna," her mother said as Anna reached the foyer, "this young man has brought you a note, and some flowers."

"From Benjamin Tayloe," the boy replied enthusiastically. He might have been 13, but short for that age. His untrimmed blond hair poked out in several directions as he held his hat in his hand.

"He is waiting for a reply," her mother said, giving Anna the note.

"Dear Miss Sigler," the writing said. "I know that this is perhaps..." Anna had a hard time focusing on the words. She did see "your great-grandmother," and "visit," and a few other things, and thought she understood what he was saying. "Thank you," she said to the boy. "Please tell him that I will think about it." She thought she detected a reaction in her mother. "Tell him that I will write him a note in reply."

"Yes, ma'am."

"And thank him for the flowers." She took them from her mother. "They are beautiful."

Anna tried to make it upstairs as the boy was going out the front door, knowing her mother wouldn't say anything with him in hearing range. She didn't move fast enough. "Anna," her mother said in a voice that sounded like an army officer's command.

Anna stopped with her right foot on the fourth step, her left down on the third. She hung her head to the side in a weak attempt to face her mother.

"Come down here. I think we should talk."

The went into the library. Rebecca closed the door as Anna plopped down onto the couch, and gazed up toward the crown molding rather than face her mother head on.

"What is wrong with you?" Rebecca seemed to tower above her.

A breath exploded from Anna's mouth, bringing with it a sound of disgust. She thought that was enough of a reaction, and this discussion could end. Her mother still stared at her as if she wanted more. "Well, let's see," Anna said slowly, trying to sound as if she were addressing a simple child. "the most important person in my life just died." She ignored her mother's hurt expression. "The boy I thought I might someday be in love with and marry, turned out to want someone else. The boy before that, who I liked, only wanted me for the money I might inherit. I am finished with my schooling; I am not allowed to go to a university; the only jobs I can get are teaching, and I am too young for that, or taking care of someone else's household, until I finally meet someone I want to marry, and who wants to marry me. Except, from the way that things have gone, I would have to believe may never happen. And you cannot figure out what is wrong with me?"

"Dear," Rebecca sat down in a chair to Anna's left front. "you are just going through a hard time right now. We all are."

The last thing Anna wanted was sympathy. She felt herself weaken, and turned away so her mother wouldn't notice.

"I am sorry things did not work out better between you and Sonny. He is a fine young man, but perhaps the two of you just did not belong together. Maybe he realized that. You should not blame yourself for that, or think that — "

"Exactly who should I blame? He rejected me. I was not good enough for him. He is a decent, honest, hardworking man, and I was not good enough for him."

"Dear," Rebecca was trying to do her best; she didn't like to see her daughter so unhappy, but it was a struggle to keep from scolding her. My goodness, young lady, she wanted to yell, do you think that you are the only girl who has ever... "you are only seventeen. I did not get married until I was twenty-two. I did not even *meet* your father until I was twenty-one. Do you have any idea how many boys I thought I wanted to marry before then? And everytime, or nearly everytime, that it did not go according to my plan, I was like you, dejected, wondering what was wrong with me, and whether I would ever find someone who would make me happy. We cannot always control the things that we feel we desperately need to control. In fact, *those* seem to be the things that go their own way."

"So I should just wait around and hope that I get lucky someday?"

Rebecca wondered why she was even bothering. If Anna wanted to be unhappy... "Do you know how Benjamin Tayloe ended up at Granna's funeral?"

Looking for free food? "No, I do not." But you are probably going to tell me.

"Granna heard about him from someone, and decided that you two should meet."

"Granna? How — "

"She went to church one Sunday about a month ago. I imagine that it was a struggle for her. She went to the Episcopal Church, the church that *he* attends. She talked to him for some time there. That is why he attended her funeral, and met you."

"Well, why didn't she just invite him…"

Rebecca seemed to shrug without any of her muscles moving. "Perhaps she did not want you to feel as if it were arranged, as if he were *her* choice for you. I have probably spoiled it you by telling you."

Yes, you have. As her mother kept talking she felt like screaming. This was awful, but she didn't know why, couldn't concentrate enough to figure it out. She began to realize that she was being goaded into a battle she might not win. Why would Maggie do that to her, she wondered. She slumped back onto the sofa realizing she hadn't, she was just concerned for her happiness, and doing whatever she could to help.

Tears began to swell in Anna's eyes, not just from the thought of Maggie's compassion, but from the chaos of it all, the confusion. There were too many possibilities, too many things that could go wrong, too much for her to think about. It was going to be a disaster. She wouldn't like him; he wouldn't like her. Everybody would be disappointed, and blame her for it all. Or, or, it *would* work out, they would fall in love and be married, and everyone would think Maggie used her power, and perhaps her money, one last time to acquire a suitable mate for her pitiful granddaughter. No, that was gossip that she was worrying about. Hadn't she told herself to fight that?

"Of course, you do not have to marry him. But, please, do see him, perhaps invite him to dinner."

Anna pulled one of the barn doors open with both hands and slipped inside, closing it behind her. The space was dark, lit only by the late afternoon sun filtering through the cracks in the siding. Hearing a sound to her left, she turned to look into the shadows "I am sorry I am late, Peter," she said. "I had trouble getting out of the house without anyone seeing."

Leaning against a stall wall, he stood upright and took a step toward her, putting him into the light.

Anna's face jumped with alarm. "You're not... Who are you?"

"I sure as hell ain't Peter Metzger. Always bin real happy bout that."

Anna bolted toward the door, now sorry she had pulled it shut. She was halfway outside, had almost escaped, when Johnny grabbed her left wrist and started to tow her back in. "I'm John..." he started to say before Anna's right hand smacked him on his temple and stunned him, causing him to lose his grip. Another shot to the head made him teeter, then stumble to the barn floor. "Wait!" he yelled as she tried to get away. He flashed his right hand out and caught her ankle, making Anna trip and fall. She smacked face first onto the ground just outside of the door with an, "Umph."

"Oh, jeez," Johnny said, shuffling to his knees beside her. "I'm sorry. I'm sorry."

Anna rolled onto her back with a moan. Her pupils went to the side of her eyes, which showed mostly the white of fear. Just as Johnny thought she was about to listen to him, she balled her hand into a fist and swung it hard against his left cheek. He dropped like child's doll. She scrambled to her feet, and raised her right foot as if to stomp it down. "Don't," Johnny pleaded, "Mattie already took care of that." The words confused Anna. The pause was all the time Johnny needed. "I'm here for Sonny!" he yelled.

"Sonny sent you over here to attack me? That —"

"No!" Johnny was starting to be sorry he did this. It seemed like a good idea at the time, but now he was wondering if maybe he should stop drinking. "No, he sent me here ta talk ta ya. What I mean — *I* came here ta talk ta you. He don't know nothin bout it. He'd probably use me as a scarecrow if he knew." Johnny felt safe enough to sit up. He could hear Anna still breathing hard above him. He dared to glance up at her face and saw that it had softened only slightly; there was still ferocity in her eyes. He watched them as he stood, and backed through the doorway into the barn. Anna followed.

"You're Johnny, aren't you?" she asked, still not ready to smile. He nodded. "Sonny mentioned you."

Johnny swung his head back and forth in a grand gesture. "That boy's miserable cause of you."

Anna's head dropped suddenly. Her gaze went toward the floor. "He is?" she said softly as she raised her head up and showed a smile. "*He* is?"

"Ya know what he thinks, don't ya?"

"Not really." Anna's head shook in short quick tremors.

"He thinks ya like Peter Metzger more than ya do him."

"Oh. That *was* it." Anna sighed.

"An he thinks yer jist seein him sos nobody'll suspect anything bout you an Peter."

"What? He thinks that?" Anna took such a strong step toward Johnny that he was afraid she was going to hit him again, and backed up. "He thinks I would do something like that, that I would be that cruel?"

"Well, he ain't sure, but he knows bout Peter climbin through yer window."

Anna's face drooped, but she went from being embarrassed to outraged in about five seconds. "Has he been spying on me?"

"Sonny? Nah. From what I hear he's bout the only one that ain't."

"Then how did he find out?"

"Well, uh, I, uh, sorta told him."

"How did you find out?"

"Somebody told me. Ain't really my fault. I was just passin long what I heard. Figured he oughta know. It is true, then?"

Anna was getting uncomfortable having this conversation with a stranger. "What other gossip have you told him?"

Johnny told her everything he heard, and what he reported to Sonny. "It's true, ain't it?" he said when he finished. "You an Peter?"

Anna shrugged. She saw no need to admit what she was feeling, or thinking to him.

"I mean, I sent ya a note ta meet here, an signed his name to it, an ya did show up."

Yes, she did. "But if there were something going on between Peter and me wouldn't I recognize his handwriting?"

Good point. "Then there really *ain't* nothin goin on tween ya two?"

"Not really."

"Sonny'll be happy ta hear that."

"You cannot tell him."

"Why not?"

"Because Sonny has to decide for himself that I want him more than I do Peter, or anyone else. It is his decision."

It was a dreary day for July. Rain came in the night before arm in arm with a cold front, and continued all morning. When Sonny awoke at dawn and looked out the cabin window he gritted his teeth and moved his lips in anger, then settled back down on the bed knowing there was nothing he could do about it. He had hoped to get the second cutting of hay started that day, but that would have to wait. There was little else he would be able to do if it kept up. He could, of course, go back to working on the new house; there was still lathe that had to be put up, or he could start the plastering on the first floor, but he hadn't stepped foot in there since the day of Maggie's funeral. Just the thought of it caused such an uneasiness that his mind quickly jumped to something else.

Sonny got up and fixed himself some breakfast — bread with butter and jam, and two eggs he boiled on the wood stove. He stood on the front porch to eat, cracking the eggs on the door jamb and peeling off the shells, the wind blown rain chilling his face. He had few thoughts then, no plans, no dreams; nothing seemed to stir him those days, not even Clarisa. He was getting his work done, wasn't angry, hadn't gotten mean, but knew it would be a while before he would ever be really happy again.

He finished eating, flipped the crumbs off of his shirt, swiped his hands clean on his trousers at his thighs, then walked inside, plopped down into a chair, and did nothing all morning.

◆ ◆ ◆

Anna stood at the window and watched the rain fall. Looking to the east, toward the Massanuttens, she could see the roof of the Cummings' old dairy barn. She thought about the conversation she had with Johnny three days before. She was surprised Sonny hadn't come by yet. She was starting to worry that Johnny kept his word and had not told Sonny what she said. She figured the two of them were friends; Johnny's loyalty would have been to Sonny, not to her. But then maybe Johnny *had* told him; maybe told him everything, including the fact that Peter had climbed into her bedroom window that night. She really should have explained to him what that was all about, why that happened, so he would know she hadn't done anything wrong, but it was all so complicated, so bizarre, she wasn't certain she would believe it herself.

It probably didn't matter. If Sonny wanted to see her, that was all right. If not, there was Benjamin Tayloe, and perhaps others. Her mother was right, she realized. That may have been the end of a romance with Sonny, but it was definitely not the end of her life.

Anna's thoughts were interrupted by a knock on her door. It was probably her mother wanting to know if she had made any progress on the note she was writing to Benjamin. "Come in," she called out, but whoever it was didn't hear, so she walked across the room and opened the door.

"We're still going, aren't we?" Junior asked.

"It's raining. I don't want to get soaked just so you can buy a baseball. Besides, you can't even play with it today."

Junior looked as if his world was ending.

"You really don't need me to go with you, do you?"

"I thought you wanted to look at dress cloth, or something. It's what you said.

"It was. But I am not going to ride all the way to Steenbergen's in the rain just to do that."

"You know they won't let David take just us to buy a baseball. We can only go if you want to."

"Okay, okay, but only if we can take the carriage instead of the wagon."

"Great."

"I'll meet you downstairs."

The trip to the west took about twenty minutes. The rain eased some on the way, seemed to stop completely, then started up again, but not as hard. When they got to the store there were no horses or wagons in front, and no customers inside. Anna looked at bolts of cloth on the table by the door, while her brothers asked Mr. Steenbergen about baseballs, and followed him to the shelves in back. She was about to see if there was anything she wanted to buy when she heard footsteps clunk on the front porch, and the door creak as it was opened. She turned her head in that direction. "What are you doing here?" she said.

Peter was as surprised as Anna. Once the shock left his face a smile showed. "Actually, I was just stopping in to get some lunch. Had to go look at some timber we're buying. I am on my way back to the foundry. This was certainly fortuitous."

Anna had several days to think about what Johnny told her in the barn. It hadn't been hard to figure out where the gossip started. She even realized the rumor that she was up in one of the bedrooms with Ian Froth at Maggie's birthday party must have come from Peter. She knew Alvis and others had gone looking for him; he had to hide somewhere. She was pretty certain it had been under her cousin Melanie's bed. She laughed when she first realized that, but it took only a little while before her anger grew. Peter tried to ruin her reputation to scare Sonny away, was the way she saw it. It was because of Peter that Sonny became so distant, and she so miserable. He caused her several weeks of unhappiness, not to mention ruined what might have been the only worthwhile romance of her life. She had been plotting revenge for several days, even though she knew there was really nothing she could do, until... "Yes," she said, "it is fortuitous."

Peter walked further inside a few steps, so Anna had to turn to face him with her back to the door. She could hear Mr. Steenbergen explaining the rules of baseball to Junior and Thomas. Mrs. Steenbergen was busy at the stove in back. There was no one else around.

Peter," she said, "I know what you tried to do. I know who you are now, and what you are like." Anna had the tone and the fire of a prosecutor that day. She chose her words perfectly, formed her arguments exactly. She was so absorbed in what she said, and so cherished the diminishing stature of Peter Metzger, that she didn't notice the sound of footsteps on the porch floor. She did detect the creak of the door as it was opened. Not yet finished with the execution of Peter Metzger, not wanting to be overheard, she took a step closer so her face was just inches from his. Somehow, even though she focused on what she was saying, she was aware that whoever it was who opened the door walked back out and closed it, and it was this act that confused her, distracted her, made her mind try to understand why. In an instant she realized who it must be.

Anna stopped her harangue in mid sentence. She hurried the eight feet to the window next to the door, getting there just in time to see Sonny start down the steps. She was consumed by panic, didn't know what to do. She wanted to chase after him, to explain, but what could she say that would do any good, that would change what he just witnessed. Halfway down the stairs, he stopped. A breath of relief poured from Anna's lips. There was hope, he might be thinking about it; he might be coming back.

Maybe he was going to fight for her. But she saw a bonneted head appear, then the face and shoulders, and realized Sonny had run into someone he knew, and was merely stopping to talk.

Anna stayed at the window and watched as Sonny had that conversation. He was turned sideways; she could see his face only in profile, couldn't see his eyes, couldn't really tell how he felt, what he thought. At first she assumed he was hurt, perhaps beyond repair, and wondered how he could have that conversation without breaking down, without showing any distress at all. She watched him for nearly five minutes — his hands didn't shake; he didn't glance nervously back toward the store, showed no concern at all. When the conversation ended, he seemed to smile at the woman, then continue down the steps as if nothing was wrong.

But something *was* wrong, Anna was feeling, something was definitely wrong. Why were her hands starting to shake?

It was over, she realized. This was surely the end. She could hear the sound of his horse as he rode from the store. She would never forget the tightening in her stomach as she felt an involuntary fear that she had done something horribly wrong by letting him get away without a word from her.

Anna walked to the carriage dazed, not aware that the rain had picked up, hearing the voices of her brothers but not the words, and being annoyed by their chatter. The landscape was a blur on their way home as if the carriage moved too fast.

"Hey."

The voice was muted by the sound of the rain on the canvas top so Anna wasn't certain who it was, and at first didn't care. She glanced over annoyed at the intrusion and was shocked to see Sonny grinning down at her.

"That was you watching me from the window, wasn't it?"

Anna smiled so brightly that the radiance from her face might have evaporated the rain before it hit the ground. "Maybe. You decide."

Sonny smiled back, then laughed. "I guess I already have."

EPILOGUE

Sonny's courtship of Anna continued from that day unimpeded. Sonny and Anna were soon seen everywhere together, in Edinburg (formerly Stony Creek) shopping, were guests at each other's churches, attended square dances and parties, and each evening when they were not out, for the rest of the summer and into the fall, would sit on the front porch of the Faraday house until sunset, then wander off toward the west fields and disappear into the corn. For the first time in his life Sonny resented the coming of harvest.

The only ugly incident of note during this time occurred the second week in September. No one was sure of its purpose until Anna explained it to them. Sonny was on his way home in the late evening darkness when a horseman, who seemed to have been waiting for him to pass, pulled onto the road behind him and began to follow. Sonny thought little of it at the time; highwaymen and rogues were rare in that part of the county, but the clop of the stranger's horse soon seemed so steady and so persistent that he began to take it as a symptom of evil intentions. Sonny sped up some; the other rider did as well. Sonny slowed; the distance between them did not change. Sonny considered stopping, letting him go by, or even pulling his horse around and confronting the intruder, but the thought made him feel as if he were being afraid for no good reason, so he continued toward his house as he had every night for weeks before.

He was almost there, was descending to a creek so small and so insignificant that no one had ever bothered to give it a name, when the rider in back began to gallop toward him. Alarmed at the sound, a little confused, Sonny yanked on the reins to get him and his mount off of the road and out of the way. Once settled in the underbrush he looked back, and was so shocked by what he saw that he exclaimed, "What in the ..." and nothing more.

The rider, now close enough to be seen in the dim light of a half moon, for some reason had pulled his coat over his head, covering it completely, as if trying to give himself the appearance of a man who had been decapitated. In his left hand, held in place against his side, was a pumpkin, small and ill-formed, a month away from harvest. As he passed Sonny he spouted a progression of sounds that could be described as beastly, or ghostly, or just plain strange.

Unfortunately, with a coat over his head he was blind to where he was going. His mount, perhaps unfamiliar with the road and the surroundings, crossed the creek with splashes and a clatter, then veered slightly to the right, up against the trees. A low branch caught the rider where his chin should have been. He was swept from the saddle like a batted ball. The pumpkin flew from his grasp, and smashed to pieces beside him.

Sonny didn't know if he should stop to help, or gallop away as fast as he could. He walked his horse slowly by the fallen rider, looking down as muscles began to twitch, then limbs moved, and a low moan came from beneath the coat. Satisfied that whoever it was still breathing and was not in any grave danger, Sonny spurred his horse and rode on home.

It was shortly after this episode that Richard Faraday called Hessie into his study on a Sunday evening. As she entered, he closed the door and instructed her to sit. Dread washed over her like a summer sweat. She had been waiting for this discussion, but was surprised her step-mother was not there to chastise her as well. For weeks she had been living with the anxiety of her guilt, causing her to spend her spare time creating excuses and explanations, trying them on like new hats, never quite satisfied with how to best defend herself. When her father spoke her body tensed, her mind raced to decide which deception might work best.

"We know that you have been meeting secretly with Alvis Clapp," her father said. "At his mill, and back in the Cummings barn. On several occasions." Here it comes, Hessie thought. "We do not understand it. Your stepmother and I are baffled that you would want to get romantically involved with someone like him, but I guess we do appreciate why you did not want to be seen with him in public, yet...

Hessie was stunned. She started to protest, but what could she say? How could she deny it without revealing what she had tried to do? She just sat there and stared at her father in shock.

"The way we feel at this time," Richard Faraday continued, "is that you might have to marry the boy to keep you, and this family, from being disgraced."

Two days later Alvis was certain someone took a shot at him as he rode home from Stephan's farm, thought he heard the crack of the gun from the woods beside the road, heard the ball as it whistled by his chin, and the thud as it smashed into a fence rail on the other side. Galloping toward the mill he tried to figure out who might have tried to do that to him. Lying under the covers in his locked room he realized that the list of possible assailants was almost endless, and that they were still out there. Three days later he left home, left the county, and according to his father, was living in a rooming house in Winchester next door to Paddy Stubbs.

Hessie got very lucky after that. Her father, concerned about her behavior and the family's good name, decided that she needed to get away from Shenandoah County for a while. He agreed to let her accompany his sister Kaster, his niece Edina, and a man servant on a several month tour of Europe. There was some discussion about whether the trip might cause her to miss Anna's wedding, but Anna insisted that she and Sonny had not made that decision yet, and besides, she had always wanted to be a June bride, and Hessie would certainly be back by then.

Anna and Sonny were married on Saturday, October 23 at Solway Court. It was now her house. As Peter Metzger feared, Maggie divided up her estate among her many relatives, and all of her employees as well. Her interests in the carding mill, the wool factory, the dairy, the slaughtering house and the wagon company were liquidated and the proceeds split among 50 of her 51 great-grandchildren. About 2,000 acres of the farm, if it could be called only that, were apportioned to the workers by length of service. The house itself, the furnishings, and the remaining thousand acres were left to Anna specifically, with no conditions.

They had not intended for the wedding to take place at Solway Court at first, knowing that any event there might attract a mob of crashers. Sonny suggested his church, but once they made an estimate of the number of attendees they realized that it was too small, as were both the Episcopal and the Lutheran churches. Richard Faraday, heeding Anna's desperate pleas that she had no intention of being a luminary like Maggie, went out and hired every strong boy and young man that he could find to act as guards around the perimeter of the farm. Even so, on the day of the wedding there were at least five hundred people crowded on the hillock where Peter Metzger had once perched, and among the sheep in the north fields.

After the wedding, according to the customs of the time, Sonny and Anna made a trip, accompanied on the first two legs to Washington and Baltimore by Rebecca, Junior and Thomas, then to Philadelphia and New York with just her brothers.

Sonny was stunned by New York City. Anna was enthralled. Even visits to the three cities to the south had not prepared them for that place. Sonny tried to understand what made people live like that, all crammed together where every action one took seemed to be immediately followed by a reaction, and more after that, until it was hard to tell who had started it all. He couldn't wait to get back to Shenandoah County.

All Anna saw were the stories, by the thousands, of dirty

faced children, of princes of commerce, painted women, warriors without wars to fight, of ordinary lives that lived on hope, promises and desperation, all right in front of her detailed and textured. She couldn't wait to get back to Shenandoah County to write about it.